# The Doll House

*Katie Masterman*

Copyright © 2020 Katie Masterman
All rights reserved.
ISBN-13: 9781720115410

# Dedication

To my partner Julian, my daughter Lily and my son Harry, without whom this book would have been completed two years earlier.

# Table of Contents

Dedication..................................................................................................3
Chapter One ...........................................................................................6
Chapter Two..........................................................................................13
Chapter Three ......................................................................................22
Chapter Four ........................................................................................30
Chapter Five .........................................................................................38
Chapter Six............................................................................................44
Chapter Seven .....................................................................................52
Chapter Eight .......................................................................................59
Chapter Nine .......................................................................................64
Chapter Ten ..........................................................................................70
Chapter Eleven....................................................................................76
Chapter Twelve ...................................................................................83
Chapter Thirteen ................................................................................89
Chapter Fourteen ...............................................................................98
Chapter Fifteen ................................................................................105
Chapter Sixteen ...............................................................................112
Chapter Seventeen .........................................................................119
Chapter Eighteen ............................................................................127
Chapter Nineteen ...........................................................................136
Chapter Twenty................................................................................144
Chapter Twenty-One .....................................................................151
Chapter Twenty-Two .....................................................................158
Chapter Twenty-Three ..................................................................166
Chapter Twenty-Four.....................................................................168

Chapter Twenty-Five .................................................................. 175
Chapter Twenty-Six..................................................................... 178
Chapter Twenty-Seven................................................................ 183
Chapter Twenty-Eight ................................................................ 188
Chapter Twenty-Nine ................................................................. 198
Chapter Thirty............................................................................. 207
Chapter Thirty-One..................................................................... 214
Chapter Thirty-Two .................................................................... 218
Chapter Thirty-Three.................................................................. 224

Katie Masterman

# Chapter One

When a person dies, they have seven minutes of brain activity left in which they see a dream-like sequence of their most substantial memories. Hence the phrase *their life flashed before their eyes*. Needless to say, as I stepped out of the road narrowly missing the speeding double-decker bus, I was slightly disappointed that my only thought was that I still had last night's pizza left in the fridge.

After living in Oxford for the whole 23 years of my life, I probably didn't appreciate the beauty of the city anymore. The lifeless modern shops intermingled between the beautiful mix of gothic and classical buildings and universities dating back hundreds of years. Today, the city centre was at its busiest. With school Christmas holidays in full swing there were the usual assemblies of people scattering the streets. Christmas shoppers; teenagers hanging outside fast food restaurants; the regular buskers showing off their talents and of course, herds of tourists.

Navigating the streets in a rush to my job interview was proving to be a task. As I battled my way through the tourists and in an attempt to avoid their cameras and rucksacks, I'd somehow managed to spill coffee all down the front of my shirt. I stopped still and checked the time on my phone. I'd never have time to get a new shirt. I groaned, pulled my jacket over the stain hoping it wouldn't show and continued in my stride in an attempt to not be late.

After a few minutes of half walking, half running I found myself standing outside of a modern looking, sandy coloured stone building. At the front were two large glass doors, with a sign over the top reading Chambers Psychology Research Lab. I pressed the intercom with an annoyingly shaky hand and spoke into the microphone.

"Hi, it's Lila Beaumont. I have an interview at 9?"

A crackly voice came through the speaker, "Yes come through to the reception area please."

One of the large doors swung open and I followed the signs to reception. I looked around, impressed with the how swanky the room was. It was empty

# The Doll House

apart from the receptionist who gave me a huge smile and told me to take a seat. So I sat down on one of the colourful leather sofas. There was a large flat screen TV showing the news and an array of refreshments, newspapers and magazines were spread out on a glass table in front of me.

I pulled my jacket over my shirt again and flicked through magazines for about 15 minutes. I looked at the time becoming impatient. Just as I leant over to nab one of the complimentary chocolates, I heard a soft male voice.

"Lila Beaumont?"

I looked up. "Yes?"

"I'm Dr Reynolds."

The man stood in front of me stretched out his hand and I shook it, unable to hide the look of surprise across my face.

The world of psychology had always been one that attracted me, especially clinical psychology. After applying unsuccessfully for several jobs, fate took charge and a letter was posted through my door with the job advertisement for the role of Dr Reynolds' Personal Assistant. He was one of the lead clinical psychologists in the country and had published a number of papers, which I had read both throughout university and purely out of interest.

I was however, expecting a serious looking older man. Dr Reynolds however had aged like a fine wine. In fact, he was extremely attractive. His face was clean-shaven and chiselled and his sandy blonde hair was well looked after. To be honest, it looked like he spent more time in front of the mirror than me when he had got ready that morning. He also had a decent fashion sense, wearing an expensive looking navy-blue suit with a white shirt and grey tie. I was impressed.

"Nice to meet you!" I smiled, still shaking his hand.

Realising I had held it for too long, I awkwardly pulled mine away and blushed.

He had a serious face and there was little humour in his eyes.

"Yes, and you. Follow me." He said.

He led me into a small meeting room where we sat down across the table from one another.

"So, why do you want to be my personal assistant?" he asked, straight to the point.

"Oh well, I find your work really interesting. Especially that paper on how unemployment is linked to mental illness. Oh, and your paper on the overlaps between Schizophrenia and Bipolar Disorder. I thought working with you would be interesting as well."

He nodded and looked down at his notepad. "Do you have any experience in PA work, or with psychology? The job role will be sort of half personal assistant, half research assistant."

I smiled. "I was hoping you'd say that to be honest. I studied psychology at university so I've conducted my own research for my final thesis and I've dealt with mental health issues personally."

His questioning eyes look up from his notepad to meet mine.

"Oh no, not me!" I stammered. "My mother." That was way too personal. I sighed.

He didn't acknowledge my statement, instead he just looked down at his notepad and said, "Where do you see yourself in five years?"

After half an hour of pretty generic interview questions, he scribbled something down on his notepad and then stood up.

"It's been a pleasure. Hopefully working alongside me will be rewarding for you." He said. I stared.

"Can you start Monday?"

"Oh, thank you! I thought you'd have loads more people to interview, but yes thank you."

"Yes well I was impressed and I couldn't turn down such a big fan." He said deadpan. Was he making a joke? I nervously laughed just in case.

"Well, thanks again. I really appreciate it." I shook his hand and he opened the door for me.

"See you Monday," he said.

Just as I turned to walk away I heard. "Oh and Lila?"

I turned around. "Yes?"

"Perhaps invest in a couple of new shirts." He looked pointedly at my coffee stain, and without another word, walked away.

He was a lot different from what I had expected. He seemed profoundly serious and intense, almost socially awkward. Throughout the interview I had expected a smile or a casual joke or two thrown in to ease the tension but there was nothing, not even the slightest hint of humour. Maybe he was in boss mode and would soften up once he got to know me.

Lost in thought and busy looking at my phone, as I turned the corner, I found myself smacking straight into someone's chest.

"Oh shit, sorry!" The word slipped out, forgetting I was in a professional environment.

When I stepped back though, I realised it was a young man dressed in builder's overalls. He looked pretty scruffy, covered in dust and paint but *damn*, he was extremely good-looking. There was something in the water around here. He was tall and had dark unkempt hair and stubble. I could see the beginning of a tattoo protruding out of his sleeve. I blushed.

"Sorry," I said again. He raised his eyebrows and looked me up and down. This was a look I had become accustomed to; I can acknowledge the fact that I'm not the most unattractive girl in the world. I've been told that I have "curves in the right places".

"Don't worry about it." He smirked and then moved passed me. As he walked away, I turned around for another look to see he was already looking back at me. As he went around the corner, I was sure I could hear a faint laugh.

After I had looked around town for a while and grabbed some lunch I headed home. I had gotten extremely lucky with where I lived. My best friend Stephanie, who I had met in school, just happened to have a millionaire family. When things turned south with my mother when I was only seven, I didn't have anywhere to live. I think I must have mentioned something at school or rumours went around the parents that social services were involved I'm not really sure, but anyway, they took me in. As children Stephanie and I grew up together as close as sisters.

Stephanie's parents owned a large property development company that built and sold houses. After university her father had given one of those houses to Stephanie with everything paid for. Whether this was purely out of generosity or to make up for the fact he was always so busy at work, she was grateful. When she asked me to move in with her I had nearly cried. It wasn't your bog-standard house share, it was an incredible, newly built, modern house and I would be eternally grateful. Eventually our two other friends Miles and Tom had moved in with us and it turned out to be the perfect set up. It had been that way for almost three years now with no hint of any of us moving on.

When I got home I told Stephanie how the interview went.

"So he's clever, rich and attractive?" she said, raising her perfect eyebrows.

# Katie Masterman

Stephanie is a girly girl. She sets her alarm an hour and a half before she has to leave in the mornings so she has enough time to get ready. Her perfect natural blonde hair was her pride and joy, and she works as a personal stylist, obviously. Although she could seem quite materialistic, she was actually really kind and down to earth.

"Well I mean I'm not sure how much a registered psychologist makes but I'm pretty sure he's rich," I replied as I took a sip of my red wine. "He was so dry though. All looks and brains and no personality."

She laughed. "Well that doesn't matter it's a good job to have, I'm proud of you. Oh! I forgot to say, someone left something for you earlier."

Steph got up off the sofa where we were sitting in our living room with a glass of wine, as we did most nights. The room was large and modern but we'd decorated it with fairy lights, candles, bean bags, blankets, cushions… everything that makes a living room cosy. She came back a few seconds later and handed me a rectangular box wrapped in blue paper with a bow on top, like a present. I looked at it with a frown.

"Who left it?" I asked.

She shrugged. "I don't know. The doorbell rang and I went to get it and there was nobody there. That was just left on the doormat."

I looked closer at the box. There was no message or clue to who or where it had come from just "Lila" written on a dainty blue name tag. I unwrapped it and opened the box.

As I looked down at the contents of the box I let out a small involuntary gasp. In a bed of blue tissue paper laid a porcelain doll. Stephanie leaned over to have a look and put on an exaggerated shiver.

"Creepy," she said.

She was right, but it was more than creepy. I couldn't drag my gaze away from the dolls wide, empty eyes. They looked so sad. I moved my head slightly to the left and then to the right. The hollow eyes followed my every move and I swallowed hard before taking in the rest of its appearance. It wouldn't have looked out of place in a Tim Burton film. Its skin was a sickly pale shade of grey, it looked as though, if it were really skin, it would be cold to touch. She was wearing a ratty old Victorian style nightgown with slippers and her dark hair looked matted and rough.

I grimaced and turned to Steph. "I don't understand, who would have sent me this?"

# The Doll House

"Maybe work? As a congratulations for getting the job?" Stephanie said, unsure.

I shook my head. "Too quick. It was here before I'd even got home." I put the lid back on the box and shrugged. "Never mind, I'll put it somewhere that won't creep me out at night."

I went into the kitchen, my favourite room of the house; it was a large, modern kitchen with a white tiled floor, matching white cupboards and black marble surfaces. An island of the same style centred the middle. The back wall was made purely of glass, with two large doors, which opened into our back garden.

I put the box on the island and didn't think anything of it all night until Miles came home.

"Who's got the weird, dead voodoo doll?" He asked as he wandered into the living room with a beer.

Miles was incredibly attractive, large built with olive skin covered almost completely in tattoos. From an outsider's perspective he looked pretty intimidating, if you had to pick a bodyguard you'd pick this guy. Really though, he was a big softie. He had the best sense of humour of anyone I knew, but he also literally couldn't take anything seriously. He'd been Stephanie's personal trainer a few years back. She had invited him for drinks with us one night and offered him a place to stay when he outgrew living with his parents and we'd all been friends ever since.

"That would be me," I answered. "It was sent to me for some reason."

"By who?" he asked. I just shrugged.

"Lila's got a stalker," he sang.

I chuckled. "Shut up. I'm sure there's an explanation."

He raised his eyebrows. "It wasn't even posted here, it was dropped off. They know where you live and everything."

I frowned, ignoring the pang of anxiety that suddenly settled in my stomach. "Yeah well if it is a stalker hopefully the gifts get better. I could do with a new watch."

Stephanie laughed as she filled her glass up. "Or some more wine!"

Miles laughed but shook his head. "It's flipping creepy though who sends someone a dead doll?"

"Why do you keep saying it's dead? She's got her eyes wide open," I said.

His eyebrows pulled together and he tilted his head to the side. "Lila, did you even look at the doll?"

"Not for long…" I said slowly. "Why?"

He motioned for me to follow him into the kitchen. I sighed but followed him anyway and watched as he lifted the doll out of the box and pushed back her dark hair.

I gasped, "What the hell? Who would send me this?"

"What?" asked Stephanie. She had followed us in and could see the look of horror on my face. "What is it?" she asked again but I was completely speechless so she came over to look for herself.

"What the hell?" she gasped.

It became apparent why the dolls eyes were so wide and why her skin was so pale. On her tiny, delicate neck were painted red and purple bruises with a small rope wrapped tightly around it. The doll had been hanged.

# Chapter Two

"I don't get it." I stared at the doll. "Why would anyone send me this?"

"I don't know, I'm sure it's just a stupid prank." Miles rolled his eyes.

I looked at him and narrowed my eyes. "It was you wasn't it?"

He dramatically put his hand to his chest. "I'm hurt. Why would you point the finger straight at me?"

I raised an eyebrow. "You once hid in the back of Tom's car for an hour just to scare him."

Miles shrugged, still smirking. "Alright point taken, but it wasn't me."

Stephanie and I looked at each other and Miles shook his head.

"What a waste of money too." I continued. "You could have at least got me a decent present."

He responded by sticking up his middle finger.

I wrapped the doll back in its tissue paper and placed it in the box. I held back a shiver as I stole one last look at its haunted face. It really was creepy. I put the doll in a high up cupboard in the kitchen and attempted not to think about it for the rest of the night.

We all cosied up together in the living room watching a film, Steph and I with a glass of wine and Miles with a beer. Tom came home at about 10pm. I had introduced him to the group during school. He was average height and small built with piercing blue eyes and a face full of freckles. His hair was brown but in the direct sun it shone an array of brown, ginger and auburn. He probably was quite an attractive lad, but all I could picture was the freckly teenager with bad acne and braces whom I had grown to love as a brother.

When Tom entered the room I looked towards Steph, whose cheeks immediately turned a bright shade of pink. She was never as close to him during school as I was and sometimes, I swear she would stare a little too long at his face and laugh a little too long at his jokes. But I hadn't mentioned anything. Yet.

# Katie Masterman

Tom worked at a bar grill called Joe's Diner, our favourite place to go to eat and drink, and he had just finished a late shift. He dropped down on the sofa next to Miles who handed him a beer.

The boys hadn't gotten along at first. There was never any problem between them, the problem was that there was *nothing* between them. When Tom moved in he was very skinny, a little too into his Marvel and Star Wars films and had a degree in computer science and Miles was... well, Miles.

They didn't have much in common and they never had anything to talk about, until one evening Tom was mugged on his way home from a late shift. It shook him up really badly and so he decided to bulk up to protect himself. Cue personal trainer Miles. If you spend enough time one on one with someone you eventually bond, you find common goals and interests and this is exactly what happened with the boys and now they get on like a house on fire. Neither of them would ever acknowledge it, but even though Tom had definitely built up his strength and muscles, Miles still felt a bit protective over his friend. I believe it triggered Miles' change in career. He had spent the next couple of years training in various martial arts and progressed so quickly he began to teach his own private self-defence classes.

"That shift was hell." Tom sighed as he gulped down half of his bottle of beer. I was on one sofa, Tom and Miles sat on the other and Stephanie, covered in a cosy blanket, sat on a bean bag on the floor. I noticed over the course of the film she had gradually inched closer to Tom until her head was resting on his knee.

I looked around at my friends and smiled to myself. Almost every weekend and every evening after work we spent together and we never got sick of each other. Of course, sometimes we got a bit snappy but we never had any arguments. We all looked out for each other and had each other's backs. We were a family.

I wish more than anything I had known then what course our lives were about to take.

The weekend passed completely without event and the most exciting thing I did was buy some new shirts. Monday morning the four of us were in the kitchen ready to go to work.

"Pour me a coffee please?" Stephanie groaned with her head in her hands.

"I told you not to have any more wine." I laughed as I passed her the coffee.

# The Doll House

We had ordered a Chinese take-out the night before and had stayed up playing board games and watching crappy tv and, of course, drinking wine.

Miles stood leaning against the counter drinking a protein shake. He shook his head. "She's just a lightweight, you had double what she had and you're fine."

Stephanie snorted. "Yeah that's because she also ate double what I had."

"Hey!" I laughed. "It's not exactly breaking news that I like wine and Chinese food."

I plucked the slice of toast that Tom had just buttered out of his hands and he chuckled and put a new slice in the toaster.

"You nervous for your first day?" asked Miles.

"With Doctor Sexy." Stephanie piped up, head still in her hands. I shook my head as I passed her a glass of water and some paracetamol.

"No, I'm fine, it will be good, I think I'm going to learn a lot."

Miles snorted as he took Tom's new slice of toast out of his hand and took a bite.

"What?" I said.

"You're his lapdog."

"Sorry?"

"His lapdog." Miles said. "You're Doctor Hot-Shot's personal assistant. You're going to be making coffee and tidying his drawers."

"I am not. There will be some of that I'm sure, but it's a steppingstone into furthering my career as a psychologist and I genuinely think I'm going to learn a lot." I said, although we all knew it sounded rehearsed.

Miles and Tom looked at each other as if I were going to be proven wrong in a couple of hours.

I frowned and looked up at the clock on the wall. "I'd better go anyway."

"Ugh, me too." Stephanie groaned and then stood up and took Tom's third slice of toast from his hand and winked at him.

We all chuckled and headed our separate ways.

I was due to start at 9 but thought on my first day I should make a good impression and so I arrived at 8:45. I was buzzed into the building and walked up to the reception in the fancy waiting room that I had sat in on the day of my interview.

"Hello, I'm Lila Beaumont, it's my first day here."

The receptionist looked up. It was the same woman from the first day but I hadn't taken much notice of her then, I must have been nervous because she was strikingly beautiful. She smiled up at me, not one of those receptionist smiles, a genuine smile.

"Ah yes I remember you from the other day. Dr Reynolds' assistant. How are you today?"

I smiled in return. "I'm good thank you, a bit nervous but I'm sure I'll settle in fine."

"Oh you will do of course!" She stood up and walked over to a grey filing cabinet behind her large wooden desk and pulled something out.

"This is your fob to come in and out of the building so I don't have to let you in every time, I'll let Dr Reynolds know that you're here." She smiled and sat down which I took as my invitation to do so as well.

At 9am on the dot the reception phone rang.

"Hello?... Yep... Okay, I'll bring her up."

We made idle small talk as I followed her up the stairs to the second floor. She ushered me into a huge office where Dr Reynolds sat at his desk. He stood when we entered and walked around the desk and leant against it.

He wore a dark navy suit with brown shoes and a light pink tie. His hair was once again groomed to perfection and he had grown a slight beard, trimmed to perfection. He looked good.

He kept his office as immaculate as he kept himself. There was no colour to the room, there were no plants or flowers, no photos adorned the wall or his desk. I took a deep breath and nearly coughed at the strong scent of bleach and air freshener. I swallowed and subtly dried my suddenly sweaty palms on my thighs.

"Hello," I said awkwardly.

"Good morning. Thank you Annie." The receptionist, Annie, took this as her dismissal and nodded her goodbye and shut the door behind her. If I weren't mistaken she gave me a look before she left as if to say *good luck, you're going to need it.*

"How are you?" he asked, as a formality rather than out of genuine interest.

"I'm good thank you. Excited to be working with you."

He nodded as if this wasn't news to him.

"Glad to see you're wearing a clean shirt today, as you can tell I like to work in a clean and tidy environment," he said with a touch of humour in his eyes.

I blushed and before I could say anything he continued, "I wish I could make my cupboard as tidy as my office, but I just don't have the time."

I followed him over to the cupboard door at the side of the room which he opened and gestured for me to look inside. There were stacks after stacks of files filling the shelves and overflowing cardboard boxes completely covered the floor. I groaned internally as I could see where this was going. Miles had been correct.

"I'd say anything dated before 1990 throw out, I have all the important old files in my desk. The rest need to be arranged chronologically first and alphabetically by patient or case name. Any that don't have a patient or case name put in a different section in order of disorder. Okay?"

*Yes sir.* "Yes that's fine, I'll get straight on it." I forced out a smile.

By the end of the day I felt almost ready to quit. I had managed to clear a section of shelves that covered the whole wall of one side of the cupboard, although I had just dumped everything on top of the piles on the already cluttered floor. I then began the gruelling task of sorting through all the piles and putting them in alphabetical order on the shelves and I was still only about a third of the way through.

I had about a hundred paper cuts, I'd inhaled so much dust I'd developed a cough and Dr Reynolds had not said a word to me all day. No, he asked me for a coffee once. I genuinely thought Miles was just teasing this morning, I didn't realise how accurate he would be but I decided I wouldn't be beaten. And I certainly couldn't let Miles know he was right. I would finish the cupboard as quickly as I could and then pester Dr Reynolds until I started to learn something. Inside his stern exterior surely there would be a softer light-hearted character? Even if there weren't I decided that I would force one out of him. I'd been so excited about this job, so looking forward to learning more, I wasn't going to give up yet.

I put the last folder of the pile in its rightful place and walked back into the office.

Reynolds looked at me expectantly.

"It's 5 o'clock," I said hesitantly.

He looked at his watch. "So it is. See you tomorrow." Then he looked back down to his computer screen without another word.

I was rummaging through my handbag trying to find my car keys when I once again slammed straight into someone. I stepped back and looked up to see it was the attractive builder from the day of my interview.

"We've got to stop meeting like this." He laughed. His voice was lower than I had expected.

"Oh God," I groaned but smiled. "How cliché."

He looked me up and down the same way he did before and smiled. It was more of a cheeky smirk than a smile. He looked like trouble.

He stuck out a paint covered hand. "Caleb."

"Lila," I said, shaking it.

He chuckled. "Most people introduce themselves as Doctor or Professor around here."

I nodded. "Not me yet. I'm just the Doctor's lapdog apparently." My tone was more bitter than I had intended it to be and he raised an eyebrow.

"Are you new then? I haven't seen you around before and I think I definitely would have remembered you."

*Was he flirting?*

"Yep, it's my first day and I've been filing a messy cupboard all day. What are you doing here?" I decided against flirting back.

"We're building an extension out the back, almost finished now though we're onto the interior. Anyway, I'd better get going, hopefully see you around." He smiled that playful smile again and I swear my heart actually fluttered a little bit.

"Yep, see you!" I said and walked away. He probably thought I was the most boring person ever. Still, I walked to my car with a smile on my face.

The week passed incredibly slowly. On Tuesday I continued tidying the cupboard, this time I asked Reynolds if he wanted a cup of coffee to which he responded with a nod so he didn't actually have to say anything to me all day. On Wednesday I saw Caleb from across the carpark, who waved when he saw me hurrying inside and that was the peak of excitement for that day. I didn't manage to tidy the cupboard as quickly as I had hoped and on Thursday Reynolds brought in four more cardboard boxes full.

# The Doll House

By Friday afternoon I had finished. My back ached and my fingers were covered in plasters but I was finished. I stood back and looked at my masterpiece. The cupboard did not have a single item on the floor.

"Would you like to come and see the finished product?" I said with a nervous smile.

He looked up as if he had forgotten I was there and then stood slowly and walked to the cupboard.

Today his hair looked a bit more natural and he wore a grey pinstripe suit and a black tie. I stared at him trying to figure out how old he was when he cleared his throat and raised his eyebrows.

I quickly looked away and stepped to the side with my arms gesturing inside the cupboard.

"Tada!" I sang.

He looked inside and then walked into the middle turning in a full circle. He *actually* smiled at me.

"This is great Lila. Thank you."

I sighed in relief. "You're welcome." I explained the order of the folders which were just exactly how he had told me to do it.

"Perfect," he said then turned and sat back down at his desk.

I thought it was now or never, get to know him and hopefully learn something or forever be the lapdog.

"So what is it that you're working on at the moment?" I asked.

He looked at me for a bit too long, clearly thinking whether to actually divulge this information or make me clean out his desk.

To my surprise, the corner of his mouth twitched into a slight smile. "Would you like to see something interesting?"

"Always."

He pulled a manila folder out from the top drawer of his desk, handed it to me and I read the two words on the cover.

*"Patient Zero."*

"I have been reviewing an old patient file recently, I call him Patient Zero to protect his anonymity, it's an extremely sensitive and confidential case and it's still ongoing so we must keep all the information discussed here today in the workplace only. Understood?"

I nodded.

"Zero was incredibly young when he developed what was diagnosed back then as Paranoid Schizophrenia, do you know much about the disorder?" Reynolds regarded me closely as he asked this question.

"A little, we touched on it at university." I was hoping he would continue talking but he just looked at me expectantly.

I continued, "I know it's the most common type of schizophrenia and each case is completely unique, diagnosed by the experience of delusions and hallucinations, particularly hearing voices."

He nodded. "Exactly. However, the American Psychiatric Association has now chosen to eliminate schizophrenia subtypes. The symptoms that were being used to categorise the different subtypes of schizophrenia were not concrete enough because of how unique each case is. The association believed that the subtypes of schizophrenia should be removed because they didn't appear to help with providing better treatments for the patients. So, we now diagnose them with generalised schizophrenia and with proper treatment, a person with the illness can have a normal and high quality of life."

I nodded but didn't respond again in hope that he would continue and this time he did.

"At an incredibly young age Zero was experiencing extreme symptoms. Paranoia, delusions that people were following him or were out to get him, hearing voices, slurred speech. He started showing symptoms at 17 and was diagnosed at 19. At 21 he was arrested on suspicion of the murder of a fellow classmate."

I gasped. "God, what happened?"

"Zero was on a high dosage of antipsychotics, his symptoms had subsided and he had been doing remarkably well. He got into university and from what I gather he was a highly intelligent young man. He was studying engineering at Oxford University and was achieving high grades. During his second year he developed a relationship with a fellow student. For the sake of anonymity let's call her Sophie. It was going well at first and then, according to Sophie's friends, Zero became overly possessive and controlling. Every time she went out he was paranoid that she was cheating, every time she picked her phone up he believed she was messaging other men or messaging her friends making fun of him. Eventually she ended their relationship after he took all the clothes from her wardrobe that he believed to be too revealing and burned them. He had come off of his medication by this time of course but apparently Sophie had never even known that he had the illness in the first place."

I was nodding, guilty to be so engrossed in the story that was somebody's real life. I realised that I had subconsciously sat down on the chair opposite where Dr Reynolds sat at his desk as he continued.

"One evening the police received a distressed call from Zero claiming that he was at her flat and that there had been an accident. They arrived and found Sophie at the bottom of the stairs in a pool of blood and she was pronounced dead on the scene. Zero was arrested on suspicion of murder but after a trial was found not-guilty because all evidence pointed to it being an accident."

"And what do you think?" I asked.

He paused and looked at me intently. It was such a strong, intense look that I almost forgot all about Patient Zero for a second.

"I'm not here to make judgements on old closed trials," he said. "The trial which took its toll on Zero and made his symptoms much worse. Eventually he was detained in a psychiatric hospital and now, here is where it gets interesting."

I leaned forward.

"Fast forward a couple of years when Zero was 23 he had evidently developed another relationship with a female patient inside the psychiatric hospital where he was being detained. They were allowed to spend a lot of their time together, their favourite was arts and craft classes where apparently Zero made her a ring and asked her to marry him, to which she said yes. Once again however, the police received a distressed call after one evening a nurse went to check on them both and give them their medication."

He paused.

"The fiancée was found dead and Zero was missing."

It was a young man, he couldn't have been much older than me. I couldn't really make out his facial features from that far away, but he was wearing a logo t-shirt, an open black hoodie and baggy jeans. When he saw me staring, he got into a black BMW and drove away. I frowned. I was probably just being paranoid because of the weird doll gifts so decided not to think too much into it. I stared at his car for a few seconds longer as it drove away when I heard Stephanie come up behind me.

"What are you looking at?" she followed my gaze.

"Nothing." I said, shaking off my paranoia and giving her a smile before climbing into the taxi.

Joe's was one of my absolute favourite places, I always felt comfortable and at home here. It was a large restaurant, themed and decorated like a vintage American diner. It had booths with red leather sofas around the outside and circular tables in the middle. At the far end under an archway was the bar area with pool tables, a dartboard, a couple of game machines and a long bar with a seating area for people not eating. Tonight was especially busy.

Tom was already sat in our usual booth when we arrived. We sat down, Stephanie next to me, opposite Tom and Miles was opposite me. We eased into natural conversation and laughter and ate our meals and drank away happily. Tom and Stephanie were definitely a bit tipsier than Miles and me, even though we had drunk the same amount. We shared an amused look.

"Lila was left another doll today," Miles said.

Tom looked at me. "Is that what it was? I found it on the doorstep when I got home last night. Don't tell me this one had a rope around its neck as well."

"No, it didn't," I said. "Somebody dropped it off whilst we were sleeping, how creepy is that."

Tom and Stephanie looked at each other frowning but Miles was still sniggering.

"I wonder if your stalker takes requests. Might leave a note on the door asking for a new Rolex."

I shook my head. "It's not funny and it's not a stalker. Probably just some kids down the road picked our house at random to have a bit of fun."

Stephanie nodded, visibly relaxing as if this was a reasonable explanation.

# The Doll House

After we had finished our meals, we went to the bar area for a few more drinks and a couple games of pool. Most of our nights here ended this way; Tom, Stephanie and I drinking and playing pool and Miles off flirting with the most attractive girls he could find. It was too predictable. Tonight, he had targeted a rather pretty blonde who was sat awkwardly with a couple who had their hands all over each other. He chose wisely.

As Tom and Stephanie were building up their liquid confidence, their flirting increased and I started to feel like a spare part. Stephanie was giggling non-stop at Tom's pretty mediocre jokes and every time she laughed she'd put her hand on his arm or his knee.

"Lila those guys are looking at you." She giggled and looked pointedly in the direction of a group of guys who looked about 16.

I rolled my eyes at her, I wasn't interested in picking up some boy in a bar. Miles wandered back over with a cheesy grin on his face.

"She had to leave but I got her number," Miles said

"Surprised you didn't just leave with her," Tom replied.

"Couldn't be bothered tonight."

We all rolled our eyes.

When we got home the boys went straight to bed but I followed Stephanie into her room. We often spent evenings in each other's rooms giggling and gossiping like we were still in school. She got into her Stephanie-style pink silk pyjamas and climbed into bed. I laid down on the end of it.

"So, c'mon then," I said. "Tell me all about it."

"I don't know what you're talking about," she said with a wry smile, still slightly tipsy.

"You like Tom." I said smiling, it wasn't a question.

"Don't be stupid, I just get on with him the same as you do," she said but her cheeks turned a bright shade of pink.

I smacked her with a pillow and she laughed.

"Since when did we lie to each other?" I raised my eyebrows.

"Alright." She sighed and began to ramble. "It's a slight crush. Maybe more than a crush, but I doubt he feels the same because we're so different, literally polar opposite personalities and also we live together so it would be too complicated. If anything were to go wrong it would ruin a great friendship and make things awkward around the house."

I shook my head. "You're mad if you think he doesn't like you, and nothing is complicated until you make it complicated."

She went to speak but I interrupted. "Don't stop yourself like you usually do, just see where things go."

She nodded. "Alright. It's early days yet."

"Steph we've lived together for over three years it's hardly early days."

"You know what I mean, early days since I've felt like this. Anyway, enough about me, what's going on with the men in your life?" she wiggled her eyebrows.

"Alright time for bed." I laughed and stood up to leave the room.

As I was leaving the door Steph said, "Miles is single."

I stopped and turned to face her. "Miles is always single."

"He likes you."

"You're drunk."

"I'm serious!"

I shook my head, laughing. "This is because you want the four of us to pair off and go on double dates."

"He's really lovely and caring, good-looking and he makes you laugh more than anyone else does."

"You can't be serious?"

"Why not?"

"It's Miles!"

She just stared at me.

I shook my head again. "No thank you. I know where he's been. Now go to sleep."

Sunday morning the four of us stood in the kitchen looking for food.

"Right this is stupid, Steph we're going food shopping," I said.

"It's the boys turn!" Stephanie groaned, once again nursing a hangover.

"No way, last time they went they came back with a whole chicken and two tins of baked beans."

The boys looked at each other smiling.

Stephanie poured herself a coffee and said, "Then we'll have to make do with what we've got." Then walked out of the kitchen.

"Fine, I'll go on my own," I said.

"You're the best. You shop we'll cook," said Miles and he kissed me on top of my head. He always did this as he was so much taller than me.

"Get all the stuff for a nice big fry up yeah?" Then he and Tom also left the kitchen.

I rolled my eyes at their backs.

We all put £10 a week in a little box on the kitchen side for food, toiletries, kitchen stuff, anything we shared the costs for. I grabbed some money out of it, took my keys off the hook and walked to my car whilst scrolling through my phone.

I stopped suddenly. I looked up and took a deep inhale of the air around me. I could smell it before I saw it.

My heart started to race but I swallowed and forced my body to relax. The soapy flowery scent of lavender was so common I told myself every time I smelt it to calm down but the scent always stirred unwelcome memories. Every time I passed a soap shop or a florist or a field full of the flower my heart would start to race. I told myself to calm down, the smell was so popular, it was just another one of those times.

I was wrong.

Placed underneath the wipers on the windshield of my car was a large bunch of lavender, tied together with a little blue bow. There was a little blue tag wrapped around it. With unwanted memories invading my thoughts, I reached out a trembling hand to read the handwritten message.

*"Lavender is for lovers true,*
*Which evermore be faine;*
*Desiring always for to have*
*Some pleasure for their paine:*
*And when that they obtained have*
*The love that they require,*
*Then have they all their perfect joie,*
*And quenched is the fire."*

I felt sick.

Katie Masterman

# Chapter Four

The door slammed behind me as I rushed back into the house.

"That was quick," Miles joked.

I just stood still as I drew in shaky breaths. I didn't understand how this could be happening, it didn't make any sense.

"Umm... I... Uh..." I stammered.

"What's wrong?" he asked, furrowing his eyebrows.

I shook my head. "Nothing. I... I don't feel well. Do the shopping yourself."

I handed him the money, pushed passed him and practically ran up the stairs to my bedroom, slamming the door behind me. I paced around the room trying to calm down. I couldn't breathe, my heart was pounding through my chest. I didn't understand. How could anyone know about this? I couldn't make any sense of the situation.

I nearly jumped out of my skin when there was a knock on my door.

"Go away!" I shouted.

"Lila, it's me," Stephanie said through the door. "Miles said that you were acting strange. He actually looked concerned which you know is not like him. What's wrong?"

"Please leave me alone." I was annoyed to hear my voice catch as I tried to stop the tears from flowing.

"Lila this isn't like you, open the door."

Realising that my annoyingly persistent best friend wasn't going to give up I wiped my eyes and opened the door. She walked in and sat on my bed without saying anything and waited for me to speak.

I looked at her for a moment and then sighed. There were no secrets between Steph and me. I passed her the note that I was still clinging to with a sweaty, shaky hand. I had left the bunch of lavender on my car.

She frowned. "What's this?"

"I just found it on my car. Read it."

She did as I said and then looked up at me.

"Is this...?"

I nodded.

"Oh Lila," she said, in a soft sympathetic voice which at this point just annoyed me.

"Don't," I snapped. "It doesn't make any sense. It was left with a bunch of lavender."

She just stared in disbelief, shaking her head.

"There's got to be a reasonable explanation," she said. "Someone else who this means something to?"

"There is no one! Just me and..." My voice caught.

She stared at me and I couldn't hold it in anymore. I let the tears flow and I cried whilst she held me and stroked my hair.

Once the tears had subsided I sniffed and sat up. "Do you mind if I can just be left alone for a while?"

"Of course, come get me if you need anything."

I nodded and climbed into bed as she closed the door behind her. I wrapped the duvet round me tightly and built up a mental wall, attempting to block the memories threatening to force their way through.

I didn't leave my room until that evening purely because I could smell food and my stomach had started to rumble. When I went downstairs, Stephanie was in the kitchen. She knew everything about my past as I grew up with her and her family, there were no secrets. But Steph was the only person I'd told every single memory down to every last detail that I could think of and so she knew the significance behind the lavender and the poem.

I sat down on one of the stools at the breakfast bar, where she had laid out a load of takeaway pizzas. A true friend.

"I knew the smell of pizza would entice you down," she smiled.

Miles walked in and grabbed a slice of pizza from in front of me but Stephanie smacked his arm and took it from him.

"That's for Lila," she said, placing it on an empty plate in front of me. "Stuffed crust is her favourite."

She rubbed my shoulder and I shrugged her off, I hated it when she made a fuss.

He gave her a quizzical look and then whispered, "Oh is it that time of the month?"

I shot him a look. "No you idiot."

"Lila received another... Um... Gift," Stephanie said.

He sniggered and through a mouthful of pizza said, "Oo was it another doll?"

I could only imagine the look that Miles received from both of us at that moment because his smile vanished almost instantly.

"It's different this time," Stephanie whispered, as if whoever had sent it was listening.

"It's nothing," I interrupted and shot her a look. "Honestly, it's nothing."

"Lila come on, we should talk about this."

"Drop it," I snapped.

Miles looked back and forth between Stephanie and me. "Okay, what's going on?"

"Please can you drop it, it's just a stupid prank and I don't want to talk about it."

"Did you get another gift?" Tom walked into the kitchen.

"If you don't tell them I will," said Stephanie. "It's gone from a meaningless prank to personal Lila."

I just put my head down on my arms as I could feel my face getting hot. I didn't want to talk about this, I didn't know how to when I didn't even understand it myself. Tears once again brewed in my eyes as I finally allowed in the memories I'd been pushing away…

"Lavender is for lovers true, which evermore be fain…" my mother sang, elongating all the notes like opera singers do except her voice was terrible.

I giggled as she continued, "Desiring for to always have, some pleasure for their pain…"

She picked me up, laughing madly, and span me round.

This was one of her good days, her happy days.

She continued spinning me around and my feet knocked the vase off the table.

"Oopsie daisies!" she laughed.

She bent down and scooped up the bunch of lavender that was now on the floor and threw it up in the air so it rained down on us. She did this again and again laughing and singing and dancing.

"And when that they obtained have, the love that they require, then have they all their perfect joie and quenched is the fire!"

Taking my silence as permission to continue, Stephanie once again lowered her voice to a whisper.

"There was a bunch of lavender left on her car with a poem written on a bit of paper," she paused, probably for dramatic affect knowing Stephanie. "Both were her mother's favourites, right Lila?"

I lifted my head up now that my tears had subsided and nodded.

I didn't really know my family history and I was too young to understand much, but from what I gathered my mother's parents had died in a car crash when she was 16 and left her the house. I guessed there was no other family to check up on her, and she lived there alone until she had me. It was small, just a little two-bedroom terraced house in Oxford but it was so cosy. The soapy, flowery scent of lavender was so powerful in the house it overpowered your senses as you stepped through the door. There must have been at least 50 vases around the house all filled with the flower. My mother even used to carry it around with her in a little pouch, I was never really sure why. The smell used to make me feel instantly at ease and at home. Not anymore.

The tears threatened to flow once again as another memory entered my mind...

I was painting a silly picture as my mother laid out on the sofa in front of me. She wasn't smiling today. She was holding a bunch of lavender under her nose and breathing heavily in and out with her eyes shut. I reached over to dip my paintbrush in a glass of water and some dripped over the carpet.

"Oopsie daisies," I giggled.

My mother jumped up and before I had time to react she grabbed the glass and poured the remaining water over my head, soaking me and the carpet around me. I gasped at the freezing water running down my face and back, clinging to my top. I looked up at her with wide eyes, teeth chattering and felt my bottom lip begin to wobble. She looked back down at me sadly, shook her head and then she laid back down and continued smelling the lavender as if nothing had happened.

"Our house was always full of Lavender," I said in a quiet voice. "On every shelf and windowsill, in pouches in all the cupboards and drawers. My mother used to carry it around with her in a little bag... You could smell it as soon as you walked in the house or even just if she was close. Her hair, her clothes, she just smelt of lavender all the time."

Miles and Tom looked at each other with different expression. Tom looked concerned and confused, Miles looked unconvinced.

"I don't buy it." Miles shrugged, "There's got to be someone who knows about that asides from you and your mother."

"There isn't!" I snapped. "In the whole seven years that I grew up in that house with my mother I never had any friends visit and I never saw my mother have any friends full stop. *Nobody* came into that house except for us. We didn't even have any family."

They were all silent. I didn't know who could possibly know about the poem or her lavender obsession.

A completely irrational thought popped into my head. Could it be her? Was she trying to communicate with me?

I shook my head, physically shaking the thought away. That was impossible, she was dead. I *knew* she was dead. Didn't I?

"Anyway, even if somebody did understand the meaning of the poem, why are they sending it to me now? I just don't understand."

Tom nodded. "Okay it does seem a bit weird at the moment but there is probably a completely reasonable explanation, we just… don't know it yet."

"I think we should call the police." said Stephanie.

We all looked at her.

"Are you mad?" I asked. "What are we supposed to say? *Oh hi, can you help I keep getting dolls and my dead mothers favourite flowers dropped at my house.*"

Miles snorted.

"Alright," Stephanie said, "but if it gets any weirder we've got to do something about it, okay?"

We all agreed.

Monday morning, I wanted to call in sick. It didn't really appeal to me to listen to Dr Reynolds talking about patients with mental illnesses but I had only been there a week. If I was lucky he'd have another cupboard for me to tidy up.

My shirts were all still in the laundry basket as I usually did the washing on Sundays but was in such a bad mood yesterday I didn't do anything except feel sorry for myself and eat pizza. I had one clean shirt which was now too small for me and was missing a top button, so not only was it low cut but also incredibly tight. I knew Stephanie only had a half day at work today so I texted her asking if she would do the washing. I looked in the mirror debating whether it was inappropriate for work and then decided I didn't really care.

"Morning," I said when I walked into the office half an hour later.

Once again Reynolds was back to dropping the niceties. "Morning. I have some handwritten notes from a lecture I attended over the weekend and I need them typing up, could you do that for me?"

I nodded and attempted small talk. "What was the lecture for?"

He looked up at me. "One of my old friends from university was leading the lecture and asked me if I'd attend as it was relevant to some research I'm currently working on."

I nodded. "Oh that's cool, what was the topic?"

"You'll figure that out when you type up the notes," he said and handed me a notebook.

It was almost an inch full of notes.

"You want me to type up the whole thing?" I asked.

"Yes, is there a problem?"

I smiled. "No, I was just making sure."

He opened a laptop and put it opposite him on his desk and pulled up a chair.

"Oh I'll be working here?" I asked, surprised.

His lips twitched into a small almost playful smile. "Lots of questions today Lila."

"Sorry." I smiled and sat down as he sat opposite me. We looked at each other for a second before we both turned our attention down to our laptops.

I wasn't sure what he was doing all day, probably typing up notes as well because he seemed to be typing on his laptop for ages. Every now and then he would mumble something to himself.

My neck and shoulders ached and I was incredibly bored. We'd hardly made any conversation at all. I took back my earlier wish and hoped that tomorrow we were working on Patient Zero again. I was only about a third of the way through the notebook by the end of the day. When I walked out of the office I was in a mood. I was bored of my job and I was worrying there was going to be something left on my car for me, so when I heard a wolf whistle from behind me in the carpark I was less than impressed.

I turned around with a death stare to see Caleb stood on some scaffolding with a couple of his builder friends who were laughing. One of them wolf whistled again. I now regretted the lowcut tight shirt. I gave them my best evils, shook my head and got into my car. I was not in the mood.

The next day at work again dragged by, but on the upside by the end of the day I had finished typing up the notebook. My previous mood had thankfully evaporated, although still bored by work, the house had done a good job of cheering me up last night. I was just about to get into my car when I heard my name.

"Lila?"

I turned around to see Caleb standing there, as scruffy and handsome as ever.

I didn't say anything and he continued, "Sorry about yesterday, my friends have the combined mental age of a 12-year-old."

I tried not to smile but I failed. "It's okay. I was in a bad mood anyway."

A playful smile grew on his lips. "I could tell, if looks could kill I would have fallen straight off my ladder."

I shook my head. "It wasn't that bad!"

I looked over to where he was working yesterday. "Looks like you're nearly finished?"

He nodded, "Yeah, I'll only be here another week or so."

I couldn't help but feel disappointed at that and just hoped that it didn't show on my face. I nodded and we stood there slightly awkwardly. He seemed to always have an amused look on his lips that made his eyes glisten.

I reached for my door handle and he said, "I was just wondering if you wanted to go for a drink?"

"Really?" I blurted.

He laughed, "Yeah. What, you only go out with Doctors?"

I snorted, "No I mean, I don't even know you."

He shrugged and smirked. "So, get to know me."

I frowned unable to keep the smile off my face and looked at him for a second. "Um, I'll give you my number?"

He nodded and I put it into his phone.

"I'll text you later then." He winked and walked away.

When I got home I was still smiling. I walked into the living room where the rest of the house were sat watching tv.

"You're smiling. What's happened?" Stephanie sat up.

"Why does something need to have happened?" I smirked.

She raised her eyebrows. "Did something happen with the sexy doctor?"

"No of course it didn't!" I laughed. "Sexy builder on the other hand..."

"I knew it!"

"He asked me for a drink and I gave him my number that's all."

She squealed excitedly and the boys rolled their eyes. "Has he text you yet?"

I had purposely not checked my phone on the way home but I did then. I was disappointed to see no text had come through.

"No not yet, but I've just got home and he only asked me as I was getting into my car."

"How romantic," she giggled and the boys rolled their eyes again.

We were halfway through a film when my phone buzzed and Stephanie squealed again making Tom jump and frown in her direction.

"I bet that's him!"

I laughed and checked my phone and saw that she was correct.

"Hope this isn't a fake number. Drinks tomorrow night after work? C."

I read the message out loud and Tom put his hand over Stephanie's mouth before she could squeal again.

"Reply!"

I rolled my eyes and said, "For god's sake Steph we're adults."

Although, I did actually feel a twinge of excitement.

I text back. "Sounds good. See you at 5. L."

Katie Masterman

# Chapter Five

Stephanie helped me get ready that morning as I would be going straight after work for the drink with Caleb. I wore a black skirt and a red strappy top with red heels, appropriate both for work and for a drink. Of course, Steph insisted on doing my hair whilst I sat listening to her rambling on about how I should act on the date. I decided I was just going to be myself.

I finished typing up the last of the notes in yet another giant notebook that Dr Reynolds had handed me that morning and looked up from over my laptop.

He was sat opposite me, looking down and continuously typing on his laptop. His beard and hair both again groomed to perfection. He was wearing a black shirt today with a black tie and I again noticed how handsome he was. I so wanted to ask him how old he was, I'd have to get it into conversation somehow.

He must have felt my gaze on him and he looked up at me.

"I've finished typing up the notes." I smiled.

"Excellent thank you." He smiled back.

"I was wondering if you had done any more research into the Patient Zero case."

He closed his laptop and pulled the file out of the drawer.

"Where did we leave it?"

"Well you told me that a nurse had found his fiancé dead and that he was missing."

"Ah yes." His eyes glimmered. "But what I didn't tell you was that a few weeks later he was found."

"Oh." I said, surprised. He must have left that out for dramatic effect. It worked.

"He was found trying to enter his old university, when the police arrived to arrest him he was almost unrecognisable. He was still in the clothes from the day he left, he was dirty and had let his beard grow out. He was rambling about how he needed to 'avenge' the only woman he had ever loved."

"He was obviously having delusions again then. Do we know about his childhood? I wonder what happened to him." I asked.

"What do you mean?"

"Well, I mean, I wonder what happened to him as a child that could have caused the onset of all of these delusions." I said, unsure.

"So you believe schizophrenia is caused by some sort of childhood trauma?" he asked.

"Well, it usually is isn't it?" I was racking my brain trying to remember the lectures from university but typically my mind went blank.

"You tell me," he sniped and I frowned at his snappy tone.

"Well obviously there must be other factors as well, but in the case of most mental illnesses they are caused by childhood events, poverty, abuse, trauma etc."

"Well not in this case. He had happy, loving childhood, his mother doted on him, he went to university and was getting good grades and he was in a relationship. So what caused the sudden change?"

"I don't know," I whispered.

"Of course, you are correct." he said and I breathed a sigh of relief, "but you have to remember that childhood events aren't the only cause of schizophrenia when there is such hard evidence pointing to a biological link."

I nodded and he continued, "That is why antipsychotics are prescribed, they prohibit the receptors in the brain from releasing too much dopamine which is linked to schizophrenia."

"Okay, that makes sense. So that must have been the case with Patient Zero? A biological malfunction?"

Was that what it was with my mother? A biological malfunction? Or maybe it's both. Maybe we all have that biological malfunction, like a gun in Russian roulette. Sometimes a trauma may not trigger anything, sometimes it does. I had always assumed the death of both my mother's parents had triggered her Bipolar, but maybe she was just always destined to have it.

"Possibly." Reynolds stared at me. "Maybe he was just misunderstood."

"He killed two of his girlfriends I don't think there's any misunderstanding there," I said.

"He was never found guilty."

"But it's obvious that he did it."

Katie Masterman

"We mustn't make assumptions." He shook his head and looked at the clock on the wall. It was 5pm already. I wanted to carry on the conversation but at least I had meeting Caleb to look forward to.

I waited in the carpark for Caleb. It felt like I waited there for ages as the fluttering of butterflies progressively worsened in the pit of my stomach, but it was probably only a couple of minutes before he arrived.
"You look nice," he smiled.
"So do you," I said and I meant it.
This was the first time that I had seen him out of his work clothes. There was no paint in his hair or plaster over his clothes. No baggy work trousers and chunky builders' boots. He was in black jeans and a white polo shirt, his tattoos showed on his biceps and forearms and I wondered how many more he had.
My face obviously portrayed my feelings about my earlier conversation with Reynolds because he looked at me and raised an eyebrow. "If you didn't want to come out with me you could have just said no."
Typical men assuming everything is about them.
I smiled and shook my head. "It's not you. I'm fine."
He looked at me with a tilted head but then shrugged and said, "Alright, I know a nice place. We both have our cars so you can follow me."

I followed him for only about 15 minutes through rural oxford until he stopped at this secluded little cottage with a thatched roof and ivy climbing up the walls. It looked like it had been taken straight out of a fairy-tale. We parked up, got out of our cars and I followed him round the back straight towards the garden. It was winter so it was already getting dark but this made the garden more beautiful. It was truly spectacular; it was full of round wooden picnic style tables with lanterns in the middle lit up with candles. Surrounding the tables were green fir trees with fairy lights entwined between the branches and there was a pond with a beautiful lit up fountain in the middle. It was cosy and romantic.
"Wow," I breathed.
"I love it here," he said and suddenly I wondered how many other girls he had brought to this place.
We ordered our drinks; he had a beer and I had a glass of red wine and then we sat at one of the empty tables in the garden. A breeze whipped

around my neck and I was thankful for the heaters placed above each table. As it got darker it got more beautiful, lit by the soft glow of the fairy lights and flicker of the warm candles.

"It really is a beautiful place." I looked around.

He nodded, "Are you hungry? They do good food."

I shook my head but my stomach decided to rumble at that exact moment.

He raised his eyebrows and then called over one of the waiters and ordered us a platter of antipasti and nibbles to share. I was impressed already.

"Do you want to talk about why you were upset earlier?" he asked.

"Not particularly. I'd like to know more about you though."

"What did you want to know?"

"Anything, I don't know anything about you." I smiled.

He took a sip of his beer as he was thinking. "I'm the youngest brother of four boys, dad died when I was 4 but our mum raised us and she's the best, comes up to about here on me," he smiled at the thought and gestured at his shoulder height and continued, "I've lived in Oxford all my life, I wanted to become a pro-footballer like every other kid but ended up in construction which is fine. My favourite colour's blue, favourite drink is beer, favourite food is Indian."

I laughed and he said, "Was that a good enough summary?"

"Definitely, I feel like I completely know you now."

"Good. Now it's your turn, take the floor," he smiled his signature playful smirk.

I sighed and paused, sipping my drink.

"I don't have any siblings, I live with three friends who are idiots but they're my family. I've also lived in Oxford all my life, I'm trying to become a psychologist but at the moment I'm just a lapdog, and yeah... that's pretty much it."

"So do you want to become like a therapist and get paid £200 an hour to listening to people's problems?"

I chuckled, "No, I want to be a research psychologist. Chambers offers a couple of people every year a grant to conduct some studies and write up the research with the chance of becoming published, that's what I'd like to do."

He seemed genuinely interested which I was surprised at so I continued, "I'm starting to see a bit of research now with Dr Reynolds. He's published some pretty interesting stuff. We're going over a schizophrenia case at the moment actually which is kind of disturbing."

We easily chatted for ages. It was all light-hearted and casual, just learning about each other. It was new and exciting and flirtatious and it was exactly what I needed to take my mind off everything going on at the moment.

It had now gotten completely dark and the warm and cosy ambience paired with the sound of the water fountain made me feel quite sleepy. A cool breeze brushed my back and I shivered.

"Are you cold?" he asked.

"Only a little." I smiled.

"I would do the cliché thing and offer you my jacket but..." He was only wearing a t-shirt himself.

I laughed. "It's fine. We should probably head back anyway, I don't really like driving in the dark."

"Bloody women drivers," he smirked and I smacked him on the arm.

"Excuse me, I witnessed your driving following you here and I don't think you can say much about mine."

He snorted and shook his head. We finished the last of our now non-alcoholic drinks and he walked me to my car.

He opened up the door for me and said, "I'll probably see you at work but we should definitely do this again."

I agreed and smiled the whole way home.

I pulled up alongside my house and stopped the car. I reached for my handbag when something caught my attention and I stopped and looked up. A young man stood across the road looking directly towards my car.

I frowned as I tried to figure out where I recognised him from. I sat in my seat looking at him for a while, neither of moving and then it clicked. I was certain that was the guy that was watching me when we were getting into the taxi the other day.

I slowly got out of the car and looked towards him. He was closer this time so I could see his facial features. He looked quite young, maybe about the same age as me if not younger. He had on a logo t-shirt again, baggy jeans and his hair looked quite greasy even from where I was standing. He stared back and I hesitantly lifted my hand and waved. He stepped towards me but then stopped and looked around hesitantly. I opened my mouth to ask if he

# The Doll House

was okay when he quickly turned around, climbed back into his black BMW and drove away.

I swallowed as a thought crossed my mind. Was that who has been leaving the unwelcome gifts? Although I didn't recognise him from anywhere, how could he possibly know anything about my mother?

Maybe it was just a resident that lived on the street and he thought I was the one staring at him. I was the one who had waved after all. I shook my head and told myself to get a grip. If I kept being so paranoid about everything I was going to drive myself insane.

I walked into the house and was greeted by a smiling Stephanie holding two glasses of wine.

We sat in the living room gossiping about the night as the boys rolled their eyes. All thoughts of mental hospitals and my mother not gone but pushed aside and I was trying to just think about my night with Caleb. He was so easy to talk to, it had been a welcomed distraction.

"Is this what all girls do?" Miles asked after taking a gulp of his beer. "You go into such detail."

"Of course," I laughed. "You boys should open up more."

"Anyway, guess what happened at work today?" Stephanie said.

"What?" I asked. "And before you say it no I'm not going to guess just tell me."

She smiled. "I got asked out on a date today."

I did my best impression of a Stephanie squeal and Tom choked on his beer and started coughing. Miles patted him on the back.

"By who?" I asked.

"It's this guy who always comes into the shop. I usually only style women but he comes in for suits and stuff and we always just casually chat and then today he asked me if I wanted to go for dinner or a drink or something." She looked into her lap as her cheeks turned pink.

"Did you say yes?" Tom asked once he had recovered.

She looked at him directly in the eyes and said, "I didn't see any reason not to." Although it sounded like a question.

He nodded and took another swig of beer, directing his attention towards the television. Miles looked at me and shook his head and I knew exactly what he was thinking. *Idiots*.

# Chapter Six

The rest of the week at work dragged by as I just did general administration jobs. Friday morning when I walked into the building Annie waved me over.

"Morning Lila. Dr Reynolds isn't in today but he asked if you wouldn't mind following these instructions." She held out a piece of paper.

I groaned and she laughed. "It's okay it doesn't look too bad."

"Thanks," I smiled and took the piece of paper and read it out loud to myself whilst walking towards the office.

"Type up notes in blue book in top drawer. Holepunch and file everything in grey cabinet behind desk. Create advert recruiting participants to take part in a study, details on whiteboard."

"You had better watch where you're going else you'll bump into someone again." I looked up to see Caleb smirking.

"True I'd better be careful, the last person I bumped into keeps asking me out. Just can't seem to shake him off."

"Oh is that how it is? I was going to ask if you wanted to come for a drink with me and my friends after work too but I won't now."

"See?" I said and carried on walking. "Just can't shake him off."

He changed his direction and walked with me towards Dr Reynolds' office.

"C'mon it'll be fun."

I feigned consideration for a minute and then smiled. "Alright but if your friends are coming can mine come as well?"

"Only if they're attractive females like yourself," he said and dodged as I attempted to swat his arm.

"We were already planning on going to Joe's diner tonight so you can meet us there?"

"Never been but sounds good." We arrived at Reynold's office and Caleb whispered, "Have fun with the doctor."

"He's not in today."

"Oo I want to see his office."

# The Doll House

Before I could say anything he had walked in before me.

"Christ, smells like a hospital room in here."

I sniggered because I agreed. "Creepy isn't it."

He looked around at the neat rows of pens and notebooks and ran his finger over a shelf. "Yeah I mean you could actually perform surgery in here. Does he have OCD or something?"

"I know have you ever seen somewhere so clean?"

Before I could react he walked over to where I was standing and pressed me lightly against the wall. He bent his head down so that his lips were unbearably close to mine and my pulse quickened.

"Maybe we should make it less clean?" he murmured, mischief in his eyes.

I pushed my hand on his chest and snorted. "In your dreams."

He backed away and chuckled, "Oh it will be."

I rolled my eyes at his caveman behaviour and he sat down at the desk. "So this is what it feels like to be rich? It's not for me I don't think. Doesn't he have any friends or family?"

I had also noticed that there were no photographs in the room. He didn't wear a ring either.

"I guess not. He's never mentioned anyone but then we don't really talk so, I don't know."

"So what are you doing today if he's not here."

I held up my piece of paper. "Oh don't worry, he wouldn't leave me without a list of jobs to do."

He got up and walked over to where I was standing.

"You can come help me on the extension if you like. We're fitting the lights today it's extremely exciting."

I tilted my head to the side. "Hm as fun as that sounds I think I'll stay here and do this."

He patted me on the head and smirked, "There's a good lapdog. I'll see you later."

After Caleb left I was in such a good mood that my incredibly boring day actually went quite quickly. When I left the office I was still in a good mood, excited to go home and get ready for Joe's. That was, until I got to my car.

This time, on top of my car, was a parcel. Again, it was wrapped in blue paper with a delicate blue bow on top. I looked around but couldn't see anyone suspicious. Hairs stood up on the back of my neck and I stiffened as

I felt eyes on me, as though whoever was responsible for the gifts was watching me, waiting for a reaction. I wouldn't give them the satisfaction. I decided not to open it, I would wait until I was home with the others.

With shaky hands I threw the unopened box into the passenger seat and climbed in, heart racing. I knew I was driving recklessly but I wasn't concentrating, my mind reeled with unanswered questions. I was trying to figure out who was sending me these gifts, why they were sending them and what the hell this new one was going to be. Were they linked to my mum or was it just a *huge* coincidence?

When I got home I walked into the kitchen. Miles was stood in his gym gear drinking a protein shake and Tom was sat at the breakfast bar on his laptop. I placed the parcel heavily in front of him and Miles came over to have a closer look.

"What is it this time?" Tom asked.

"I don't know. Where's Steph?"

"She's having a shower."

I just nodded and chewed on the inside of my lip.

"Do you want me to go and get her?" he asked.

"No, it's fine."

I stood still, my eyes never straying from the beautifully wrapped parcel.

"For god's sake Lila just open it or I will," Miles said. "You're thinking too much into this, it's just a prank."

I huffed and then ripped open the present. When I took the lid off the box the smell of lavender instantly attacked my senses and my heart thudded painfully in my chest. I held my breath and looked into the box then gasped and covered my mouth with a trembling hand.

Miles put his hand on my shoulder and looked in. We looked down at yet another doll, laying in a bed of blue tissue paper. There was no rope or bruising around this dolls neck. This time, the dolls eyes were closed, its long eyelashes flailing out across its rosy cheeks. It looked much more peaceful than the others and yet looking down at its face still sent a shiver down my spine. She was wearing normal clothes, just a black dress and black pumps.

Around her head however, this doll had a headband made purely of lavender entwined intricately together. Once again, a memory of my mother flashed in my mind…

# The Doll House

I was lying in bed when she came bouncing in, grinning wildly. Today my mother was having a good day.

"Good morning, Princess," she sang and sat next to me stroking my head. I could smell lavender as soon as she sat down, it made me feel safe. At home. I snuggled my head into her lap when she pulled back.

"Look what I made us!" She beamed at me, and from behind her back pulled two matching headbands made of lavender. She placed one on her head and then the other on mine.

"We match mummy!" I giggled.

"Exactly. Two headbands fit for a queen and her princess. These will keep us safe."

I didn't know what she meant, I was simply happy to have a pretty flowery headband.

"What is it Lila?" I wasn't sure which one of the boys asked.

I just shook my head, unable to speak.

Stephanie came in at this moment, dressed in a pink dressing gown with her hair wrapped in a towel. She looked into the box and then looked up at me. I had completely forgotten about this memory so hadn't mentioned it to her before, she wouldn't understand the meaning behind this doll.

They were all silent and I took a breath and swallowed.

"My mother," my voice came out as a whisper, "she used to make us these headbands."

They all exchanged glances and Stephanie said, "We should call the police."

In unison we all shook our heads.

"Whoever is doing this isn't breaking the law." Tom said, "None of the gifts are threatening in any way and they haven't even trespassed or anything to get them to Lila."

Miles made a noise of agreement and took my hands in his. "I know it's creepy and it's bringing back horrible memories and we will get to the bottom of who is doing this, but the police won't be interested."

"I just don't understand." I sniffed. "Of course I miss my mother every single day, but I hadn't properly thought of her in years and now all of a sudden I'm receiving all these gifts significant to her? It doesn't make sense."

"Are you sure there is nobody who knew your mother like you did? What about –" she stopped and looked down at her hands, playing awkwardly with her fingers.

"What about...?" I prompted.

She looked up at me and then down again, not meeting my eyes. "What about your dad?" she almost whispered.

I shook my head. "I'm almost certain my father was just a one-night-stand and has no idea that I even exist and like I said before, my mother didn't have any friends."

We were all silent, I thought for a while whether to tell them my theory behind it all, but I decided against it. They would think I was being ridiculous, and I almost definitely was. There was no logical explanation that ended in these gifts being sent from my mother and yet I couldn't get the thought out of my head.

"There's nothing else we can do at the moment," said Miles, his hand squeezed my shoulder. "We just have to keep ignoring them until they get bored and stop, which I guarantee they will."

I nodded. Stephanie chewed her fingernail and looked up at me with concerned eyes, so I forced a smile.

"You're right, I'm sure it's nothing. Probably all just a coincidence." I sounded as though I was trying to convince myself more than them.

I couldn't bring myself to look at the doll and I turned away from it to get a glass of water. I told myself to breathe and calm down, we would figure this out. Tom was right, there was nothing threatening about the dolls, they hadn't broken the law. Whoever it was, just wanted me to have some gifts.

I could hear the sound of tissue paper rustling and I turned around to see Tom clearing the parcel away.

"Thank you." I smiled.

I flinched as my phone buzzed on the countertop. I was so on edge all because of a couple of dolls, it was ridiculous. I picked up my phone and read the text that had come through and even in the midst of everything I still couldn't hide my smile.

"Oo is that sexy builder?" Miles mimicked Stephanie's voice and she slapped him on his massive arm.

"It is actually. I forgot to mention but Caleb and his friends want to meet us at Joe's tonight."

Miles gave Tom a look and said, "You think Caleb and his friends want to meet us?"

"Well I said if his friends were going I wanted to bring mine and he seemed up for it..."

Miles snorted. "Yeah that's probably because he thinks your friends are girls Lila."

Stephanie said, "Oh well, I'm up for it."

"Me too I'll go," said Tom a bit too quickly and then looked away.

Miles rolled his eyes and I said, "It's okay Miles you can come say hello and then prey on some defenceless girl like usual."

He nodded seriously. "Sounds like a plan."

"Taxi's here!" Miles called up the stairs.

Stephanie was in my room and had just finished curling my hair. She stood back to admire her work.

"Perfect," she said.

I was perfectly capable of curling my own hair and she knew that but she insisted on doing it anyway, as well as my makeup and helping me choose what to wear.

I had gone with black high waisted jeans, black heels and a baby blue low-cut top. I looked at Steph who looked drop dead gorgeous as usual, she wore a pink leather skirt, white heels and a white top.

As we walked downstairs I gave her a playful smile. "So, who are you trying to impress tonight?"

She gave me a look. "Nobody."

"Mm-hmm," I laughed, we both knew it was for Tom.

The boys were already waiting for us in the taxi when we climbed in.

"Well don't you ladies look lovely," Miles said.

"Don't we always?" Stephanie flicked her hair.

The journey to Joe's was only a couple of minutes but we could never be bothered to walk, especially in heels. When we arrived, we all climbed out and I pulled out my phone to text Caleb to say we had arrived.

When I looked up, I stiffened as I saw the same black BMW as before. I looked around and then mentally shook myself, I knew I was just being paranoid. There were thousands of black BMWs in Oxford.

"Are you coming, Lila?" Miles called, but I was staring as the front door of the car opened and out climbed the same young man as before.

He hadn't seen me yet, he was standing with the driver's side door open looking at his phone. I felt Miles walk up beside me.

"What's up?" he asked, and then followed my gaze to the man. "Lila?"

"That guy is following me," I whispered.

I almost heard his eyes roll. "You're being paranoid because of the dolls Lila."

Somehow, this time I knew I wasn't. He was following me.

I took a step towards him and Miles placed a strong hand on my upper arm and pulled me back, I looked up at him. "Miles, he's following me. He was outside our house the other day and now he's here. What if he's the one that's been leaving the dolls?"

He looked between me and him, sighed and then called, "Excuse me mate?"

For god's sake. The man in front of us had potentially been stalking me and gifting me creepy dolls connected to my dead mother and Miles calls him *mate*.

He looked up, looked at me and nearly dropped his phone. He then quickly got into his car, slammed the door and drove away.

I glared at Miles. "Great, thanks."

He snorted. "He can afford a new beamer and yet all he gives you is a couple of crappy dolls and some lavender?"

I frowned at him and then walked away and he followed me.

"Lila..."

"This isn't funny." I snapped, still walking. "I know you think it's a joke but it's not."

I stopped suddenly and turned around to face him and he almost ran into me.

"Something just doesn't feel right about all of this Miles. It doesn't add up and it's more serious than you're making it out to be I can just feel it." My voice grew louder. "How can it possibly not be personal?"

"Alright Lila if you say so." He reached out to pull me into a hug but I stepped back.

He rolled his eyes. "Oh come o-"

"No Miles, it's all too coincidental to be a prank you've got to see that."

He reached out to me again but I slapped his hand away.

He huffed. "Lila-"

"Is there a problem here?"

# The Doll House

We both turned to see Caleb. He looked as good as always except his usual playful smile was replaced with a cold stare, his lips pressed together and his jaw tensed. His eyes were fixed on Miles.

"Oh hi, Miles this is Caleb," I said quickly. "Caleb, this is Miles. We live together. Not just us, with two other people. We're friends."

The corner of Miles' mouth twitched and Caleb raised an eyebrow.

Miles shook Caleb's hand. "Nice to meet you mate, I'll see you both inside." His eyes briefly met mine before he jogged towards the bar.

"Lovers tiff?" Caleb smirked.

"It's not like that." I snapped.

"I know I'm only joking." His eyebrows pulled together. "You okay?"

I sighed and turned away and stalked towards Joe's. "I need a drink."

Katie Masterman

# Chapter Seven

Caleb had brought three friends with him, one of which had brought along his girlfriend. We had completed our introductions, bought drinks and sat happily chatting in the bar area of Joe's, by the pool table. It wasn't awkward at all, Stephanie and Tom were sat chatting away to the couple whom I now knew were called Liam and Eve. Miles was talking to the other two of Caleb's friends, Max and Dom, about football and I was sat with Caleb. I couldn't help but notice Miles' gaze kept flicking in my direction.

I took a sip of my red wine that Caleb had insisted on buying for me and sighed.

"You seem to always have something on your mind," he said.

"I know, it's only recently, I'm not usually so... cloudy." I shrugged.

"Cloudy?" he raised an eyebrow in amusement.

"Yeah, cloudy, you know." I gestured to the invisible cloud of gloom that I imagined was around my head.

"Do you want to talk about it?"

I considered it. I did want to talk to him about it but it was quite personal and a lot to tell someone you didn't really know yet.

I shook my head and smiled, "No I'm okay."

"So this is the lovely lady you've been banging on about."

We both looked up to see Max and Dom smiling down at us. Max was a very good-looking guy, not as good-looking as Caleb, but still attractive. He looked about my age, had dark hair and dark eyes and a nice olive complexion. He was wearing black jeans and a plain white t-shirt and he wore the same playful smile that Caleb seemed to always have on his lips. Dom was less strikingly attractive but he was cute. He had long floppy blonde hair and was wearing camel coloured chinos with a black turtleneck. He had a nice smile too, more kind than playful.

I looked around for Miles who was talking to them before. I didn't have to look far, he was stood at the bar chatting up a busty brunette. My stomach tensed which I put down to my earlier annoyance at him.

"I only mentioned her once," Caleb argued and I looked back towards them.

"Want to play pool?" Max asked him.

By this point I had a few glasses of wine so my confidence was at a higher level than normal.

"Why don't we play doubles?" I said.

They shrugged and set up the pool-balls as we gathered around the table.

Max snorted and patted Caleb on the back. "You can have the girl on your team."

Caleb looked at me with uncertainty as if I was another one of those girls who didn't know how to hold a pool cue.

I played along. "They're just scared we will beat them. So what's the aim of the game?"

Caleb rolled his eyes but smiled his playful smile that I liked so much. "We've just got to pot all our coloured balls with the white ball, but don't pot the white or the black okay?"

I nodded, trying not to laugh. *Men.*

"Shall we make it a bet? Next round is on the losers?" I said trying to keep a straight face.

Dom snorted, "That sounds like a great idea."

Caleb sighed and then he bent over the table, smacked the white ball into the triangle of balls and potted a yellow. Max potted a red and then narrowly missed the pocket on his next shot. He looked towards me and said, "Just try your best okay?"

I looked at Caleb and winked and he narrowed his eyes at me. I took the cue and went on to pot three yellow balls and then sneakily hide the white behind another yellow so that they were snookered.

I batted my eyelashes at the boys and put on a fake girly voice. "Was that good enough?"

Caleb snorted, "You know how to play."

We went on to win the game. Caleb patted Max and Dom on the back and said, "That will be a pint of lager and a red wine for the winners please."

We sat with our drinks and fell easily again into chatter and laughter. These boys were funny together, bouncing off each other's jokes and bantering each other. I was trying my best to feel at ease and push all my worries out of my mind. It definitely helped that Caleb's hand had gradually made its way to my knee and sat halfway up my thigh. He gave it a light squeeze.

"You've made a good impression tonight," he purred into my ear. "They like you."

I smiled to myself and tried to hide my shiver of pleasure at his voice in my ear.

"Now it's your turn," I grinned as Tom and Stephanie pulled up chairs to join us.

I could tell Stephanie had grabbed Max's attention straight away. He was looking at her with lust-filled eyes and rightly so, she looked incredible.

"Lila you didn't tell me your best friend was so beautiful," Max said.

Stephanie blushed and let out a small giggle. "Thank you."

Tom stuck his hand out. "I'm Tom."

Max shook it and looked between them. "Ah I see, are you the boyfriend?"

"No!" They both said at the same time.

"Then I can buy you drink?" he asked as he looked back at Steph with a playful smile on his lips.

Steph actually looked towards Tom as if asking for his permission. If anything told the world she liked him it was that and if this boy had any sense he would use the moment to finally admit to his feelings.

But Tom just looked away, focussing intently on his beer.

Hurt flashed across her face but she shook it off and gave Max her most flirtatious smile and then they left towards the bar together. Tom watched them walk away with a scowl.

"Sheesh I wouldn't let that one get away mate," Dom said.

Tom's eyes flicked to mine as a signal to change the subject but I joined in. "You are being an idiot Tom, I can't believe you let her go and get a drink with him."

"Can you just drop it." He looked away.

"Just a warning mate, if Max buys a girl a drink he usually ends up making them breakfast the next morning if you know what I'm saying," Dom said.

Tom's innocent eyes widened. "Yes I know what you mean thanks."

"She likes you, you idiot," I said.

"You think I don't know that?" he snapped, meeting my eyes now. "Look at her, Lila."

I frowned and looked over to her. She was stood at the bar with Max in that wonderful outfit that hugged to her curves and made her legs look a mile long, her silky blonde hair flowed free down her back. Max said something and she put her hand on his arm and laughed musically at whatever he said.

"I've never met someone as beautiful as her and she doesn't even know it, she doesn't use it and act like she owns the place even though she could. She's kind and thoughtful, she cares about everyone she meets as if they're her own family and I've never heard her say a bad word about anyone. She's seemingly innocent and yet has a wicked sense of humour and when she laughs..." he looked away from her and shook his head and then seemed to remember where he was. His cheeks went red and he looked up sheepishly.

I looked at the way his adoring but sad eyes were watching her. *Oh.* This wasn't just a crush. He'd fallen in love with her.

He sighed. "Then look at me, I'm not enough for her. She needs someone like Max," he groaned, "I can see the outline of his six pack from here."

"You're an even bigger idiot than I thought," I said and he looked up at me. "You've just said it yourself; she's the most kind, thoughtful and pure person we know. You think she needs someone with bulging pecs and the confidence of a naughty schoolboy?" I shook my head. "She needs someone like you Tom, your kindness, your sincerity, the way you look at her as if she lights up the room, your subtle little qualities. That's what makes her love you."

Caleb's hand squeezed my thigh again and Dom shook his head. "I think I'm going to be sick," and then he excused himself to go to the bar.

"Just give it a chance mate, can't hurt can it?" Caleb said and it warmed my heart that he was making the effort to comfort my friend.

"I will when I'm ready, thanks guys." Tom smiled and gave my hand a squeeze. I think I'm going to head home. I'll see you later."

Stephanie, Miles and I stayed until Joe's shut and stumbled through the door around 1:30am. I was surprised to see Tom was still awake, he was in the living room watching television in the dark. I think he was checking to see if Stephanie came home alone, if at all, because he headed to bed as soon as we got home.

Tom and Miles had to work over the weekend. I text Caleb asking if he wanted to do something, but he said he was busy. Instead, Stephanie and I stayed in and had a nice, chilled, girly weekend. We painted our nails, put face masks on, ate lots of chocolate, watched a couple of cheesy chick flicks.

I heard Stephanie's phone buzz a few times and when I grilled her about it she just said, "Oh it's just Max, he's really lovely but he's just not my type."

I tried to get her to talk to Tom but they were both as stubborn as each other. Nothing unusual happened, no gifts were left although I had kept looking for them and so I attempted pretty unsuccessfully to keep all thoughts of my mother out of my mind.

Monday morning came around too quickly. I had woken up a few times in the night for no apparent reason, so I felt exhausted.

"Good morning. You look tired." Reynolds said when I entered his office.

"Thank you," I chuckled.

"Busy weekend?" he asked.

I stared at him. "Dr Reynolds are you making small talk?"

He chuckled lightly. "I am human you know."

Relishing in his rare good mood I sat down at his desk. "Not really, just had a chilled weekend with my housemates. Didn't sleep well last night though." I yawned.

"You know, studies show that yawns are contagious in about 65 percent of people, but it occurs most often in people who score high on measures of empathic understanding, the same way they mimic a smile or a frown."

"So you're saying people who catch yawns are empathising with the person for being tired?"

"Exactly." He nodded.

Hm interesting.

"What did you get up to this weekend?" I attempted small talk back and to my surprise he played ball.

"I attended a couple of lectures, watched a couple of documentaries, I'm sure you'd find it all very boring."

"Do you have a family?"

He was silent but had a small almost playful smile on his lips. "Now that's a bit personal, don't you think? I don't ask you about your familial life."

I knew by his smile that he wasn't annoyed so I continued, "So you're not married?"

He shook his head and stared into my eyes, "No I'm not married, are you?"

The intensity of his stare made me pause for a second before I stammered, "No, I'm way too young."

"Oh but I'm old?" he said with humour in his eyes.

"How old are you?" I questioned.

"I'm 40 this year," he said.

"You look good for your age. I mean not that you're old! I just mean you look good, I mean young, like closer to my age." I blushed.

"I don't think 23 is too young to be married," he said.

"I do... I'm sort of seeing someone though, that's enough for me at the moment."

He nodded and slid a notepad towards me. "Anyway I've got some more notes I need to be typed up."

I frowned and joked, "We're back in work mode now are we?"

"Exactly." he said and turned his attention back down to his laptop.

I was still confused by Dr Reynolds' conflicting behaviour when I finished work. When I got to the carpark Caleb was waiting for me by my car.

"Are you stalking me?" I smiled.

He chuckled, "Just wanted to say sorry about this weekend. I was just really busy."

He looked away and I noticed that he didn't mention what he was busy doing but I let it slide. He had no obligation to tell me where he was or what he was doing.

"That's alright, another time." I smiled.

I looked at him properly then. He looked tired and he had dark circles under his eyes. I touched his arm.

"Hey," I said softly, "You okay?"

"Yeah of course," he smiled but it didn't quite reach his eyes.

"You're not acting like yourself."

He surprised me by leaning forward and kissing me on the forehead. "Come on don't psychoanalyse me now, I'm fine I promise."

I frowned and was about to protest when I saw something move out of the corner of my eye. I turned my head towards what had caught my attention and saw the same black BMW that I had seen outside my house and at Joe's. My heart instantly started to pound in my chest. The front door opened and out stepped the same young man and I knew then I wasn't being overly paranoid at all. When I looked at him then closer up I realised he was younger than I'd thought.

I looked towards Caleb, unable to hide the concern on my face.

"What's wrong?"

"This sounds crazy I know but I think that guy is following me. I've seen him outside my house twice and he was there that night we were at Joe's and now he's here too. That can't be just a coincidence can it?"

Caleb frowned and before I could say anything he strode over to the young man who was stood by his car, staring towards us. Caleb grabbed him by the collar and pulled him close.

I hurried over to them. "Christ Caleb!"

"Alright kid, you better tell us why you're following Lila," he demanded.

"S-so you are Lila B-b-eaumont?" he stammered, looking towards me.

He was shaking like a leaf and sweating through his clothes. Up close he looked even younger, he was just a kid. Caleb and I looked at each other and he obviously had the same thought because he let him go and stepped back.

"Yeah that's me," I said.

He relaxed a little when Caleb let him go. "I'm sorry that I was following you. I'm n-not good at speaking to other p-people. I don't leave my flat much." He looked between us and then bent down to reach into his satchel which had some sort of comic book print on it. He stood up and with trembling hands handed me a bunch of letters tied together with string.

"My names Robin. I h-have these for you, they're from your mother."

# Chapter Eight

At that moment I wished more than anything that Caleb hadn't been standing next to me.
I swallowed hard and tried to keep a steady voice. "You must have a mistake, my mother died years ago."

I felt Caleb's gaze shift towards me but he didn't say anything.

"No, I know. My mother was in the same hospital as your mother. They were f-friends." He took a deep breath as if he was trying to stable his voice and continued, "I used to visit my mother weekly and she always spoke about your mother, Kendra, she was very fond of her. She said she always spoke about you."

I could feel the tears as they began to fill my eyes but I forced them back. "You were allowed to visit? You must have only been young?"

He nodded and looked confused. "Yes, my dad took me to see her every week. Why? Were you not allowed to see your mother?"

I shook my head. "Did you ever see her?"

He nodded. "A couple of times I think, I was too young to remember it properly now."

He held out the letters. "Anyway, my mother was released a couple of months back and the hospital just sent her some of her belongings. It seems like these letters from your mother got mixed up in her stuff and she asked me to give them to you."

I took them from him and whispered, "Thank you. So, you didn't leave anything else for me?"

Both Caleb and Robin looked at me with confusion now.

"No, why?"

I shook my head. "It doesn't matter. Thank you. For the letters."

He nodded and picked up his bag. "Sorry about your mother. My mum was incredibly sad when she died."

He turned around to walk away when I said, "How did you know where I lived?"

He shrugged, "Um... I'm a bit of a computer nerd. I looked you up on Facebook, Lila Beaumont isn't a common name. I saw where you worked and then hacked the lab's database, your address was stored on there. P-please don't tell anyone. I'll leave you alone now, it was only because we thought it was important."

I nodded and smiled at him. "It's okay don't worry. Thank you, I appreciate it."

He breathed a sigh of relief, gave an awkward little wave and then walked back to his car.

Caleb and I watched Robin drive away in silence. The letters felt heavy in my hand.

"I didn't know your mother had died." he said softly.

"It's not exactly something I go shouting from the rooftops."

He ignored my remark. "Do you mind me asking how?"

I sighed, I couldn't exactly lie. I met his eyes for a second but then looked away. "She was admitted to a psychiatric hospital when I was seven and three years later she killed herself."

"Oh, Christ. I'm so sorry."

"It's okay, it was 13 years ago. I don't know why it's all coming back up now."

"That kid said his mother was just being released, does that mean she's been in the hospital for like, 16 years?" he said eyes wide, horrified at the thought.

"Probably in and out... Scary isn't it."

He nodded. "Do you want me to come with you...to read them?"

I smiled at his thoughtfulness. "No it's fine. I need to read these alone. I'll probably be blubbering everywhere."

"You're right I wouldn't want to see that mess," he joked and then turned serious. "You know I'm only a phone call away if you need me okay?"

I nodded and he kissed me on the forehead again although I barely felt it. I numbly climbed into my car and put the letters on the passenger seat. I was tempted to rip them open right here. I wondered what she would have to say. Would they make any sense? Would she be wondering why I never went to visit? I had tried to but I was never allowed. She'd probably been so upset with me. The thought made me not want to open the letters, but I knew I had to see what was inside. I drove home as quickly as I could and stormed inside into the kitchen. Stephanie and Miles were already in there.

# The Doll House

"I'm making fajitas for dinner!" Stephanie beamed.

"Tom's favourite." Miles wiggled his eyebrows at me but I couldn't bring myself to smile.

His eyes dropped down to the letters in my hand. "Did you get another gift?"

Stephanie's head shot towards me so quickly I was surprised her neck didn't snap.

"Not exactly..." I sighed and sat down at the breakfast table.

I explained to them all about Robin and the letters.

"See I told you I knew he was following me." I shot Miles a look.

"Alright, I'm sorry." He reached out and pulled me into a hug and this time I hugged back.

"I'm going to go and read these alone guys okay?"

"Of course." Stephanie looked at me with sad eyes. "Let us know if you need anything."

I sat on my bad staring at the letters until my eyes started to sting. I blinked, took a deep breath and with a trembling hand opened the first letter. It was dated 16 years ago. I worked out the maths in my head. It was the year that my mother was put into the hospital, I would have been seven. My mother would have been 23, the age that I am now. That was a frightening thought.

*21st May 2002*
*Dearest Princess Lila,*

*Mummy misses you ever so much. I'm so sorry that I had to leave you, but the doctors told me that coming to the hospital for the proper treatment would be the best thing for me. I think they were right. I'm thinking clearly again, I haven't felt this calm and well, normal, in years. I'm going to get my head straight in here darling and then I'm going to come home. You're still so young, I'm not going to send you these letters until the time is right, but I promise you I will write as often as I can. I'm thinking about you every minute of every day.*

*I want you to know that I have told social services that I don't want you to visit me. It's not because I don't want to see you. It breaks my heart to think of how long it will be until we see each other again but I can't stand for you to see me like this.*

*It won't be long sweetheart. I love you more than you know.*

# Katie Masterman

*Mummy xxx*

I put the letter down as the tears ran freely down my cheeks. I had always wondered why I was never allowed to see her. I missed her every single day but now suddenly the ache for her hurt my chest more than ever. I drew in a shaky breath. I wasn't sure I could carry on but I needed to hear more. I put that letter to the side and picked up the next one.

*1st June 2002*
*Dearest Princess Lila,*

*I'm getting better. I am seeing the world in a completely different light. I miss my ridiculously happy days but I know they were not normal. I do not miss my depressed days, I'm glad to be rid of them. I'm just calm, happy but I'm at the right level. I have asked when I will be able to leave, and they said soon but I know it won't be as soon as I would like.*

*I miss you so much sweetheart. I was so happy to hear social services had followed my request for you to live with your friend Stephanie and are being well looked after by her family. I can't wait to see you.*

*Mummy xxx*

I didn't understand. She sounded normal, she wanted to leave. What could have changed over the next three years? I wiped the tears from my cheeks, took a deep breath and opened the next letter.

*21st July 2002*
*Dearest Princess Lila,*

*I am still missing you terribly.*
*I've made a couple of friends, they're keeping me sane in here.*
*Veronica is a lovely lady, she's about my age. She has manic depression and she's had a couple of episodes since she's been in here and has had to be sedated but on her good days she is so kind and incredibly interesting. She has so much to say. Her baby Robin and husband James come to visit most weeks. He's adorable, not as cute as you were though of*

## The Doll House

*course. At first it made me want to allow you to visit, it made me miss you so much it hurt. But then seeing what she was like on the days after he had left was horrible, it was almost like every time they left she was being tortured. She probably was. She'd cry and scream for hours after they left. I'd probably feel the same if you came to visit and then had to leave. Hopefully I will be out soon.*

*My second friend is called Samuel. He's very charming and incredibly handsome. He makes me laugh so much. I've told him all about you, he said he would love to meet you one day and I think I would like that too.*

*See you soon sweetheart.*

*Mummy xxx*

The tears burned in my eyes again and I decided that that was enough I could handle for one day. One thing I was sure of though. These were not letters written by a woman who wanted to kill herself.

Katie Masterman

# Chapter Nine

I got up and left for work an hour early the next morning. Partly because I couldn't sleep, partly so that I didn't have to speak to the rest of the house. I wasn't in the mood. I knew they meant well but they'd want to know what was written in the letters and I couldn't bring myself to talk about them yet. My mother had wanted to come home that part was clear. I just had so many questions.

What happened? Why was she there so long? What could have possibly happened that made her want to end her life? Was it the hospitals fault, did they keep her there too long until she couldn't bare it anymore? Or did she just relapse?

I again attempted unsuccessfully to push all thoughts of her out of my mind for the day. I picked up a coffee on my way to work and when I arrived at Chambers, I looked at the clock in reception: 8:30am. I was an hour early. I wandered to the office suddenly feeling tired, maybe I could have an hour's nap before Dr Reynolds got in.

I walked in looking at my phone in one hand, taking a sip of coffee with the other.

"You're early."

"Christ!" I jumped and the lid came off my cup, spilling hot coffee all down my chin, chest and shirt.

I set the coffee down and picked up a bunch of tissues from the box on his desk and quickly cleaned myself up as the heat rose to my cheeks.

"Guilty conscience?" Reynolds asked.

"What?"

"You're very jumpy," he laughed and I looked at him quickly.

"What?" he frowned.

"That's the first time I've heard you laugh since I started working for you and it was because I spilled coffee all down myself!"

I rolled my eyes still dabbing at my shirt. It was no good, I was covered.

He shook his head and walked over to a small cupboard behind his desk which was next to the cupboard I had cleaned out for a week. I hadn't seen

# The Doll House

what was inside this one. He rummaged through it for a minute and then pulled out a grey shirt on a hanger.

"Here."

I stared at him and he shook the shirt at me.

"Put this on."

"Umm..." I hesitated, feeling embarrassed at putting my boss's shirt on.

"You're not sitting in a wet, coffee-stained shirt all day. Just put this on." He said seriously.

"It's fine honestly it will dry quickly." I brushed him off.

"Lila... it's see-through."

"What?"

"I can see through your shirt," he looked pointedly at my chest and I covered it with my hands. I looked down mortified and then huffed and snatched the shirt from his hand. He was trying not to smile.

I went to the bathroom, cheeks still flushed from embarrassment, and changed into his shirt. I stood and looked in the mirror. He was almost a whole foot taller than me so you could barely see my black skirt from underneath his shirt, it looked more like a dress and for some reason it made my legs feel exposed. The shirt was incredibly soft on my skin, it was probably awfully expensive. I lifted the collar to my nose and breathed in a whiff of fresh detergent. I looked at myself in the mirror. My hair was scraped into a messy bun, I had horrible black bags under my tired eyes and I was wearing this stupid shirt. Today was not going to be my day. I stared at myself a minute longer, tugged down on my skirt and then sighed and headed back to the office.

He looked up at me from his desk and I saw his eyes brush over my face down my body and then back up to my face. He looked away quickly.

"Lovely. Now if we can do some work that would be great."

I sighed, hating how he could switch back to boss-mode in a second. "What do you need me to do?"

After a few hours of typing up notes I sat up and stretched. I looked at Reynolds who had his earphones in and was typing up an interview that he had recorded. He really was good looking. It was hard to believe he was going to be 40 this year. He was wearing a plain white shirt today with grey trousers and a matching grey tie. His face was set in its usual serious expression. Dark and mysterious. He never fully smiled, never fully let his expressions show so he always had a tone of mystery about him. But, when he did let a slight smile show it always reached his eyes and made me want to smile back.

He must have sensed that I was staring at him because he looked up at me.

"Can I help you with something?"

"No, no I was just... having a break." I stammered.

He leaned back in his chair and stretched his arms behind his head. I noticed instantly that this movement pulled his shirt tight on his arms. I looked away quickly.

"Why were you in so early this morning?" he asked as though it had been on his mind.

"Oh I couldn't really sleep and I couldn't really face speaking to my housemates." It surprised me that the truthful answer came out.

He leaned forward, resting his elbows on his desk. He looked torn as though it was completely against his nature to ask what it was that was clearly on his mind.

"Something serious?" he said.

I looked at him and pondered for a minute. There was something about his serious face and rare smile that made me want to open up to him. He was a psychologist after all, if anyone was going to understand it would be him.

I sighed, "13 years ago my mother killed herself whilst she was in a mental hospital and yesterday a boy who has been following me for the past week came up to me and gave me some letters that she had written whilst she was in there."

Reynolds' eyes widened and he raised his eyebrows and sat back again letting out a deep breath. "Do you mind me asking what her diagnosis was?" He'd probably use my life as a research project.

"Bipolar Disorder. She was really happy some days and other days she..." I trailed off, knowing he knew what the disorder was.

He nodded in understanding. "Did you read the letters?"

"Only the first couple, I couldn't bear to get through the rest. She seemed normal... happy. She wrote that she was going to come home to me, that I was keeping her going, but I never saw her again before she..." I trailed off again.

"She obviously loved you very much."

I nodded. "I thought so, but it obviously wasn't enough."

## The Doll House

Reynolds now looked extremely uncomfortable and it dawned on me that I was unloading all my personal issues onto my already awkward boss.

I laughed nervously, "I'm fine though, sorry for oversharing."

He looked at me for a second and then nodded and looked back at his computer.

What a day.

When I left work in my ridiculous shirtdress I was already in a horrendous mood. This was made 10 times worse when I saw the present wrapped in blue paper sat on top of my car. I had cried too many tears recently over something that I didn't understand and the way I felt then was not upset. I was angry. I was fed up. I was done. I just wanted all of this to stop and to go on with my normal life.

I stormed up to the car and ripped open the present to see another stupid doll staring up at me. I didn't allow myself to look at its features or its outfit because I was saw red.

I threw it back in the box and onto the floor and then stamped on it over and over again, hoping that whoever had left it on my car was watching. I then picked up the doll by its hair and slammed it into my car over and over again until suddenly somebody grabbed by wrists and pulled me into them.

I was stood breathing heavily looking into Caleb's eyes. He held my wrists tightly to my side and looked at me with wide eyes as though as I had gone mad.

He let go of my wrists suddenly and stepped back, pushing me away from him as he did so. He looked me over: hair a wild mess, tears in my eyes, wearing my boss's shirt, stamping on a present on the floor and I instantly realised what conclusion he had jumped to.

I shook my head. "It's not what it looks like."

"Right, because it looks like you just did the dirty with Dr Cleanliness and then got thrown out of his office with a present as a thank you?"

"Yeah it's definitely not what it looks like." I stormed away from him, picked my phone and keys up off the floor and threw my car door open. As I sat into the driver's seat Caleb climbed into the passenger seat beside me.

"So what's going on?"

I leaned my head back on my headrest and closed my eyes, breathing heavily.

"Lila… talk to me."

I looked over to his troubled expression and swivelled in my seat so I was facing him.

"It started a few weeks ago when I came home from my job interview to find that a present had been left for me..."

It seemed like it was a day of oversharing because once I'd started telling him what was going on I couldn't stop. I told him all the details about the dolls and the lavender and the poem and the link to my mother and the letters and how I thought it was Robin leaving the dolls.

"So, there we go. Run for the hills because I have one messed up life right now."

He snorted and brushed a tear off my cheek with the back of his fingers. "To be honest that's a lot better than when I thought you were sleeping with your boss. I thought I was going to have to go and kick his ass."

I let out a watery laugh.

"Stephanie thinks that we should call the police."

He shook his head. "There's no point yet, not until they actually break the law else there's nothing the police can do."

I nodded. "I know we told her that. I just don't understand any of it. I literally can't even take a guess at who is doing this. It's not like they've actually done anything threatening or even done anything wrong, it's just starting to creep me out that's all."

"It is strange... You're sure there isn't anyone you can think of that could be doing this?"

I shook my head again, "I've honestly racked my brain a thousand times over. I thought my mother never had any friends or family, maybe I was just too young to remember. Either way, I still don't have a clue who could be doing this."

"And why? Who is one question yeah, but why? What are they gaining from this?" He frowned. "Maybe they think they're being nice. Like actual nice meaningful gifts?"

I pursed my lips. "I don't know... maybe. I can't shake the feeling that its more than that. Something more sinister." I put my head in my hands.

"If there was anything I could do to help I would, you know?" he said.

I lifted my head up and sighed, "I know, there's nothing you can do."

His eyes, full of concern, dropped from my eyes to my lips. I gave a slight smile as way of consent. He leaned forward and gave me a light but lingering

# The Doll House

kiss that made the heat rise in my cheeks. I sighed into him, he smelt incredible. He pulled back and then smiled a naughty smile.

"So, what's with the walk of shame shirt?" he asked playfully.

I let out a small laugh. "I spilt coffee all down my shirt so Dr Reynolds let me change into a spare one he had in his office."

He raised his eyebrows and snorted. "Of course he has spare clean shirts in his office."

He leaned forward and kissed me again. He moved his hand onto the inside of my thigh and breathed, "As good as you look I'd much prefer it if you were in one of my shirts."

I chuckled lightly as I pulled away and removed his hand from my thigh. "Maybe one day. I'd better get going."

He laughed and shook his head. He opened the car door and stepped out and then leant down, flashing me a mischievous smile. "Hopefully one day soon."

# Chapter Ten

When I got home and walked into the kitchen with a slight smile on my face, Stephanie and Tom both looked at me as if I was about to snap.

"I still feel like crap. I can't stop thinking about the letters and I had to spend the day in my boss's shirt but I just saw Caleb and he made me smile okay?"

Not wanting to ruin my okay mood the others didn't bring up the letters that night. Stephanie and I giggled about Caleb and what had happened in the car whilst Miles rolled his eyes and made annoyingly childish gagging noises. They all made fun of the fact I was wearing Reynolds' shirt all day and then we settled down to watch a film as though everything was normal. I must had drifted off during the film at some point because I woke up with a start to see Miles laughing at me. I looked at the clock, it was only 9pm.

I stretched and yawned. "I think I'm going to have a bath, they're supposed to be relaxing right?"

I hadn't had a bath since I was a child but Stephanie had them weekly.

"Oh my gosh," she squealed. "Can I run it for you? It will be amazing, you'll never have felt so relaxed in your life!"

She bounced off the sofa and hurried upstairs, Miles shook his head taking a sip of beer and Tom's eyes followed her, smiling at the way she got excited over such little things.

About 20 minutes later she called down the stairs, "Lila your bath's ready!"

I walked into the bathroom to see a beaming Stephanie.

"Tada!" she sang and I looked around and couldn't help but laugh.

Our bathroom was big and modern like the rest of the house. It had marble flooring and everything in it was white. The bathtub sat right in the middle; it was a ridiculously sized round bath that could easily fit three or four people and had a feature that turned on jacuzzi bubbles.

Stephanie had filled it to the brim with steaming hot water which you couldn't even see through the amount of bubbles that were piled high on top and were almost flowing over the edge. She had lit candles all around the tub and dimmed the lights giving the room a warm and cosy ambience. Soft music played through the speakers in the ceiling and she had lit an incense stick in the corner which made the whole room smell of... Stephanie. I took a deep breath in.

"It's lemon-grass and chamomile, the most popular scents in aromatherapy. You'll feel relaxed and sleepy in no time," she smiled.

"Thanks Steph." I hugged her. "This looks amazing."

She smiled with pleasure and left the room.

I got undressed hanging my clothes over the heated rack on the wall and lowered myself under the bubbles, letting out a long sigh. The water was so hot it made my stomach tense but when I got used to the heat I relaxed into it. I laid my head back and covered myself in the bubbles, breathing in the rich aroma of all the scents that were going on in the room. It really was relaxing.

That was until Stephanie came back in the room.

"How is it? Oo it looks so relaxing I might have one after you! I just thought I'd bring you your dressing gown for when you got out," she said and hung it up for me.

"Thank you," I said and closed my eyes.

"Christ it looks like Stephanie exploded in here." I heard Miles' laugh.

My eyes shot open and I frowned. "Excuse me I'm naked under here."

"It's nothing I haven't seen before," he said as he pretended to try and look through the bubbles.

I flicked water at him and laughed. "Stop being such a perv!"

"What are we all doing in here?" Tom said wondering in and I sighed.

"I was just thinking I might join Lila in the bath," Miles said.

I stared at him. "No you bloody well won't!" But to my dismay he started to take his clothes off.

"Miles, I swear to god if you get in here whilst I'm naked I will get you arrested for sexual harassment." I warned but he wasn't listening. He stripped down and climbed into the other end of the tub which to be fair was big enough so that he wasn't actually touching me.

"Oh for Christ sake!" I huffed, using my arms to cover as much of my dignity as possible.

Stephanie giggled and hurried out of the room and then bounced back a couple of minutes later wearing a bikini. She threw my bikini at me and then climbed in between me and Miles. I quickly put my bikini on, relieved to have something to cover myself with and then felt Tom climb in beside me. Thankfully, he kept his boxers on.

"Unlike Miles I didn't want to get in whilst you were naked. No offence," he said.

"Absolutely none taken," I laughed.

In pure Stephanie style she reached over to a box by the bath and pulled out a bottle of champagne and some plastic flutes. When she noticed us all staring at her she shrugged. "For emergencies."

"Right whoever is tickling my foot you better stop before I kick you." I snapped and then gasped as the hand suddenly grabbed my ankle, pulled on it and dragged me fully under the water. I sat back up, gasping out of the water as Miles was killing himself with laughter.

"So much for relaxed and sleepy," I groaned.

"Just pretend we're not here." Miles sniggered.

"Yeah we'll all have a relax," said Tom.

I laid my head back and closed my eyes and then sighed about 30 seconds later because of the giggling that was going on around me. I looked up to see the three idiots I call my friends sat giggling with bubble beards on their faces. I couldn't help but laugh.

We sat in the bath drinking champagne and laughing about stupid stuff until the water got too cold to sit in anymore. I smiled at my friends. Stephanie was just Stephanie, she had the most kind and genuine heart of anyone I'd ever met. Miles was an idiot who liked to act tough but we all knew he cared about us more than anything. Tom was awkward and shy but kind and considerate and funny in his own way. They were all so special to me. They were all so understanding and supportive, I really didn't know how I got so lucky.

I walked to my bedroom and threw my coffee stained shirt and jeans in the white-linen laundry basket that sat in-between mine and Stephanie's rooms and then climbed into bed.

The bath was supposed to relax me but the splashing and the laughing and the buzz from the champagne was keeping me awake. As I laid in bed alone in the silence I couldn't help but think about *literally* everything.

My thoughts somehow drifted to Dr Reynolds. He was serious and intelligent and slightly awkward, yet underneath I could tell he had a hidden,

# The Doll House

dry sense of humour. I didn't fully understand him yet, I couldn't work him out but I hoped that I would eventually.

My thoughts then landed on Caleb. Caleb was confident, fun and playful but I felt like there was definitely more underneath the surface and I was excited to find out more about him too.

My thoughts then surprisingly drifted to Miles. We'd always had a flirtatious friendship but it would never be more than that. Although I'd be lying if I said I hadn't thought about it a few years back but things had changed since then. While he did act jealous sometimes, I assumed it was in a protective brother way before anything else. I shook my head, unsure why I was thinking about this I forced my thoughts elsewhere.

They inevitably drifted to everything that had been happening recently. I was just so confused; nothing was adding up. I was sure there were links between everything, and it would all make sense in the end but I just couldn't think what it could possibly be.

Who on earth could be leaving the presents? Why were they leaving dolls? How did they know about the lavender? What was the link to my mother?

With all these unanswered questions floating through my mind I somehow eventually drifted off to sleep.

It didn't feel like long before I woke with a start. I sat up, pulse racing, wondering what had woken me up. I didn't think I was having a dream. I laid back down, but my heart was pounding so hard in my chest I could feel it in my ears. As I laid there every noise from outside my window or every creak from inside the house was putting me on edge.

I heard a creak, almost like a footstep directly outside my door and a sliver of ice slipped down my spine. I sat up.

"Steph?" I called. No answer. I waited a few minutes, but it was all silent. My mind was definitely playing tricks on me.

I laid my head back down, willing myself to calm down. I laid there for about 20 minutes. I tossed and turned and tried to put everything out of my mind but it was no good, I couldn't get back to sleep. I decided to get up, stretch my legs, get a glass of water and then try again.

I walked downstairs and turned the kitchen light on, squinting as my eyes tried to adjust to the light. Now that everything was quiet, the house was eerie. I had never been scared of the dark, scared of the house or getting up alone at night. At this moment however, I felt scared and I didn't know why.

I forced myself to get a grip and grabbed a glass from the cupboard. I filled it with water and took a sip and then I leant against the breakfast bar taking a deep breath.

One of the walls in our kitchen was made completely out of glass with two double doors that opened into our garden. I stood still, staring out into the darkness. Standing in the light of the kitchen, it was impossible to see anything except pitch black. Anything or anyone could be out there, staring back at me, watching me and I would have no idea. I swallowed and the hairs suddenly stood up on the back of my neck.

I turned to refill my now empty glass when there was a huge crash from outside. It startled me so intensely that I let out a scream and dropped the glass from my hands which smashed loudly into pieces on the tiled floor. I huffed and shook my head at myself, annoyed that I was acting like a paranoid mess. It was probably just a cat trying to get into our bins or something. I *had* to get a grip.

I grabbed the dustpan and brush and swept up the broken glass off the floor. I held a hand to my chest where my heart pounded furiously beneath my trembling fingers. I was *definitely* not going to be able to sleep after this.

I finished clearing away the broken glass and reached into the cupboard to get another one out. As I reached in, the movement sensor lights in the garden suddenly lit up making me jump again. This time I jumped so powerfully that a couple of glasses fell out of the cupboard, making several piercing smashes against the counter and floor.

My attention was drawn to the sudden light outside and I spun my head towards the garden.

My knees almost buckled.

"Lila?" Tom had walked in behind me but I didn't reply. I didn't move. I didn't even let out a breath.

I could hear the sleep in his voice. "Lila what's going on?"

He reached my side and looked at my face and from the corner of my eye I saw his gaze follow mine towards the garden.

"What the hell?" he exclaimed. "Holy crap!"

He ran out of the kitchen and yelled loudly up the stairs, "MILES! Get down here now!"

I heard Miles' bedroom door open and slam shut and then his footsteps speeding down the stairs but my eyes still didn't move from the garden. The garden light suddenly switched off and I managed to take a breath.

# The Doll House

"What's going on?" Miles said as he followed Tom into the kitchen.

Tom walked past me to the glass doors which he unlocked and shoved open, causing the sensor to light up the garden once more.

"What the fuck?" gasped Miles. "Lila?"

They both looked at me and then back at the garden from which my eyes still had not moved. I didn't know what to think, I didn't know what to say or do. Because looking back at us, hanging from a tree branch by a rope wrapped around its neck, was a *life-sized* doll. This doll had a recognisable face, hair style and an outfit I knew all too well.

The doll was supposed to be me.

Katie Masterman

# Chapter Eleven

The boys worked together to get the doll down from the tree. They shoved it inside a black bin bag and left it outside where I couldn't see it. When it was out of sight they both came and joined me at the breakfast bar where I was sat chewing my nails and involuntarily bouncing my leg up and down. I didn't even need to look up to know they were giving each other a look.

"Did you see who did it?" Miles asked me softly.

"I have that outfit," I whispered.

"What? Lila, did you see who hung the doll outside?"

I spun around to face him. "That doll was supposed to be me, Miles! It had on an outfit exactly like–" I stopped suddenly.

"Oh god," I breathed.

I ran upstairs as fast as I could. Mine and Stephanie's bedrooms were next to each other and in-between them was the white linen laundry basket that we shared. I tipped it upside down and rummaged through it, throwing clothes everywhere. The boys had followed me upstairs and watched me, speechless.

"Someone has been here!" I panted. I stood up and looked at them both. "Someone has been in our house. Tonight!"

I ran back downstairs and into the kitchen. They were both still following me around like I was some sort of mentalist, but they didn't understand yet.

I swung open the large garden doors again and heaved the bin bag back into the kitchen with a grunt. The doll was heavier than I had expected. I knelt and pulled it out of the bag onto the kitchen floor whilst trying to avoid looking at its face. I searched until I finally saw what I had been looking for and then I stopped and leaned my head back against a cupboard, breathing heavily.

Miles was looking at me as if I had gone mad. Tom looked at the doll and then at me and said, "Can you please tell us what's going on Lila?"

I breathed heavily in and out, trying to make sense of it all.

"The doll was supposed to be me. It's got the same hair and the exact same outfit. I thought that whoever this was had just copied my style but look..." I pointed out the large coffee stain on the front of the shirt.

"This is my exact shirt, I spilt coffee on it literally today and put it in the laundry basket with my skirt before we all went to bed. They aren't in the basket anymore, they're here on this doll."

"What?" We all turned our heads to the sound of Stephanie's voice. She stepped into the kitchen. "So, you're saying that somebody has been in our house to steal your dirty clothes, put them on a mannequin intended to look like you and then hung it up by its neck in our garden, all whilst we've been sleeping?" Her voice was trembling.

I nodded and then looked at Miles and said with a flat voice, "What, no jokes this time?"

He shook his head without taking his eyes off the doll.

Stephanie and I argued about calling the police.

"You're being ridiculous Lila! Someone has literally broken into our house whilst we've been sleeping, and you don't even want to call the police? What are you not telling us?"

"I'm not hiding anything! Please Steph, I can't explain why I just don't want to involve the police yet I just don't. I have a feeling that we shouldn't, not until we understand what's going on."

After a while of back and forth she huffed and threw her hands up in defeat. We made sure that all the doors and windows around the house were locked, but Stephanie was insistent that she still felt unsafe.

"I'll sleep in with you if you like?" I said.

"We all will," Tom said. "Why don't we all sleep in the living room?"

Stephanie nodded. "We can get our duvets and pillows from upstairs. That's really sweet of you Tom." She stood on her tiptoes and gave him a kiss on the cheek.

As much as I'd like to think he was being a considerate friend I was sure he was just looking for an excuse to spend the night in the same room as Stephanie.

"Very sweet," I said dryly, giving him and Miles a knowing look.

We dragged down enough duvets and pillows for all four of us to lie on as well as use as cover. Miles grumbled the whole time.

"I don't know why we're doing this when we have perfectly comfortable beds upstairs." But I knew his complaints were for show and that he wouldn't go and sleep upstairs even if we told him to.

By the time we had moved the sofas to the edge of the living room and settled down in our sleeping positions it was almost 5am. We laid in a row, the order being Miles, myself, Stephanie and then Tom. I turned to face Stephanie and met her eyes for a second before she rolled and turned her back to me, laying with her head on Tom's shoulder. Feeling as though I was intruding on something, I rolled over to face Miles who was already snoring loudly. I smacked his face with a pillow and whispered at him to shut up. I didn't sleep a wink that night.

The next morning the four of us all called in sick to work, sometimes it just needs to be done. We laid on the floor in the living room in our makeshift beds and made small talk, but there was no laughter or humour in the room this morning. We didn't mention anything about the night before.

My mind was still reeling. I thought back to the doll hanging lifeless by its neck in the garden, swinging in the wind. My pulse instantly quickened and my palms clammed up. Who the hell was behind all of this? I swallowed hard and shook the images from my mind.

Stephanie, being the wonderfully altruistic human that she is, went to the kitchen and made us pancakes. She never could stay mad at me, or anyone for that matter, for too long. She laid them out on the breakfast bar with bowls of fruit, lemon juice, sugar and chocolate sauce. We ate hungrily and then went back to our slummed-out positions in the living room for the rest of the day.

It was exactly what I needed. I knew they probably could have all made it to work but they had obviously made a silent agreement to stay home with me which I appreciated. Sometimes I needed to be alone but today I was glad I had them.

For some reason Stephanie was teaching Miles how to plait hair and was using me as a model. I didn't mind though, I loved having my hair played with, it could relax me to sleep. Or so I thought. When Miles attempted the plait, I felt like he was trying to rip my hair out. Luckily my phone buzzed from across the room so I could move away from his heavy hands.

When I checked the screen, I saw there was a text from Caleb.

# The Doll House

"Hey, your car isn't in the carpark today, just checking everything's okay?"

I smiled to myself, secretly happy that not only had he noticed but cared enough to ask. I typed a quick reply.

"Hey, yeah I'm okay. Called in sick, I'll explain when I next see you."

His response came back instantly.

"What's your address and what's your favourite take-out?"

I typed back a response with my address and with the obvious answer. Pizza. I smiled to myself. "Does anyone mind if Caleb comes over?"

"Oo Lila's having a boy over!" Stephanie giggled, wiggling her eyebrows at me.

"Grow up." I rolled my eyes as I threw a pillow at her.

I assumed he would finish work, go to his house and get changed and then pick up the pizza which meant he'd probably be here in just under two hours.

Miles looked at me and chuckled. "As good as I personally think you look right now you might want to go and take a shower. Unless he likes the homeless look?"

I looked in the mirror, my hair was a mess, I was in the baggiest most unflattering pyjamas and I had makeup smudged all around my eyes.

I showered (and shaved) and blow-dried my hair and tied it up into a messy bun and then got changed into figure hugging gym leggings and crop top. Cute but casual.

I was just finishing putting some mascara on when the doorbell rang.

I jogged downstairs but Steph and Miles reached the door first.

Steph opened the door, Miles stood behind her and through them I could see Caleb standing at the door with a slightly taken aback expression on his face. He had a bottle of wine in one hand and a couple of pizzas in the other.

"Hi, Caleb! I'll take that," Stephanie sang as she took the wine and then skipped away.

"Yeah and I'll take them, thanks mate." Miles said, taking the pizza and following Steph into the living room.

I rolled my eyes trying not to laugh and walked to the door.
"I did come baring gifts, but I guess I'll have to do," Caleb said.
I smiled at him. "That's good enough for me."

Caleb clearly hadn't been expecting the others to hang out with us, but he didn't complain, just apologised for not bringing enough pizza and wine.

"Oh we always have spare wine." Stephanie smiled at him, pulling a bottle of red out of the cupboard and pouring herself a glass.

Tom and Miles sat on one sofas and Stephanie sat on the floor where the makeshift beds from the night before were still laid out. Caleb and I sat on the other sofa, I was leant into him and he had his arm around me. Just as before at Joe's I couldn't help but notice Miles' gaze keep flicking over to our direction. I suddenly wondered if he was jealous but then realised with everything going on he was probably just feeling overprotective of me.

Everyone was feeling slightly tipsy by this point. The boys were getting louder, Stephanie was getting gigglier and I was getting sleepier.

Caleb was nodding along with Tom as he was telling him something about a new super-hero film coming out and I smiled to myself at how much he was humouring him.

"C'mon don't bore the poor boy." Stephanie laughed and Tom look hurt.

Caleb nodded towards the duvets and pillows. "So what, did you guys have a sleepover last night or something?"

The room went silent and I swallowed. I sighed. I was trying to put last night out of my mind but it was impossible. I stood up and pulled him by his hand towards the kitchen.

"Did I say something wrong?" he asked.

"No, I just feel like I should explain," I said as I climbed onto one of the stools at the breakfast bar. He followed suit and sat on a stool opposite me.

I explained what happened and his eyes widened. It sounded so ridiculous to even be saying it out loud.

"Christ Lila! Did you see who it was?"

I shook my head.

"Did you call the police?"

I looked away.

"Why the *hell* would you not called the police?" he demanded. There was no way I was going to admit to him that I thought it could be my mother. Even though it was impossible, I couldn't shake the feeling.

"I... wish I had an answer to that. I just didn't think it was necessary," I said shyly.

Caleb shook his head in disbelief. "I know I probably don't know all the details but none of this makes sense to me Lila."

I scoffed. "You think that you're confused? Imagine how I'm feeling."

He stood up and walked around the breakfast bar so he was stood in front of me. "So let me get this straight... Someone, we don't know who, is stalking you and leaving you creepy dolls and flowers and poems that have a meaning that you believe only your mum, who died 13 years ago, would know about. Now that person has broken into your house whilst you were sleeping, rummaged through your dirty laundry and hung it on a doll, supposed to be you, by its neck in your garden?"

It was serious. I knew whatever was happening should not be taken light-heartedly and I had been feeling so crappy about everything. Yet, after hearing him piece it all together and say it out like that, I couldn't help but burst out laughing.

"Okay it's official, you've gone mad." Caleb was looking at me as if I actually had.

I breathed to stop myself from laughing, my head still a bit woozy from the wine. "No, I know it's serious. It's just hearing you say it like that... it just sounds so ridiculous!" I started laughing again and this time he joined in.

"You surprise me all the time you know that? Not one day has been the same since I met you and I don't know how you're taking all of this so well."

I sobered then. "Maybe it's just the wine... I don't know what else to do, there's nothing I can do about it except laugh. Anyway, that's why we all slept in the living room last night, Stephanie and I didn't feel safe sleeping alone after some creep was in our house."

His smile turned playful. "Well I can stay over with you tonight... For you know, protection reasons obviously."

"Hmm... well you've been drinking so you can't exactly drive home can you?"

"That's a good observation, really you'd be doing me a favour."

"Alright you can stay, we have a very comfortable couch," I teased.

He walked towards where I was sat on the bar stool and positioned himself in-between my legs. He braced his hands on the breakfast bar behind me and trailed light kisses down my neck, sending a pleasurable shiver down my spine.

"The couch is where you want me to sleep?" he breathed.

"Mmhmm yep..." I moaned defiantly and yet tilted my neck so he could have better access.

His kisses moved up from my neck and onto my lips.

"Are you sure?" he teased and I giggled.

His kiss then got harder and more heated, I moaned into his lips. He kissed me passionately and pressed his body into me wrapping my legs around his waist and at that moment I couldn't think about anything else.

I laid with my head on Caleb's strong muscly chest and he stroked my back lightly with his fingers. I traced over the tattoo on his chest that reached over his bicep and all the way to his forearm.

I sighed as I thought about the night. It had been... nice. Was it passionate and heated and everything that I had imagined it to be? Maybe not. But I had a lot on my mind. That's what I needed at the moment, a nice, simple distraction. Caleb had a way of making me feel relaxed, as though I didn't have a worry in the world.

We laid there like that for ages in a comfortable silence until I felt his hand stop moving on my back and his breathing became slow and heavy. I knew he had fallen asleep, instantly making me feel safe and relaxed. Eventually, listening to the rhythm of his heartbeat, I managed to fall asleep.

Out of nowhere my eyes jerked open and all I could see were dolls heads floating around me. They all had their eyes wide open, some had ropes around their necks. Their eyes were haunting, staring deep into my soul making my insides feel instantly cold. I felt like I couldn't breathe. I gasped for air, reaching my hand up to my neck and felt a rope squeezing the life out of me. I pulled at the rope but as I pulled and struggled, the rope only squeezed tighter. I tried to scream and then–

I jolted awake with a start. I rubbed my eyes, breathing heavily attempting to calm myself down. I reached my arm over to feel Caleb laid next to me but all I found was an empty space. I opened my eyes assuming he had just gone to the bathroom. I waited for what felt like an eternity and reached my arm out again. The sheets were cold.

Nobody had been laid there for a while.

# Chapter Twelve

After realising Caleb had gone home, I couldn't sleep. I tossed and turned in bed for several hours before I sat up and looked at the time on my phone. It was 3:27am. I sighed and rolled over shoving my face into a pillow. Was the only reason Caleb had stuck around through all the craziness to get me into bed? He seemed so nice and genuine but was obviously another one of those guys with only one thing on the brain. He could have at least waited until the morning to leave, at least said goodbye instead of sneaking out in the middle of the night after we had slept together. My life was a mess enough at the moment without him adding to it and he knew that.

I didn't know what time it was when I eventually fell back to sleep but I woke up in the morning feeling like absolute crap. When I went into the kitchen I was relieved to see it was just Steph in there. She beamed at me, obviously excited to hear about my night with Caleb and passed me a cup of coffee.

"So come on spill the beans! How did it go?"

My eyes betrayed me and filled with tears and she instantly rushed to my side and pulled me into a hug.

"What did he do?" she demanded. "You wait until I get the boys in here they'll kill him!"

I just shook my head and chuckled through my tears. "It's fine let's not kill anyone just yet."

"So what happened? And drink up you look terrible." She pushed the coffee towards me.

I explained what had happened in detail and she giggled and sighed in the right places of the story.

"It was nice and we fell asleep together and then I woke up in the middle of the night to find that he was gone." I put my head in my hands.

"Gone?" she gasped.

I nodded. "Gone."

I felt a couple of hands on my shoulders and twisted round to see Miles. Heat rushed to my cheeks.

"I'm sorry I know I shouldn't have been listening," he said. "But any guy that sneaks out in the middle of the night after spending it with a beautiful girl like you is an idiot."

My eyes filled with tears again and I hugged him and then he shrugged. "That or you just weren't very goo–OW!"

Steph had smacked him.

I pulled into the carpark at work to see Caleb stood chatting to his builder friends by his van. I saw him glance over to me so put my head down and hurried into the office without looking at him. He didn't try to stop me.

I slammed the door a little too hard when I got to the office and Reynolds gave me a questioning look. I sighed and sat down in the chair.

"Are you feeling better?" he asked.

"Yeah much better thanks."

"Something on your mind?" he asked as unlike him as this was, I wasn't in the mood to overshare so I just shook my head.

He pointed towards a few boxes filled to the brim with paperwork. "You can holepunch and file all of those today."

When I left work I was glad that I didn't see Caleb and by the time I got home I was absolutely exhausted both physically and emotionally. I had dinner and watched some tele with the others and then said goodnight and headed to bed early.

For the first time in ages I actually managed to drift off to sleep without any problems so I was slightly annoyed when I was woken up by the weight of someone sitting next to me on my bed. I assumed it was Steph checking on me because I had been quite upset when I had gone to bed. I kept my eyes shut, whoever it was brushed my hair off my face with a delicate touch and then it hit me.

The unmistakable smell of lavender was as strong as if I had a full bouquet of the flower right in front of my nose. My eyes shot open and I sat up, backing as far into my headboard as I could and saw a black figure moving away from me in the darkness.

I screamed and I kept on screaming until all the breath in my lungs had ran out. It was too dark to see the person in my room but whoever it was

# The Doll House

obviously panicked and decided to flee. I heard them run down the stairs and then I heard the front door open and slam shut. I sat pressed against the headboard breathing erratically.

Miles ran into my room looked around. When he saw no immediate threat he sat down on the bed beside me and tried to pull me into him. He whispered, "Shh it's okay it was just a dream." I shook my head and shoved him away.

Steph had walked in and sat down on my other side stroking my hair. "It was just a dream Lila."

Uncontrollable sobs racked my chest. I wanted to tell them what had happened, but I couldn't get the words out. I gradually forced myself to calm down and I levelled my breathing until I was able to talk.

"There was somebody in my room!" I cried.

"You were just dreaming; a lot has been happening recently it's understandable," Miles said seriously. There was no smile on his face, no jokes were going to be made, he was looking at me with genuine concern.

"No!" I cried. "Please believe me. There was someone in my room, they sat here and stroked my hair and then when I screamed, they ran away!"

Steph and Miles looked at each other but then Tom entered the room. "She's right."

They looked at her frowning.

"I heard the door slam," he said. "I thought it was one of you but when I went to check outside you were all up here."

"I told you!" As my eyes were adjusting to the darkness of the room I sat up suddenly and gasped. I shoved myself off the bed and flicked the light switch on.

We all squinted at the sudden light and then Miles stood up and looked around.

"Oh my god," gasped Stephanie.

My room was an absolute mess. The drawers had been pulled out, everything in my wardrobe was on the floor, everything on my shelves was dumped in a pile underneath them, even my bin had been tipped upside down.

"How didn't I hear this?" I gasped.

"Whoever was in here was looking for something," said Miles.

I suddenly had a thought and leapt onto my bed reaching under my pillow. I relaxed when my hand felt the pile of letters from my mother.

Stephanie looked at me and placed her hand on my arm. "Lila, I think we should call the police now."

The four of us were sat in the kitchen when the doorbell rang.

Miles went to answer it and then came back into the kitchen followed by a policeman and a policewoman, both in uniform. The woman was tall and slim and she had a kind face. The man was the opposite, he was noticeably short and wide and had a pissed off expression as if he'd just been woken up.

The policeman nodded towards us. "I'm Police Constable Rogers and this is PC Pawlyn."

Stephanie did the introductions and then offered them a cup of tea or coffee, which they both declined.

"I understand you have had a break in?" PC Rogers said.

The house looked towards me and so I explained what had happened.

"Was there anything missing from your bedroom?" PC Rogers asked as he took a notepad and pen out of his pocket.

I shook my head.

"Was there anything missing from the rest of the house?" he asked.

I looked towards Miles who shook his head. "I did a quick once over around all of the rooms and nothing appears to be missing or out of place."

"Did you get a look at who it was that was in your bedroom?" he asked.

I shook my head again and him and PC Pawlyn shared a look.

"It was dark, and I had only just woken up," I explained.

"Can you give us the best description possible?" he asked.

"Umm..." I hesitated, I had been so petrified that I genuinely didn't even get a slight look at whoever it was. "It was very dark, I only saw the back of them as they ran out of my door. They were tall, I think it was a man. I don't know what else to tell you."

PC Rogers sighed and put his notepad away without writing anything on it.

In a soft voice PC Pawlyn said, "Do you mind if we take a look around the house?"

"Go ahead," I said.

They left the room together and we sat in silence until they came back. My hands were still shaking and for some reason I felt like we were just wasting their time.

## The Doll House

When they came back into the room PC Rogers said, "There doesn't seem to be any signs of a break in or forced entry. Are you sure you locked the doors?"

We all looked at each other, knowing full well that most nights we did go to bed forgetting to lock the front door.

"It's possible that the front door was unlocked but even so, coming in here and ransacking my bedroom is still illegal right?"

PC Pawlyn nodded, "It is. Do you have any idea of who would have reason to search in your room?"

I looked away, shaking my head.

"Tell them about the dolls Lila," Stephanie said.

I looked at her and rolled my eyes. "I'm sure that isn't relevant."

"Lila, if you withhold any information, even if it doesn't seem important to you, then it could prevent us from finding anything," said PC Pawlyn.

I sighed. "Well I have been left a few um... gifts recently. Some flowers and a few dolls, the first one had a rope around its neck and another had a hospital gown on." I purposely left out the details about the lavender and the links to my mother, I wasn't ready to go into that yet.

The police looked at each other again, looking more serious now, "Have they all been left here at the house?" PC Rogers asked.

I shook my head. "No, a couple were left at my work too."

"There was another doll hung up by its neck outside," said Stephanie giving me a look. "It was wearing Lila's clothes that someone would have had to come into the house to get."

The police looked at each other again and then looked towards me, PC Pawlyn frowned. "So they have broken in twice? Why did you not deem this important to tell us?"

I stared at them, knowing I couldn't tell them the honest answer. "Well... I didn't think they were doing anything wrong, it was just a few gifts I thought it was a stupid prank or something but now they're watching me sleep and ransacking my bedroom it seems a bit more serious, don't you think?"

"I would have said that hanging a doll supposed to be you was also quite threatening don't *you* think?" snapped Stephanie.

PC Rogers nodded and said, "Yes and if they know where you live and where you work they haven't picked you at random, they seem to be targeting you. Have any of the presents had any relevance at all?"

I shook my head, silently praying that Stephanie wouldn't say anything and she didn't.

"Okay. I think we have all we need for now. We will check the CCTV in the area and get back to you. Call us if you need anything at all okay?"

Stephanie looked at Tom in panic and then back at the police. "What, that's it?"

"Unfortunately, we don't have a lot to go on at the moment," said PC Rogers. "There isn't any evidence of a break in. It's not even clear if the person who entered was the same person who has been leaving these *gifts*."

"Call us if you remember any details."

Miles showed them out and them came back into the kitchen, "Fat lot of good they are."

I shrugged, "What else could they have done, they didn't have any evidence, there wasn't a break in, nothing was even stolen."

"You should have told them about the lavender" Stephanie said quietly.

I shook my head and turned towards her, "how can I explain something to them that I don't even understand myself?"

# Chapter Thirteen

We all decided to sleep in the living room again that night although it wasn't as cosy and friendly as the first time. They didn't understand why I wasn't being completely honest with the police and I could tell they were annoyed with me. To be honest, I wasn't completely sure why I wasn't telling them everything either. There was no possible way that it was my mother behind all of this and I was sure it hadn't been a woman in my room, yet I still couldn't get the thought out of my head. It wouldn't make any sense for it to be her. I'd never seen any proof of her death, I'd never had any closure. Maybe that was what I needed.

I listened to the others all gradually fall asleep but I knew I wouldn't be getting any sleep that night. I was still awake when the alarm on my phone went off at 7am and I'd never been more grateful for it to be the weekend. I must have drifted in and out of consciousness all night but didn't get any proper sleep. It was stupid, I was almost purposely not falling asleep to listen out for anything, and every single noise made me hold my breath in fear that someone was trying to come in again. A horrible nervous sick feeling had made its home in my stomach and refused to fade and I physically couldn't make myself relax. I couldn't even see properly I was so tired. I looked over and Stephanie was asleep, cuddled into Tom's chest. I smiled to myself.

I rolled over under the covers and into the warmth of Miles' back. He rolled over to face me with his eyes still closed but I could tell by his breathing that he was awake. He put his arms around me and pulled me closer to his chest and I actually started to relax. His hand started to lightly trace circles on my back, it felt so good I almost let an embarrassing sound escape my lips. His hand continued its circles, with each trip it made its way lower down my back until it was toying with the waistband of my *very* unsexy pyjama bottoms. My pulse quickened as his touch started to feel anything but relaxing and suddenly I pushed myself away and sat up.

I frowned down at him but he smirked up at me, his eyes glistening with mischief.

"Stop being weird," I said.

He pulled a face of mock innocence. "Just being a comforting friend."

"Why are you guys making noise it feels far too early," Steph groaned whilst sitting up.

"Lila's stupid alarm woke me up but now we're all awake come on, get up and changed. Both of you," Miles said as he sat up.

Me and Steph frowned at each other from our snuggled positions, not wanting to go anywhere.

"Not in the mood I just need to be a hermit for the day Miles," I said as I laid back down and pulled the blanket tighter over my shoulders.

Miles smirked as he leant down and grabbed the blanket and yanked it off me. I groaned as the cold air hit me.

"Miles-"

He cut me off. "Look, you girls are weak and tiny and useless, that much is clear. You're coming with me to a private defence class. I won't even charge you... much."

"Miles," I rolled my eyes. "I'm pretty sure whoever is doing this is a man, a fully grown creep, I'm not going to fight him for Christ's sake."

"That's the point of my class genius, that's why people pay me good money. So that they can do exactly that, petite young women don't go to defence classes in case they're attacked by a bloody child, now come on get changed."

I huffed and looked over to Steph for back up but she was smirking looking between Miles and me. She stood up and shrugged. "I think it's a good idea, I'd feel a lot safer at least."

40 minutes later we were all in our gym gear in a private studio at Mile's gym and I was trying to take no notice of how Miles' very tight gym top accentuated all his muscles. I'd seen him topless and in his gym gear almost every day so I wasn't sure why it was any different now.

"Right, we've only got this room for an hour so I'm going to get straight to it. Grab an exercise mat and a punching bag each."

We spent about half an hour weight training and then half an hour punching a bag that barely even moved when either of us hit it. We were both sweaty messes, although Steph definitely looked more dignified than I did and Miles was barely even out of breath. This session had been child's play to him.

"This is stupid," I huffed, "I'm not going to suddenly know how to punch a weirdo stalker in my bedroom because I've been punching this bag."

Miles rolled his eyes. "This is just about building strength in your punches, we'll deal with the technique later, because at the moment neither of you are doing any damage with these things."

He snorted as his lifted Steph's arm up and dropped it.

I smiled as she pulled away frowning and then lifted her chin and continued pounding her tiny ineffectual fists into the punch bag in-front of her.

"Yep that's it," Miles encouraged and flashed me a smile she didn't see.

It annoyed me that that simple action caused the heat to rise to my cheeks. I looked away quickly, focusing my attention on my punch bag. I punched and punched, left fist, right fist, trying to focus on my stance, my technique, my breathing. Anything but Miles. It seemed to be working as I hadn't noticed him come up behind me.

He slid his hands onto my waist and pulled me gently to the side as he said softly, "You needs to stand more side on rather than facing the opponent directly."

I complied, breathing heavily, as he kicked my ankle lightly and pushed my leg with his knee. "And you need to have your legs further apart," he whispered into my ear sending a pleasurable shiver down my spine.

"Else you'll fall over," he said louder as he stood back and walked back over to Steph. Again, I couldn't help the smile that forced its way onto my lips.

Maybe I was thinking too much into things but Miles seemed to be flirting with me and I seemed to be enjoying it. I clearly wasn't thinking straight because of all the disturbing things that had been going on because it was *Miles*. I'd seen the way he treated girls; many, *many* girls. He was never disrespectful but he'd always made it clear to them he was only after one thing and I'd just experienced that with Caleb. Miles was off-limits.

The next morning I considered calling in sick for work again but I needed the money and I was sure that if I had any more days off Reynolds would replace me without a second thought. I had a quick, cold shower to wake myself up, although it didn't really work, and then begrudgingly dragged myself to work.

When I walked into Reynold's office, he took one look at me and said, "You look... tired."

I nodded and yawned as if on cue. "I haven't been sleeping very well recently."

"Ah I see... Well I won't make you work too hard today." He gestured to the papers he had spread out on his desk. "I was just having another look at the Patient Zero case."

I walked over and sat down at his desk, staying silent but looking interested so that he would continue.

"Do you know the treatments for schizophrenia?" he asked.

"Umm, antipsychotics which work by blocking the effect of dopamine on the brain, and behavioural therapies like counselling?"

"Exactly. Patient Zero was receiving both treatments. His medical records show that he was experiencing some serious side-effects of the antipsychotics. Vomiting, dizziness, weight gain, muscle twitches and spasms, blurred vision... it can't have been pleasant."

"Gosh..." I shook my head sadly. "You'd have thought by now they would have achieved a more humane treatment. What's the point in being sane if you feel like that all the time?"

I suddenly wondered if my mother had been experiencing these symptoms and going through that all alone. The thought made me feel quite sick.

Dr Reynolds nodded. "Unfortunately it's quite common. Anyway, Zero was there for such a long time that, by look of it, he made quite a friendship with one of the nurses who allowed him to take his medication himself."

"That's against the regulations surely?" I said.

"Of course. He probably stopped taking them," Reynolds nodded. "That or she felt so sorry for him that she allowed him to stop taking them. She was fired from Sherwood when they found out." He turned to put the file away in his filing cabinet.

My heart stopped and then beat so hard in my chest I thought it was going to explode.

"What did you say?" I asked.

He looked back around at me. "I said she was fired from the hospital when they found out."

I shook my head and stood up. "No, where did he go? Which mental hospital?"

"Sherwood."

# The Doll House

I turned around, shaking my head. This couldn't be happening. There was too much going that I didn't understand, too many coincidences that weren't adding up in my brain.

"How long ago was he there again?"

"13 years ago," he answered, frowning. "Why?"

"I have to go," I said. "I'm not feeling well."

"Lila what's going on?"

"Nothing!" I snapped. "Sorry. I just... I need to go. I don't feel very well, I'm sorry."

I grabbed my handbag and hurried out of the office as fast as I could, ignoring Reynolds calling my name and not caring if I was going to get fired.

I got into my car and slammed my hands on the steering wheel swearing loudly. I put my hands in my hair and rested my forehead on the wheel and then jumped wildly when I heard a knock on my window. I looked up to see Caleb looking down at me.

I pointedly locked the doors and looked away, willing my tears to subside. He knocked again.

"Lila? Are you okay?"

I looked straight ahead unable to speak.

"Look I'm sorry about the other night, I didn't mean to upset you. Please can you please let me explain?"

I rolled my eyes. That was the least of my worries. I slammed my hands on the steering wheel again as frustrated tears burned in my eyes.

"Lila? What's wrong?"

I looked towards him and just shook my head. I couldn't tell him, not after the other night. I didn't even really understand what was going on myself.

I continued to ignore him but he knocked again lightly. "Lila please talk to me, I will stay out here until you do."

I looked at him and saw a face that usually showed an amused and playful expression now filled with concern. I softened and sighed and then silently unlocked the doors. He walked around the car and slid into the passenger seat beside me and put his hand on my knee but I pushed him off. He stayed silent.

"I don't even know where to begin." I sniffed.

"Try me. I'm a surprisingly good listener."

I sighed and weighed up whether I should tell him or not.

"It's just a strange coincidence I'm sure but with everything that's going on at the moment... I just don't understand anything."

"Just try and explain..." he said softly.

"Dr Reynolds and I have been reviewing a case recently. He calls him Patient Zero. It's a really interesting case actually... he has Schizophrenia and may or may not be involved in the deaths of two women. Anyway, I just found out that he was at the same psychiatric hospital as my mother."

He raised his eyebrows. "Oh wow that is a coincidence."

"But it's even weirder." I met his eyes and studied his face. "They were both there 13 years ago. They were at the same hospital at the same time. They may have spoken, they might have known each other, and now I'm reviewing his case? It's just odd to me."

I could tell by his face he was adding it all together the same way I was. All the links to my mother but with no final conclusions that made any sense.

"None of it adds up Caleb," I sighed. "I haven't thought about my mother properly in years and suddenly all these links to her are appearing everywhere."

Caleb frowned. "Okay. Piece it all together, what's actually happened?"

I rolled my eyes. "You know what's happened."

"I know I do but just say it all out loud and something might click and suddenly make sense."

"Um, okay... So, I'm receiving random anonymous gifts which include creepy dead dolls and my mother's favourite flower and poem. I'm only now receiving letters that she wrote 13 years ago. I've had someone break into my house and hang a doll supposed to be me in my garden and ransack my bedroom. And now the patient I'm researching at work happened to be at the same mental hospital as my mother at the same time?"

We sat in silence for a little while before I said, "Nope it just sounds even messier out loud."

"You didn't tell me that when he left a doll he ransacked your bedroom too?"

I looked at him. "Firstly, we don't know if it's definitely a 'he'. Secondly, it wasn't the same night. Whoever it was broke into our house again and searched my bedroom for something but nothing was taken."

"What? Why didn't you tell me?"

"I didn't exactly have the chance to did I?" I gave him a look and then sighed. "I woke up to them sat on my bed stroking my hair."

# The Doll House

"That is really disturbing... You didn't see who it was at all? Surely you could tell if it was a man or woman."

I shrugged. "It was dark Caleb, I genuinely didn't see anything. I suppose they were quite tall, a bit too tall to be a woman."

"I suppose they don't want to hurt you then. They had the chance to and they didn't."

I shrugged again. "I don't know, I woke up because I could smell lavender, and then I screamed and they ran out."

"So there's another link to your mother then," he said and I nodded.

He shook his head and then suddenly frowned and lowered his voice to a whisper. "Is he still there now?"

"What?" I frowned, confused.

"The patient that was at the hospital with your mother, is he still there now?"

I didn't like where he was going with this.

I nodded slowly. "Yes... he escaped for a little while but then was found and taken back."

"Oh okay..." he said. "Because I thought mayb–"

"It's not. It can't be," I interrupted and he didn't argue.

We sat there in another silence for a couple of uncomfortable seconds before he said, "Look, about the other night."

"I don't want to hear it," I said. "Not now."

"Something important came up and I had to rush out, I'm really sorry."

"And you couldn't have woken me up or even sent me a text?" I snapped.

"I was just in such a rush when I left and I didn't want to wake you and then I thought you'd be mad and a text wouldn't make up for it."

"Why were you in such a rush in the middle of the night?"

He hesitated and then said, "It was just a family emergency. I had an amazing night with you Lila, I wouldn't have left unless I had to."

I looked towards him now and he seemed genuine. I sighed.

"Look, why don't I make it up to you. Are you free tonight? We can go to that bar we went to that first night?"

I sighed, unsure.

"Come on Lila, I'd like to try and cheer you up." His irresistible playful smile was back and I couldn't stop the smile that formed on my lips, which he took as a yes.

"Okay, I assume you're going home," he said and I nodded, "but I have to finish work and then go home and get changed so I'll pick you up at eight."

I pulled into my road thinking about everything that had happened over the last couple of days and tried to add it all together to create some sort of link but I couldn't. There were still a couple of pieces missing from the puzzle and I wasn't completely sure that I wanted to find them. I was fairly sure I was just being paranoid anyway. Sherwood was such a prevalent mental hospital, one of the largest in England, of course it was going to come up some point if I was working in psychology. Any other day, before all of this mess, the mention of the hospital would have brought back memories of course, but I wouldn't have thought too much into it. It was purely because of everything else that I was overthinking it and trying to find connections in places that I wouldn't normally.

When I walked into the house I could hear someone watching television in the living room. I knew Stephanie and Miles were at work so it had to be Tom. I went into the kitchen and put the kettle on, a cup of tea would fix everything.

"I thought I heard someone come in, how come you're home early?" Tom asked, walking into the kitchen.

I sighed and sat at the breakfast bar. He sat opposite me apparently noticing that something was wrong so I explained everything that happened at work.

"It's probably just crappy timing," he said. "Sherwood had to come up at some point during your career, it's the largest institute for miles. Even I've heard of it, they've filmed documentaries on some of the patients."

"I know you're right, it's just with everything going on..."

"Exactly, with everything going on it probably seems more coincidental than it actually is."

I put my head in my hands and sighed.

He placed a comforting hand on my arm. "You know when detectives look at something and then they suddenly have a light-bulb moment and then everything makes sense. That will happen to us soon I'm sure."

I looked up at him and couldn't help but smile. "You watch too many films."

"I know." He nodded seriously. "Come on, let's be detectives."

# The Doll House

He jumped down and opened the doors to the garden and dragged in the black bin bag which still had the human-sized doll in it.

"I don't think this is a good idea," I frowned. "I don't want to look at that thing."

He ignored me and pulled it out of the bag. It was slightly damp where it had been raining outside and it was still in my clothes, its wet hair clung to its face. I shivered and looked away. He then reached into the top cupboard where I had hidden the first two dolls that I had received and he put them on the breakfast table.

"Okay," he said. "These are the only dolls we kept, I think the others and the lavender you threw away?"

I nodded and he said, "Okay so what do these have in common?"

We stared at the dolls in silence.

"So, one is in... What is this? A hospital gown?" Tom asked picking up the doll and I nodded.

"Okay so one is in a hospital gown, which could be linked to your mother if they had to wear these gowns at Sherwood?" I shrugged and he continued talking more to himself than to me. "And we know how the doll with the lavender headband was linked to her and the poem obviously... so what about these..."

He sighed looking back and forth between the two dolls and then picked up the smaller one on the breakfast bar, brushed its hair back and looked at the rope wrapped around its neck. He then looked towards the life-sized doll, also with a rope around its neck and then slowly looked towards me.

I already knew what he was about to say.

"Lila," he whispered. "How did your mother kill herself?"

Katie Masterman

# Chapter Fourteen

I had been on the phone with the receptionist at Sherwood for only about five minutes, but she wasn't giving away any information about my mother. To be honest I knew they wouldn't have been able to over the phone, but I thought I would try.

The woman's high-pitched and clearly false telephone voice was irritating me. "If you want any information you will have to come in with a valid form of identification, I'm afraid."

I sighed and thanked her and hung up and then looked at Tom.

"I'll drive." He smiled.

We got into Toms car and as he pulled out of the drive I breathed heavily to calm myself down.

"You nervous?" he asked.

I nodded. "I don't want to find out how she killed herself and I especially don't want to go to the place that she did it but... I know we have to."

Tom knew I was in no state to be making small talk, so he turned the radio on and we spent the rest of the journey in silence. After about 25 minutes he pulled into a gated carpark, parked up and then we climbed out of the car. I stood still for a second as I looked towards at the lifeless building.

It was a huge stone building, it looked incredibly dated except for the bright white windows and doors which looked out of place, like they had been recently changed. From the outside it looked like you'd expect a mental hospital to look, it was literally just a big square building with a few windows. There was nothing exciting or exceptionally characteristic and there was certainly nothing that made us want to go inside.

We looked at each other and then made our way to the entrance. There were two doors. The left one read "Sherwood's Main Reception" and the right door read "PICU - Psychiatric Intensive Care Unit". I looked at Tom and swallowed hard, glad to be going through the left door.

We pushed it open and entered the main reception. It was incredibly plain and again looked exactly like I was expecting it to. It was a small square room painted a sickly yellow shade. There were a few wooden chairs against the

# The Doll House

two side walls with the receptionist's desk against the back wall, although there was nobody sat at it. There was a wooden door on the back wall which I assumed led to the rest of the hospital, where all of the patients were. I breathed in and it smelt... clean. There was no other way to describe it. The smell brought back a rush of familiarity, but I wasn't sure why.

We walked up to the desk in silence. It was almost empty except for a few files, a pen and a computer. There was a note on the top that read, "Please ring bell for assistance." Tom rang the bell and was just about to sit on one of the chairs when two women came through the door on the back wall. One woman looked mid-forties, she had dyed bright red hair, wore a pearl necklace and giant matching pearl earrings and her makeup was sloppy. The other woman looked older, perhaps mid-sixties. She looked like you would expect a cute old lady to look with curly silver hair, glasses and an ankle length dress and boots. In each hand she held a beautiful bunch of colourful flowers.

The two women were chatting to each other and when they noticed us the older woman smiled, gestured to her flowers. "I'd better sort these out anyway."

The other woman nodded and walked behind the desk and sat down, obnoxiously taking her time to turn on the computer in front of her and line up her pen with her notepad before she eventually looked up and said, "How can I help you?"

I smiled falsely, recognising from her voice that she was the woman on the phone. "I spoke with you earlier regarding my mother's records, you said I needed to come in with a valid form of identification to get any information."

She nodded, she didn't have the friendliest face and her overdrawn lips still showed no hint of a smile. "What is the patient's name?"

"Kendra Beaumont, um, she died a few years ago."

The woman looked up at me and raised her eyebrows.

"I'm sorry to hear that. What information is it that you would like to know?"

"Um... Well, I was only young when she died. It was 13 years ago so nobody told me anything that happened, only that it was suicide. I just..." I looked at Tom who nodded encouragingly. "I just wanted to know, how she did it?"

"Well Dear, some things are best left in the past."

"I know but... I'm old enough now, I just want to know," I lied. I didn't want to know at all. I *had* to know.

"Well, I'm really sorry to tell you but after the patient has deceased we only keep their records for ten years on our system and then a hardcopy is made and placed in the archives. You can apply for the records of course but it may take a few weeks."

I didn't have the energy to argue. I just looked at Tom and shrugged, defeated.

"Here's the number to apply," she said, as she wrote down a number and handed it to me.

"Okay, thanks for your help..."

We walked away and headed back out to the carpark. Tom put his hand on my shoulder and said, "It's okay, we'll apply and then when we find out we will go from there. I'm sure it won't take as long as she thinks."

I was just about to respond when I heard a voice from behind me.

"Excuse me?"

I turned around to see the old lady from the reception. She had on a pair of green gardening gloves and an apron covered in mud. She slowly walked over to us and smiled and I could instantly tell she was a nice woman.

"Sorry to bother you and I didn't mean to eavesdrop. I'm Edie." she said, her voice was soft. "Did you say your mother was Kendra Beaumont?"

I nodded, frowning.

"Well, there can't have been two patients here with such a beautifully unique name so I am sure I knew your mother. She was a lovely woman, it was terrible what happened to her."

My voice caught in my throat when I tried to respond and Tom stepped up beside me. "Yes it was sad, how did you know her?"

"Well I've worked here for almost 30 years as a gardener and florist. Studies show that flowers naturally reduce stress. Adding a few flowers to the patient's daily life can reduce their levels of depression and anxiety and also boost their creativity and productivity." She smiled proudly at her knowledge and then continued. "Anyway, I used to put a bunch of flowers in every patients room and got talking to some of them. Your mother always requested–"

"Lavender?" I smiled and she smiled back.

"Yes lavender, her room always smelled so strongly of the flower. She said it relaxed her, she always requested more on days that she was feeling upset or was missing you..." She looked sadly at me. "She told me that she didn't allow you to visit but she missed you terribly. I thought she was ever so brave."

I swallowed the lump in my throat and blinked back the tears in my eyes. "I still miss her now. I wish that I got to see her before she..."

She put her had on my arm and nodded in understanding. "I know Dear, it is incredibly sad. It..." She paused, took her hand away and averted her gaze.

"What were you about to say?"

"Oh I'm not sure you would like to hear it my dear." She shook her head.

"I would... please? I'm trying to find out more about her death."

She studied my face and then looked between Tom and me and sighed.

"It was just... a bit unexpected is all. She seemed quite happy, I know I shouldn't say this but she seemed *normal*. She always took her medication and she seemed to understand that she had to stay in for a while longer so they could monitor her progress and she was doing everything she could to get better so that she could see you again."

I nodded. "I had some letters from her and I thought the same. They didn't read like they were written by a woman who wanted to kill herself."

"Yes, but I suppose we can never know what is going on inside someone's head."

I nodded and was about to thank her and say goodbye when Tom said, "I'm really sorry to ask this but... do you know how she killed herself?"

"Oh," she said in surprise. "You don't know?"

We shook our heads in unison and she said the words that I was expecting but still sent shivers down my spine.

"I'm sorry to be the one to tell you this but, well, she hanged herself."

We had drove home in silence. Every time Tom tried to speak I shook my head. It felt like my mind was racing and empty at the same time. I numbly walked into the house; everything was a blur. I was sat down in the living room with Stephanie Tom and Miles around me and I didn't even really remember how I got there. I knew they were all talking about me and what had happened at the hospital but I wasn't even listening. I couldn't hear anything. It was like I was in my own bubble.

"Lila! Hello, Lila?"

I looked up and my bubble regrettably popped. Stephanie was knelt down in front of me with her hands on my shoulders, staring at me with an anxious expression. I looked around to see that Miles and Tom's expressions matched Stephanie's and I shook my head.

"Sorry guys," I tried to speak strongly but my voice came out as a whisper. "I... My brain isn't really working at the moment, what did you say?"

"We were speaking for about ten minutes," Miles said with an eyebrow raised and I shrugged.

"I'm worried about you Lila, I'm worried about *everything*!" Steph said, her voice raised a few pitches.

I sighed and just looked at her not knowing how to respond.

"You can't just ignore this Lila. What do you think this means?"

I put my head into my hands and ran my fingers through my hair. I sat up and breathed and rested my head against the back of the sofa.

"I think it means that whoever is doing this to me was in the hospital with my mother. I think they know her, they know about her obsession with lavender because she used to have it in her room and they know about her suicide because they would have been there."

I looked up and they were all nodding and then Miles said, "But why are they doing this to you? And why now after all these years?"

I shrugged. "I don't know. I really just... don't know."

"I mean, it doesn't bode well does it?" Miles said.

"What do you mean?"

"That the person doing this has spent time in a nuthouse."

I glared at him and began to speak when Steph said, "I think we should call the police again."

"Do whatever you want," I said. "I don't care anymore. I've decided I'm going to ignore the problem and hope that it disappears."

"I'm not sure that's the best idea," said Steph.

I sighed and abruptly changed the subject. "Caleb is picking me up at 8 to make up for leaving the other night, I feel and look like crap so are you going to help me get ready?"

She softened and smiled. "Of course."

We picked out a cute little outfit, white jeans, a black top and black heels, and Steph plaited my hair.

"I love your hair in two plaits, it really suits you."

# The Doll House

I looked into the mirror in front of me, still feeling like crap. "Maybe I should cancel."

She walked around in front of me and said, "Don't you dare. He's a nice guy and he's sexy as hell, he will give you a valid explanation about why he left and you will have a great night which you deserve after everything that's been going on. Okay?"

I smiled a genuine smile at my best friend and nodded. Steph looked me up and down and grinned, she seemed satisfied. We walked into the living room and Miles let out a wolf whistle.

"Caleb is a lucky guy," he said. His eyes looked seriously into mine and I ignored the unwelcome feeling in my stomach that had been occurring far too often for my liking. Stephanie giggled next to me, completely unaware of my confused state. I gave him a smile and looked away.

I sat down on the sofa next to Tom and looked at the time on my phone which read 19:58. Caleb should be here any minute and he'd better have a reasonable explanation.

The more time passed, the more my stomach sank. After what felt like an eternity I looked at my phone again. The time now read 21:37 and Caleb was clearly not coming.

The others looked at me sadly. I looked so pathetic I wanted the floor to swallow me up. I was humiliated. I wished the rest of the house were out and hadn't had to see me waiting for him, looking at my phone every minute for 2 and a half hours. He'd probably forgotten or had something better to do. Either way, I was done.

I stood up. "Right that's it, I'm going off the rails. Who's coming with me?"

Miles chuckled and said, "I'm in." Then followed me to the kitchen where I pulled out a couple of glasses and a bottle of red wine from the seemingly endless supply we kept in the cupboard.

Miles stepped up behind me and put his hands on my waist.

He leant down and whispered in my ear, "He doesn't know what he's missing."

I could hear the smile in his voice and I turned to look at him, but he stepped back and looked away as Steph walked into the kitchen. I narrowed my eyes at the back of his head and wondered why he was acting like this with me all of a sudden. Why was I enjoying it? This was *Miles* for Christ's sake.

Steph pulled two more glasses out and I smiled at her and filled them all, emptying the bottle.

We all sat in the living room with our favourite music playing, silently agreeing not to talk about anything that had been going on. We had gotten through a few bottles of wine and some tequila shots and it was now in the early hours of the morning. My stomach hurt from laughing and I actually felt okay. I decided alcohol was a great way to numb the world around me.

Steph stood up and then giggled as she nearly fell straight back down. "I've got to go to bed, I can't afford to take any more time off work."

She kissed me on the forehead and then headed up to bed. Tom followed suit. I was rather drunk and doubted that I could walk to bed so I laid down on the sofa and closed my eyes.

Miles stood up and picked me up easily as if I weighed no more than a bag of flour. "Come on, let's put you to bed."

"Alone," I murmured half asleep. His only response was a light laugh.

# Chapter Fifteen

My alarm went off on my phone and I snoozed it, ran to the bathroom and threw up. Then I threw up repeatedly. My throat burned, my head span and I still felt nauseous. I was never *ever* drinking that much alcohol again especially on a work night.

I *literally* crawled into the shower and stayed sat down, worried if I stood up I'd either pass out or throw up. The cold water made me feel a little better. I got ready ridiculously slowly, accepting the fact I was going to be late to work. Hopefully Dr Reynolds would be in one of his nice moods.

When I walked into the kitchen I saw Stephanie leaning against the side with a coffee in her hands.

When she saw me, she sniggered. "Well, you look about as rough as I feel."

"Why do we drink wine?" I asked.

"Because it numbs the pain?" she laughed, handing me a cup of coffee. I took a sip.

"Where are the boys?" I asked.

"Still in bed I think, Tom is on the late shift and Miles doesn't have a class until this afternoon."

I shook my head and gulped down the rest of my coffee. "Lucky for some. I'm just hoping I don't throw up whilst driving."

Steph laughed and wished me good luck as I headed towards the front door. I stopped just before I opened it, racked by a sudden rush of anxiety. My hands began to shake, I just had a feeling there was going to be something out there, on the car or on the doorstep. Another doll or some flowers or a note or something. I just had a feeling. I decided then that if there was something out there I was going back to bed.

I took a deep breath and then opened the door and looked around. Nothing on the doorstep. I walked out to my car to see there was nothing on there either. I was so on edge. I breathed a sigh of relief, although an excuse to go back to bed would have been nice.

# Katie Masterman

When I arrived at work my day got even better. Dr Reynolds was on a conference. Not only would he not know that I was half an hour late, but I didn't have to act like I wasn't hungover. I slumped down in his chair at his desk and read the note that he had left me.

"Lila, please can you take the document printed out on my desk and create a PowerPoint presentation from it. I have to present next week and I don't think I will have time do to it myself. Thank you."

I spent the first couple of hours of the day recovering, scrolling through various social media pages on my phone and drinking lots of coffee. When I felt a little bit better I decided to actually do what Reynolds had asked me to do. It didn't take me long so I was finished by 2 in the afternoon. I didn't really have anything else to do so I decided to let myself have half a day off. He wasn't here anyway so what did it matter?

As I was leaving the office I once again felt that anxious, nauseas feeling creep into my stomach. I was expecting one of two things to be by my car when I went outside. A gift or Caleb. I wasn't sure which was worse. I once again took a deep breath and walked out to my car to find that nothing unusual was there. I had started to get used to this paranoid feeling.

When I got home the house was empty, I assumed they were all at work. I still felt pretty rough from the night before so I decided I would go upstairs to have a nap. I changed into comfortable leggings and a vest top, pulled my hair into a bun and when I climbed into bed I fell asleep as soon as my head hit the pillow.

I wasn't asleep for long before I heard raised voices.

I got out of bed and crept to my door, opening it slightly to listen.

I heard Caleb's voice. "Look I'm sorry you feel like that mate but really this has nothing to do with you, I just came here to apologise."

"This has everything to do with me!" Miles growled. "You think we enjoy seeing her all excited, dressed up, watching the time, waiting for you to come and pick her up only to realise that you weren't coming?"

I physically cringed.

"I can explain but I don't need to explain myself to you. Her car is outside so I know she's in."

I heard Stephanie's voice. "Do you not think that she is going through enough right now?"

## The Doll House

"I know you guys are trying to protect her and I get that but I think that she would want to talk to me. If you could just let me in–"

"Miles!" I heard Stephanie yell. I jumped and opened the door to see that Miles had grabbed Caleb by neck of his top.

"Miles!" I echoed Stephanie as I ran down the stairs. "What are you doing?!"

Miles let go of Caleb and they all turned to look at me, as though I was a poor damaged little girl who was going to break. I plastered a defiant look on my face, I was stronger than they thought.

"I'll get him out of here," Miles said, turning back to Caleb who took a step back. Caleb was tall, muscular and strong and yet stood next to Miles he looked tiny.

I stepped forward, pulled Miles' arm back and looked up at him. "It's okay. Really. I want to talk to him."

There were a few moments silence in which nobody moved so I said, "Alone."

Steph and Miles both glared towards Caleb and then walked away to the living room. I gestured with my head for him to come inside and then I closed the door behind him. We went into the kitchen for some privacy. I sat down on one of the stools, remembering the last time we were in this kitchen together and I sighed.

"Lila, I never would have stood you up on purpose I hope you know that."

"No, I don't know that," I snapped.

"Something came up, it was important."

"Is your phone broken?"

He looked down. "No, it's not. But I was just... I was busy, I didn't have time to look at my phone. I know I should have let you know but I got distracted and by the time I remembered I was already two hours late. I thought I'd let you cool off and then I would come around today."

"How thoughtful of you," I said flatly.

"Look, I've got a lot going on at home Lila. I am deeply sorry that it slipped my mind but I just... I'm sorry, okay. I'm not going to beg. I made a mistake and I'd really like you to give me another chance."

I sighed and thought for a moment.

"One more chance Caleb," I said.

He smiled and walked over to kiss me on the forehead. "Good choice. I will meet you at the bar tomorrow at 8 this time, okay?"

I nodded and he looked me up and down. I had scrubbed my makeup off before my nap and my hair was up in a messy bun. "You look beautiful like this by the way."

"Alright you don't need to suck up." I shook my head. "I already said I'd meet you tomorrow."

He smirked and followed me to the front door passing the living room along the way where he shouted, "It was a pleasure to see you as always Miles!"

I smacked him on the arm. "He's just being a good friend."

"Hmm...I'll see you tomorrow okay? I won't be late."

I woke up the next morning feeling slightly more relaxed. I felt optimistic, as though the plan was working. Ignore the problem, don't give them a reaction and the problem will go away. Whoever was doing this would eventually get bored and leave me alone. I felt good.

I walked into the kitchen to get my morning coffee to see Steph, Tom and Miles already in there.

"Morning," Steph sang, but she averted her gaze.

"Morning," I said back. I went to reach for the coffee and noticed that the blinds in the kitchen were still shut.

"Why is it so dark in here?" I asked, leaning forward to pull them open.

"No!" Tom jumped pulling my arm back. "I just –" He put his hand to his head and squinted. "I have a migraine. The light is really hurting my head."

"Oh right okay," I frowned as I took a sip of coffee. Both Stephanie and Miles were unusually quiet. They were normally annoyingly chirpy in the mornings.

"What's going on?" I asked.

"Nothing," Stephanie smiled but I could tell it was forced. "Everything's fine."

"Are you mad at me for forgiving Caleb straight away? I just thought one more chance won't hurt and with everything going on right now I think I deserve a distraction, don't you?"

"We're not mad at you Lila," Steph rolled her eyes. "You do deserve it. If he stands you up again though Miles will hurt him."

# The Doll House

I looked to Miles who just nodded in agreement.

"Okay..." I chuckled lightly and drank the last of my coffee. "Anyway, I should get to work."

"Are you sure?" Steph looked at the time. "You're a bit early aren't you?"

I looked and frowned. "Not really? I don't want to be late anyway..."

She nodded but began to chew her nails. I turned to walk away still looking at her curiously.

"Wait! Umm... I–" She looked at the boys and then looked at me and suddenly put her head in her hands and burst out crying.

"Steph what's wrong?!" I gasped, walking over to her and pulling her into a hug.

She sniffed and said, "Oh it's nothing, I don't want you to be late for work."

"It's okay Reynolds will understand, just talk to me."

She sniffed. "Well um – I just, I've been feeling so upset lately..." She trailed off looking around the room, when her eyes met Tom's she let out a small sob. "Because of him!"

The boys looked at each other with wide eyes and I said, "What? What has he done?" I looked at Tom. "What have you done?"

He shrugged and looked between everyone and opened and closed his mouth. I narrowed my eyes. *Hmm...*

I pulled Stephanie into a hug again and then pulled her face up by the chin to look me in the eyes.

"You never were very good at pretending to cry," I said flatly.

She stopped instantly and sighed.

I shook my head and demanded, "Will somebody tell me what the hell is going on?"

They all just looked at each other but still nobody said anything. I threw my hands up with a noise of frustration, grabbed my keys off the side and then headed towards the door. I pulled it open about an inch before Miles had caught up with me and slammed it shut, making me jump. He stood in front of the door blocking my way out.

"Oh for god sake Miles! What is wrong with all of you this morning?"

Stephanie just sighed.

"We didn't want to tell you... We thought it would be a bit... much." She nodded towards Miles who looked at me and then stepped aside.

I whispered, "What am I going to see when I open this door?"

Steph dropped her voice to a whisper as well. "It must have happened over night, I don't really know how to explain."

I took a deep breath and opened the door so that she didn't have to.

I gasped and took a step forward.

Our entire front garden was *completely* covered in bright purple lavender. There wasn't even an inch of space left. It wasn't just thrown onto the garden either, it was all fresh lavender, planted neatly in rows and rows right up to the fence. A soft breeze blew the scent of the flower towards me and I breathed in. It wasn't as strong because it was fresh but it still made my stomach tense up.

I turned back around to face the others who were all stood behind me staring at the garden in dismay.

"I really just don't even know what to say," I said.

Miles put his hand on my shoulder and said, "We'll get it cleaned up whilst you're at work."

"No," I said. "Leave it. Ignore it. We ignore the problem; the problem goes away."

"I'm not sure that will work they seem pretty persistent," said Steph.

"They're just looking for a reaction and I'm not going to give them the satisfaction. They'll get bored eventually." I looked around at the garden. "It's weird though isn't it? Whoever is doing this isn't *exactly* threatening me are they? Yes they're being a bit creepy, coming into our house, giving me dolls and my dead mothers favourite flower... but they haven't threatened me or tried to hurt me. What are they trying to achieve?"

"Um, Lila" Tom said, "There was a doll, intended to look like you, hanged outside in our garden. Your mother was... well, she hanged herself too... do you not think that is a threat? Maybe like, you next?"

"Tom!" Steph gasped and I swallowed.

"I'm sorry to say this, girls," Miles said. "But the thought has crossed my mind too. I know I didn't take this seriously to begin with but then when we saw that doll hanging outside, knowing that's how your mother died..." He trailed off.

I shook my head. "But it doesn't make sense. Who would want to hurt me? I haven't done anything."

"I think you need to speak to the police again," Steph said. "Tell them everything, the links to your mother, they will be able to look into her history.

# The Doll House

You probably don't remember everything about who she was friends with because you were so young when she was still alive."

"No," I argued. "I remember her, I remember everything. She had nobody and even if this was one of her *friends* what the hell are they trying to do by sending me all these weird gifts and messages?"

"That is what the police would find out."

I sighed. "Right, I have to go to work. Don't touch the garden, ignore it and they will get bored, I know it. If anything else threatening happens I will call the police okay?"

I didn't wait for a response before I turned and walked away.

Katie Masterman

# Chapter Sixteen

When I got to work I saw Caleb standing by his van chatting to his friends who were smoking, as usual. He smiled when he saw me and jogged to my car. He looked impeccably attractive this morning, with his scruffy hair and tight t-shirt that accentuated his muscles.

"Morning," he said and surprised me by giving me a quick peck on the lips which prompted a series of wolf-whistles and woops from his friends. It made me smile despite my foul mood.

"Do you guys actually do any work?" I joked.

He shrugged smirking. "Hm, not really. We just stand around preying on attractive women who park here."

I rolled my eyes. "I'm going to be late. You'd better show up tonight okay?"

"Yes ma'am." He saluted to me and then jogged back to his friends.

I shook my head, realising how similar him and Miles were. They were both cocky and overconfident and made a joke out of everything unless it was deadly serious.

When I entered the office Reynolds was sat at his desk. He looked up at me and raised his eyebrows. "Nice of you to turn up."

"I'm really sorry I'm late I just – I have a lot going on at home and I was really distracted this morning and then Steph my housemate starting crying and–"

"Fine," he held his hand up to cut me off. "Your life is like a soap opera you know that don't you? Did you do the PowerPoint for me yesterday?"

I laughed because if I didn't I would probably cry. "I know trust me, I know. And yes I emailed it to you."

He gave a curt nod and then studied my face. "I hope you don't mind me asking, but you seemed to leave my office in quite some distress the other day after we had been discussing Patient Zero."

I sighed, I was hoping that he wasn't going to ask. "Right, sorry about that. It was just a little close to home that was all."

# The Doll House

"The mental illness?" he asked.

"More where he was sectioned. Sherwood... My mother was there too before she died."

"Well, that is a slight coincidence," he said. "But I suppose a lot of my patient's case files come out of Sherwood."

"I know, I just thought too much into it that's all." I said. I didn't feel the need to divulge any more details than that.

He stared at me for a second so intently I began to feel uncomfortable. Then he nodded and put his head to his laptop, without looking back up he said, "I'm emailing you across some documents, I need you to print and file them."

I just nodded and we spent the rest of the day in silence.

When I got home and parked up my stomach tightened at the sight of the lavender all over the garden. I walked into the house and the smell of Stephanie's cooking greeted my senses instantly, making my stomach growl. I walked straight to the kitchen.

"Mm... What's cooking?" I asked.

"Lasagne," Stephanie replied. She was stood by the oven with her hair in a messy bun and her bright pink apron on. I stood behind her as she was stirring the lasagne sauce and rested my head on her back.

"What if he stands me up tonight Steph?" I asked.

"He won't."

"But what if he does?"

"Then you won't speak to him again because you deserve better than that and there would be hundreds of guys dying to take you out for a drink," she said sternly and then she giggled. "Then we'd set Miles on him."

"I heard my name." Miles said walking in. "What's cooking?"

"Lasagne," Steph said. Miles walked over to where we were standing by the cooker and went to dip his finger in the sauce but Steph smacked his hand with the back of her spatula.

"Excuse me, I see you sitting on the sofa with your hands down your pants. I don't want that or your sausage fingers in my lasagne sauce thank you very much."

He put his hands up in the surrendering position and then backed away laughing.

# Katie Masterman

We ate dinner in front of the tele, but I had just picked at my lasagne. I couldn't eat much as the nervous feeling was grew gradually stronger in my stomach. I knew it was time to go and get ready and I once again considered cancelling.

"Come on, I want to put your hair in plaits again," Steph said getting up. We went upstairs to her bedroom and sat on her bed where she pulled my hair into plaits.

"Okay, now you're going to borrow this," she said as she walked to the wardrobe and pulled out her famous little black dress. "Trust me once he sees you in this you'll never be able to get rid of him."

I sat down at the bar and ordered myself a gin and tonic. Although Caleb probably thought that I had forgiven him, I hadn't. I did like him, he was a happy distraction from the shit show my life had become, but he still had some serious explaining to do. I kept telling myself that he did like me and was a genuinely nice guy else he wouldn't keep trying to make it up to me. I was sure there was a reasonable explanation as to why he didn't turn up the other night and why he would leave my house in the early hours of the morning.

I sighed and downed my drink and quickly ordered another one. Who was I kidding? Maybe he had a girlfriend at home he had to get back to. I barely even knew the guy, I didn't know what had made me give him a third chance.

I looked at the time, he was already 20 minutes late. This was his third and final chance, there was no way I was going to forgive him if he didn't turn up tonight. I really didn't need this at the moment. I had a crazy stalker who had some sort of weird connection to my dead mother and now I had *boy* troubles. He knew everything that was going on and all he was doing was adding to it.

He was 45 minutes late. I ordered another drink, pulled out my phone and rang his number. No answer. I decided to send him a text.

"Just to let you know I have been here 45 minutes and will be leaving in 15."

As soon as I pressed send I regretted it. I reeked of desperation. I had already been waiting for him almost an hour, completely stood up by him the night before and now I was giving him more time.

With everything that had been going on I just felt exhausted. I wasn't sleeping, I wasn't really eating, I felt sick with nerves most of the time and I just wanted a little time out. Time to not think about anything, just have fun and enjoy life like I used to.

I pulled out my phone and text Steph.

"Just so you're aware of my mood when I get home Caleb stood me up again. I'm going to drown my sorrows away, have the wine ready."

My phone vibrated on the bar but I turned it over so the screen faced downwards. I couldn't bring myself to read a sympathy filled message.

I sighed and ordered myself another drink and then another. The anxious feeling in the pit of my stomach eased as increased amounts of alcohol flowed through my body. It was nice actually. I relaxed, not caring if he was going to turn up or not.

I tried to look at the time on my phone and was surprised when I had to squint and wait for the screen to adjust. Why was the time moving around so much? I couldn't be that drunk could I? I suppose I didn't usually drink gin and I hadn't eaten anything substantial for a couple of days so it made sense. But I felt okay. I felt *almost* happy... Relaxed.

I wasn't sure how long I sat there on my own, drinking my sorrows away but I knew Caleb was definitely not coming and I was in a bit of a mess.

I noticed a man staring at me from across the bar, I hiccupped and waved my glass in his direction. He laughed and ordered two drinks and then came over to where I was sat at the bar.

"What's a beautiful young lady doing in a bar like this all by herself?"

"Numbing away my pain..." I giggled and took another sip of my drink, not caring that my voice was slurred.

I looked at him now he was up close. He was wearing blue jeans, a white shirt and had ridiculous sunglasses balancing on his head. He was slightly chubby; he had tried to clean shave but hadn't done a particularly good job of it. He had almost non-existent thin pink lips, quite a large nose and I saw nothing but hunger in his eyes. I hiccupped.

"Well, cheers to that!" He laughed. "I'm Clive."

"Lila." We clinked our glasses together.

By now my head was completely fuzzy and I knew if I tried to get up and walk anywhere I would fall over. Yet I still didn't care. It was the most carefree I had felt in weeks, I didn't want the feeling to end.

"So, are you supposed to meeting someone here?" Clive asked.

"I was, but that was at 8," I slurred. "What time is it now?"

He looked at his phone. "It's almost midnight, looks like you've been stood up darlin'. I'm much better company anyway." He smirked but it wasn't a nice playful smirk like Miles'.

Regardless of my drunken state a feeling of unease suddenly washed over me. I rubbed my temples.

"God, is that really the time?" I yawned. "I should probably order a taxi."

He nodded. "Alright, lets finish these drinks and then I'll help you order one."

My drunk brain took over and I gulped down the last bits of my drink. I couldn't help but notice it tasted slightly different and left a horrible powdery sensation on my tongue. I looked towards Clive who was hungrily watching me finish my drink and my stomach clenched. Well *shit*.

I wondered if my life could get any worse.

I swallowed and said, "I just need to go to the bathroom."

My plan was to make myself sick, ring Miles and everything would be okay. Of course, nothing in my life was that simple.

As I stood up, I swayed and almost tripped over the barstool which gained the attention of the other people sat around the bar. He grabbed my arm and hissed loudly, "For god sake honey, I told you not to drink that much again. Come on, let's get you home."

The people around us looked away in embarrassment. I began to protest when my vision momentarily went black. I forced my eyes open but the room in front of me had a dark haze around it.

I was going to pass out.

I willed myself to stay alert, I tried to pull my arm back but I felt so weak. I couldn't even stand up straight. My brain wasn't functioning properly so I just let Clive pull me outside into the carpark even though my gut was telling me I was in trouble

"You've drugged me," I slurred.

"Shut up," he hissed. "You did this to yourself."

I forced some strength into my voice. "Was it you? The dolls and the lavender? Have you been following me?"

He looked down at me utterly perplexed as beads of sweat rolled down his forehead. I realised then this wasn't targeted, I'd just been an impulse victim for him and I'd made it too easy.

# The Doll House

His grip tightened on my arm and he dragged me through the carpark. I heard a jangle of keys and my stomach clenched. I knew this was dire and I knew no matter what I did I could *not* let him get me into his car. I searched around desperately for help, but the carpark was empty aside from us. In my search I spotted a drain on the ground. Through squinted, blurry eyes I searched for his keys. They were in his left hand, his right was leaving finger bruises on my arm. In one final surge of adrenaline before the drugs completely took hold I lunged forward. Catching him off guard I managed to snatch the keys from his hand and threw them towards the drain in one movement. They skidded along the floor and landed on top of the drain and balanced precariously between two bars. We both lunged for them at same time and in the process one of us, I'm not sure which, knocked them down the drain.

I didn't have time to feel a sense of relief before I was roughly pulled upwards by my plaited hair.

"You stupid bitch!" he snarled.

He pulled me, stumbling over my own feet, around a corner and pushed me up against a wall. I thought we were behind the bar; my fuzzy brain couldn't really tell, I just knew it was dark, quiet and there was nobody around.

He pushed me against the wall again and this time my head slammed against it, sending a shock of pain all the way down my body. He crushed his lips onto mine. He tasted bitter, like a horrible mix of cigarettes and alcohol. I jerked my head away and tried to scream but he put his hand over my mouth.

"Don't even tell me this wasn't what you were asking for," he hissed into my ear. "I saw you, getting drunk on your own in that tiny dress. You were asking for this all night."

I whimpered against his hand and started to cry. I jerked my head away again and managed to let out a scream before he slammed his hand back over my mouth again. He roughly span me around so I was facing the wall and slammed my forehead against the brick and my vision almost blacked out. I felt the warm sensation of blood dripping down my face and into my mouth.

From behind me I heard the sickening sound of his buckle undoing on his trousers and my knees gave way but he forced me back up against the wall.

"No please," I begged. "Please don't do this."

I cried and whimpered and tried to scream but he was too strong and I was too weak. The bile rose in my throat as I felt his rough hand start to make its way up my thigh and force its way up my dress when he was wrenched away from me with such sudden force that I fell harshly to the ground.

I looked up and nearly sobbed with relief when I saw Miles. The fury in his eyes was enough to make any man tremble with fear. Clive took a step back and began to hold his hands up in defence when Miles leaned back and punched him square in the jaw with such force he stumbled backwards. Clive recovered quickly and threw his fist forward but Miles grabbed his wrist mid-air with ease and twisted it, forcing him to double over. He lifted a knee and slammed it into Clive's stomach causing him to cough and splutter.

Clive reached behind him and pulled out an object, its metallic silver edge glinted in the light and my heart nearly stopped.

"Knife!" I cried. It was all I could manage. I tried to get up but I was too weak. My vision began to cloud over and I knew the drugs had fully made their way into my system.

Clive swung the knife madly but Miles was too quick and far too strong. In a move far too quick for my drugged-up vision to comprehend Miles had snatched the knife and thrown it away from them. With pure strength he threw Clive on the ground and practically straddled him. Clive punched upwards, managing to land one measly hit to the side of Miles' neck that affected him no differently than if it were a fly swatting against him.

He tried to get up but Miles flung him back down, he landed fists in his face over and over. I flinched at the crack of every blow. Miles stood up breathlessly and looked at the bloodied man lying on the ground.

He whimpered, "Please, stop! I'm s...sorry! I didn't know she had a boyfriend!"

Miles spat in disgust. "That's not why you should be fucking sorry." He delivered a couple of blows with his foot into Clive's side, who yelled out in pain and then went still.

Miles hurried over to me, panic in his eyes and put his hands on my forehead that I could feel was bleeding heavily. "Christ Lila I–"

I didn't hear what else he said. Knowing I was safe with Miles I finally succumbed to the drugs, alcohol and pain and my world went black.

# Chapter Seventeen

I woke up and tried to sit up but the pain in my head was so severe I instantly laid back down. I groaned and opened my eyes.

"Hey, you're okay Lila." I heard Stephanie's voice and I could tell she had been crying. "You're okay. You're home with us and you're safe."

I looked around. I was in my bed, Steph laid next to me, Miles on the end of the bed and Tom on the floor. Miles and Tom both sat up and moved closer when they realised I was awake.

"What happened?" I asked. "What time is it?"

"It's 10am."

"But what happ-" My hand went to my mouth and Stephanie quickly held out a bucket which I immediately threw up into.

"You've been doing that all night." She said sympathetically as she rubbed my back.

I took a sip of water that she handed to me and then closed my eyes. Memories of the night before flooded back in.

"If Miles hadn't got there in time..." I trailed off as bile threatened to rise in my throat.

"I know, he told us everything," Stephanie teared up and stroked my hair.

I looked to Miles who said, "Steph said you'd text to say that dick Caleb hadn't turned up and then it got late. I drove out there to see if you were okay and give you a lift back." He shook his head. "Lucky I did too. *God*, I could have killed that son of a bitch. I called the police who took him away and an ambulance which brought us back here. They stitched up your forehead and made sure you didn't need your stomach pumping or anything like that... They said you'd be okay in the morning."

"I don't feel okay." I groaned and my hand went up to my forehead where I felt a series of stitches. It hurt to touch but wasn't nearly as bad as the pain inside my head.

I reached out for Miles' hand which I noticed was red, swollen and bruised. I met his eyes and forced down the lump in my throat. "Thank you. For being there."

He opened his mouth to speak but then appeared to change his mind and settled for a nod.

"Caleb called your phone this morning," Steph said. "I explained everything. He thinks it's his fault. He was so upset. He gave me his number to give him regular updates on how you were doing. Shall I tell him you're awake?"

I shook my head. "No." If he didn't care enough to actually show up then I was done with him and I was over it.

"Okay if there's anything you need..."

I nodded and pulled the covers over my head in an attempt to block out the world.

When I woke up I felt horrendous. I was still shaken up from what had happened the night before and I felt like I had the world's worst hangover. I felt like I was going to be sick again. I took deep breaths in and out until the nausea subsided. I hated being sick.

I tried to shake the images of the night before but it was impossible. I shouldn't have got that drunk, I knew it was my fault for drinking so much but... if Caleb hadn't bailed on me I never would have done that. That man never would have – No. It was *his* fault. He was a disgusting horrible predator and if it hadn't been me he would have preyed on some other poor girl that night anyway. I was just lucky that Miles had turned up when he did.

I looked outside to see that it was dark so I had obviously slept until the evening and I could have easily gone back to sleep. I cuddled my pillow into my face ready to sleep and shut off from the world again when my hand touched something hard underneath it. I pulled out my mother's letters, wondering how I could have forgotten they were under there.

I was feeling crappy enough so I supposed reading the rest of the letters wouldn't hurt. I put away the top three that I had already read and then opened the next one.

*7th July 2002*
*Dearest Princess Lila,*

*Mummy still misses you ever so much. I feel like I have been in here forever. I wonder when they will let me out. I wonder how you're doing. I just need to know if you're okay. You must be on your summer holidays now. I hope you're having a good time.*

# The Doll House

*Veronica has taken a turn for the worst which has made me a bit sad. She had a couple of episodes and tried to harm herself. It was terrible, we were just getting close too. She has been moved to a different part of the ward.*

*At least I still have Samuel, my lovely Samuel. He was ever so comforting about what happened with Veronica, he makes me smile most days. I cannot wait for us both to get out of here and you can meet him.*

*See you soon darling.*

*Mummy xxx*

Still, she sounded normal. Like she really did want to be released, I again wondered what could have changed. I wondered who this Samuel was, was he still in there? Had he been released now? Did my mother fall in love with him? He seemed to be making her happy. I sighed and ripped open the next envelope. I frowned as I noticed the huge jump in time.

*20th November 2002*
*Dearest Princess Lila,*

*Sorry it has been so long since I have written, but every time I try to write I seem to get distracted by Samuel. Sometimes I wonder if he is doing it on purpose. I don't think he has anyone at home to write to so I think he might be jealous. I don't really like to write these in front of him. I hope you don't think I miss you any less though. I think about you every day.*

*Samuel is ever so clever. We spend a lot of time in craft classes and he makes the most amazing things. Today he made me a bracelet its lovely. I might ask him to make you one.*

*See you soon darling.*

*Mummy xxx*

I sighed again. The letters were getting harder and harder to read. I missed her so much. It took a few moments before I could bring myself to open and read the next one. There was yet another time jump.

*14th April 2003*
*Dear Lila,*

*I have seen another side to Samuel. He's ever so possessive, he gets angry when I try to write to you or even when I talk to the other patients here. He shouted at me and left a bruise on my arm when he found me speaking to a lovely lady whilst I was supposed to be in craft class. I am starting to wonder if he was behind Veronica's episode.*

*I voiced my opinion to the nurses but I am afraid I made a terrible mistake. They think I'm paranoid but I'm not. Am I? I thought I was getting better, perhaps I was wrong. I really hope I do see you soon.*

*Mummy xxx*

My heart sped up at the sudden change of tone. I swallowed hard as I looked down at the next letter in my trembling hands, wondering if I was finally about to get some answers.

*25th July 2003*
*Dear Lila,*

*I have been in here for so long and I don't know what to do. When I try to talk to the nurses about it they up my dosage and look at me like I'm going crazy but I'm not Lila. Please darling will you show this letter to someone, a teacher or Stephanie's parents?*

*Tell them that Samuel is dangerous. He has become violent and abusive both verbally and physically. I don't feel safe in here but nobody will believe me because he is so good at acting. He's incredibly manipulative, nobody sees the bad side to him they just see the nice, caring side.*

*Every time he is horrible to me he cries and apologises and says that he won't do it again but he does. He keeps crafting me things to make me forgive him but even they are becoming increasingly sinister.*

*Everyone I get close to in here seems to suddenly get worse and end up in the psychological intensive care and I'm scared.*

*I know you're only a child sweetheart but please do something.*

*Mummy xxx*

My heart thumped wildly and my hands shook as I held the last letter. There were no more after this. I didn't want to read it but I knew I had to, to know what happened. It was the last letter she wrote before she died. I read it quickly and afterwards I dropped it on the bed. I felt sick. Everything was starting to add up, everything was starting to finally make sense.

I snatched the letter back off the bed and ran downstairs as quickly as I could, trying my best to ignore the dizzy feeling in my head.

Breathing heavily I burst into the living room where the others were all sat watching tv.

"What is it?" Steph stood up. "Are you okay?"

"No," I panted. "I was just reading these letters from my mother, I forgot I had them. I had only read the first few and she seemed happy and normal. It looks like she got in a relationship with someone called Samuel and he started to get a bit weird... and then remember I told you about that case I was studying at work, Patient *Zero*, he got into a relationship with someone at Sherwood and then they ended up dead."

"Lila..." Stephanie hesitated. "Are you sure you aren't just connecting the dots where you want to? I know a lot has happened recently, you've been through so much but it—"

"No," I interrupted. "This is the last letter... Listen."

I took a deep breath and tried to steady my voice as I read out loud. "Dear Lila. Samuel found out that I was writing to you. He was furious. He thinks because I'm getting better I am planning to leave him for you. He thinks it's your fault, he's blaming you for making me want to get out of this place but of course I want to see you, you're my daughter! He's said he's never going to let me leave. I explained if we both got better we could leave together, become a family but he doesn't want that. He wants me all to himself. I'm afraid he's going to do something stupid. He keeps making these dolls," I paused as Steph gasped. "They're all supposed to look like me. He says he likes to keep them with him when I'm not around so it's like I'm with him all the time. At first I thought it was sweet but now it just seems crazy." I took a deep breath and read out loud the last line of the letter.

"Please Lila if you're getting these letters tell the police, if something happens to me tell them. Tell them it was Samuel Zerox."

I had barely even finished reading the letter before Stephanie was on the phone to the police and I didn't blame her. Eventually the doorbell rang and the same policewoman from before walked in. She was followed by a man I didn't recognise, he was tall and stern looking and he wasn't in uniform.

He held out his hand. "DI Myers."

"DI?" I questioned, giving Steph a look. They had obviously escalated the case.

We all sat in the living room and explained as much as we could, down to every single detail this time.

PC Pawlyn, looked to me directly. "Why didn't you tell us all these details before? The links to your mother are crucial information."

I looked down at my hands that were sat in my lap. "I know... it's so stupid but... I thought maybe it was her, trying to contact me... I know she's dead. It was just a stupid idea and I wanted to be sure it wasn't her... but obviously it's not." I shook my head, annoyed at myself for being so stupid.

"So we are all thinking the same thing right? I mean... it's obvious," Miles said. "This Samuel psycho was in love with Kendra to the point of obsession and when she wanted to get released he killed her to stop her from leaving him and now he's after Lila because he blames her."

I nodded, it was obvious now. The final piece of the puzzle had slotted into place and created a picture that I was not prepared for.

"It is looking that way but we can't jump to conclusions," DI Myers said sternly.

I shook the letters at him. "She literally writes that he was crafting creepy dolls supposed to look like her, what other evidence do you need? And I know who it is, I've been studying his case... Its Patient Zero, Samuel Zerox. He was arrested for the—"

"Sorry, Samuel Zerox?" DI Myers said, he stood up and looked towards PC Pawlyn with a grave look on his face.

"Yes," I snapped. "I told you that."

"You just said Samuel."

"Well his name was Samuel Zerox, she writes it all here!" I said shaking the letter towards him again. He took it and read it and then folded it up and put it in a plastic bag that he took out of his briefcase.

"We're going to need to take this in as evidence." He looked towards PC Pawlyn, gave her a slight nod and then said, "I need to go and make a call."

"Will someone tell us what is going on?" Stephanie said.

"You recognised the name Samuel Zerox, didn't you?" said Tom.

"I think you should all sit down," PC Pawlyn said as she took a seat on the sofa opposite us.

"What is—" I went to ask but she held her hand up.

## The Doll House

"I'm going to explain." She took a deep breath and then continued. "When you mentioned on the phone about the dolls the case was flagged which is why DI Myers was assigned. Now you've confirmed it. Samuel Zerox has been a high-profile case for a long time. I don't know how much you know but he was arrested when he was only a teenager under the suspicion of murdering his girlfriend at the time. He was found not guilty because there was no conclusive evidence but he was sectioned for his own well-being. As you know, he was sectioned at Sherwood. We know that whilst he was there he had a relationship with a woman who was found hanged whilst Samuel went missing. Again, no evidence pointed to foul play so it was written off as a suicide and it was assumed that Samuel was so distraught from grief that he had another breakdown and escaped. I think we can assume that woman was your mother."

None of us spoke, we were all taking all of this information in although we'd pretty much already worked it out for ourselves and I had heard most of it at work.

PC Pawlyn continued, "He was found and sectioned again a few weeks later. Someone called the police because they thought a homeless man was trying to enter their university but it was Zerox, he hadn't exactly been looking after himself."

"So, if he has been sectioned for almost thirteen years... how could he be sending me dolls and breaking into my house?"

PC Pawlyn looked at all four of us now, as if she was wondering whether to continue. She sighed. "I will probably get in trouble for disclosing this sort of information but—"

"PC Pawlyn I think that's enough for today," DI Myers interrupted as he walked through the door.

"No!" I stood up. "No. I have had enough, I have been stalked and harassed and my life has been hell for weeks because I don't know what's going on and I am finally learning the truth, it is finally all making sense and you still want to keep secrets? I deserve to know, we all do."

"Alright you need to calm do—"

"It's for their own safety, sir. I think it would be unprofessional and unwise to keep this information to ourselves when it is possibly their lives at risk."

He shook his head and sighed but his eyes softened. "It's on your head."

PC Pawlyn nodded, taking that as permission and sat down again. I sat back down opposite her, waiting for her to say the words I was already expecting.

"Zerox *was* sectioned again. A few months ago, we got the call to stay on alert. One of the nurses had gone to give him his evening medication when he attacked her and knocked her unconscious. The whole hospital was searched but he had somehow escaped again and... well... he still hasn't been found."

# Chapter Eighteen

The police requested that we ring them if I was left anymore gifts or anything else unusual happened. They said they were glad they had all this new information, which was incredibly helpful to their case, and that they would handle everything from now on.

Once they had left, we sat down in the living room. The boys were sat on one sofa and I was sat on the other with a soft blanket over me. We sat in silence for a few moments before Steph came in carrying a tray with four hot chocolates on, each topped with cream, mini marshmallows and chocolate sprinkles.

"I thought we all needed a little pick-me-up. You can't beat a good hot chocolate." She knew I wouldn't have been able to stomach any alcohol.

She placed the tray on the table in between us and sat down on the sofa next to me. I leaned forwards and picked up a mug and took a sip. Steph never made hot chocolates too hot so that we could drink them straight away. She also made them with pure melted chocolate and milk, they were honestly the best thing in the world but contained about a whole day's worth of calories. We all made "mmm" sounds as we swallowed the warm, velvety liquid.

"How are you feeling?" Steph asked me.

I took another sip and then sighed. "I really don't know. I feel almost relieved I suppose that we know what is going on now. Everything makes sense, everything has finally added up... But, if it wasn't for him my mother would still be here so I guess I feel a bit–" heartbroken, devastated, overwhelmed, afraid "– angry."

She nodded in understanding. "I know what you mean. It is awful, but now the police know everything he will get what he deserves."

I nodded, there was something else bothering me though.

"Don't you think it's all a bit coincidental?" I asked.

They all just looked up silently, waiting for me to continue.

"I get a job as a research assistant and we just happen to be researching the case of the person that is potentially trying to kill me?"

Tom shrugged. "I don't know, I suppose if he's only just escaped again they might be asking loads of officials to review the case, psychologists, detectives, everyone they can to help find him?"

That did make sense. I still felt unsure for some reason. Could I trust Dr Reynolds? Probably. Was I just being completely paranoid because of everything that had happened recently? Most likely.

"Maybe I will ask him at work on Monday."

Steph looked at me as if I'd just said I was going to turn him in to the police. I frowned. "What? It can't hurt to ask him, right?"

"Last night you were attacked and nearly..." She cleared her throat. "And now there is a psychopath on the loose trying to kill you and you're going to *work*?" Her voice was even more high pitched than normal at the end of her question.

"Okay first of all, we don't know that he's trying to kill me. Second, I can't lie here all week feeling sorry for myself wondering what he's going to do next. I also cannot lose my job over this and I need to talk to Reynolds about everything anyway."

She was about to argue but I cut her off. "I am fine. I promise. End of conversation."

This time Steph huffed but didn't argue. My phone buzzed and I switched it to silent, knowing it was Caleb who had been blowing up my phone with calls and texts all day. It was silent in the room whilst Steph sulked and I tried to focus on anything but how much my head felt like it was about to explode. That was, until Miles flicked a chocolate covered marshmallow at Steph which bounced off of the tip of her nose and made her laugh and the tension in the room eased off.

The next morning I was hiding out in my room when I heard a clumsy knock on my door and Miles opened it without waiting for my invitation.

"How do you feel about a one on one defence class today?" he asked.

I frowned, my head was pounding and I'd barely slept from holding back tears all night. "You're kidding?"

"Oh come on," he rolled his eyes.

"Miles, I don't feel like it okay? I ache everywhere and I'm just not in the mood."

"Lila, only God knows why but you're attracting all sorts of creeps at the moment. It would really make us all feel a lot better if you knew how to defend yourself. I'll go easy on you."

I suddenly realised this was a house decision and I sighed. "Fine, let me get showered and ready then."

45 minutes later we were set up in the gym classroom.

"Right I've said it before, you're not going to be able to do much damage. This is all about defence and getting out of dangerous situations."

I nodded, I knew I wouldn't be beating up any men anytime soon.

We spent ages going through various moves that mostly included me attempting and failing to get out of some sort of hold that Miles had me in. We repeated the moves over and over and I started to get into it.

Miles had my arms pinned painfully behind my back and I struggled but his grip tightened. I took a deep breath and imagined Miles was Zerox. I imagined he had been watching me, enjoying taunting me with all those crazy gifts. I threw my head backwards and connected with Miles' nose, but only lightly as he'd taught me the move so had expected it. It did, however, cause him to loosen his grip on my arms. I yanked them away and twisted out of his vice as he'd taught me and quickly span around and attempted to knee him in the groin. It didn't work.

In one swift motion I was slammed onto my back on the exercise mat as Miles' body came down on mine, his strong hands pinned my arms either side of my head. All of the air rushed out of my lungs in a sharp huff and I groaned and began to laugh until I met Miles' eyes.

For once, there was no humour in his expression as he looked down at me, breathing heavily. His eyes were hard as they read mine and his gaze dropped down to my lips.

I sucked in a breath and frowned. "Miles..."

Before I could process what was about to happen his lips crushed down on mine. I tried weakly to push him away as I waited for it to feel unnatural, but as he kissed me harder I surprised myself by kissing him back. His hands loosened from restraining to exploring and mine made their way to his chest, feeling every ragged breath he took.

He pushed his body harder onto me, his kiss almost consuming me as if I'd been waiting for this for years. I didn't even know I'd feel like this.

Because this was Miles.

This could ruin our friendship.

This was wrong.

I thought back to our lesson and all in one movement I shoved my hands hard against his chest, lifted my left leg up into a tight grip around his waist and pushed off of the floor with my right leg. Taken off guard I managed to flip him onto his back with ease and I sat up, straddling him.

"See, at least I learnt something," I said breathlessly.

Miles blinked, his expression still serious as though he had surprised himself with his actions but he replaced it quickly with a smirk. "Sure but I'd have had time to kill you at least five times before you pulled that move."

His hands moved to my thighs but I cleared my throat and jumped up. "Don't you, um, have another class soon or... something?"

His lips twitched and he sat up shaking his head. "Not until later this afternoon, plenty of time to–"

"I think I'm done for the day actually."

He sighed, "Lila..."

"Seriously Miles it's just... it's too much." I grabbed my coat and hurried out of the gym before he had the chance to say another word. Of course it was only as I got outside that I remembered Miles had driven.

About two minutes later Miles came out of the gym and walked over to stand in front of where I was leaning against his car. I looked up at him with pursed lips and narrowed my eyes when I saw his eyes full of humour. His lips were pressed together as if he were trying not to laugh.

I rolled my eyes. "Take me home please Miles."

He unlocked the car and I yanked open the door and climbed into the passenger side. I crossed my arms and stared out of the window as he climbed in his side and began to drive away.

"I don't know why you've got your knickers in such a twist it takes two to tango."

I stared at him incredulously. "Um excuse me you were the one who… in fact, we're not talking about this."

He shrugged and we spent the rest of the car journey in an uncomfortable silence. When we got home I hurried up to my bedroom and locked myself in.

Monday morning my alarm went off and I got dressed for work and looked in the mirror. I had done as much as I could to cover up the bruises that were starting to form around the stitches just above my eyebrow but it was no good. The stitches still looked red and fresh anyway so there was no point.

I finished off my coffee in the kitchen and was just about to leave for work when I noticed a pen knife belonging to Miles on the side. It was small and thin and wouldn't do much damage to anyone but still, I slipped it into my back pocket. I felt incredibly stupid for doing so, but also safer.

When I walked into the office I was surprised to see that Dr Reynolds was not there. His laptop was however so I knew that he was around somewhere. I sat down, preparing myself for what I was going to ask when temptation took over. I stood up and walked over to where his laptop was sat open on his desk. I wiggled the mouse hoping that it was unlocked but I was disappointed.

I couldn't even hazard a guess at what his password would be. I didn't know anything about him or his family. I realised then I didn't even know his first name. I was about to type something into the password bar when I heard the office door slam. I jumped and moved away from his laptop.

"What were you doing?" he asked.

"I… Um…" I stammered.

"Well?" he asked.

"I... I'm looking to buy a new laptop so I just... I thought I'd see if I liked yours." I internally cringed at my crap excuse. He frowned looking completely unconvinced but then his eyes moved upwards to my forehead. He took a couple of long strides over to me, standing closer than he ever had before. He was much taller than me so I tilted my neck to look up at him. He gently pushed a piece of my hair back from my forehead and I swallowed.

"What happened to you?" he asked.

My hand instinctively reached up to touch my stitches and I winced in pain. "Um, it's a long story you probably don't want to hear it."

He stepped back suddenly and sat down at his desk looking up at me. He actually looked concerned.

"You'd be surprised. What happened?"

"Well... I was at a bar and I had a little too much to drink and... well basically I was attacked."

His eyes widened and he asked again. "What happened?"

I sighed. "Like I said I had a little too much to drink, I was on my own and some creep noticed and tried to… take advantage."

He shook his head. "Jesus, Lila why are you at work?"

"Well... because a lot more has happened than that and honestly that's the least of my worries. I needed to talk to you about something."

He frowned. "Go on."

"It's about Patient Zero," I said, studying his face for a reaction but he just frowned. "I know who it is... Its Samuel Zerox isn't it?"

A look of surprised flashed across his usually expressionless face but it disappeared quickly.

"I'm afraid I'm not at liberty to disclose that information," he said sternly.

"Look I'm just going to be honest with you. My mother, Kendra Beaumont, was at the hospital with Zerox. She was the one he fell in love with and she was the one who ended up dead."

This time, he didn't look surprised.

"But you already knew that didn't you?" I accused.

He took a step towards me but I took a step backwards and he sighed.

"I figured it out. Lila and Kendra Beaumont are quite unique names, I only made the connection after I hired you."

"So you knew? This whole time you knew and didn't tell me? Did you know he had escaped?"

"I couldn't tell you, it was strictly confidential."

My mouth actually dropped open. "It doesn't make sense to me. Don't you think it's a coincidence? That we just happen to be studying the case about my mother?"

He took a step towards me and I took a step back. My hand moved to my back pocket.

He stopped. "Lila, I am the leading psychologist in the district. The police have asked me to review his case to try and understand his motives and where he would go. I didn't want you to worry so I made it out to be an old research case."

"But you didn't tell the police anything about me? The two police officers that came around after I found out were surprised when I mentioned Zerox by name."

"They're probably not the officers working on the case Lila. There is only a small team searching for him and I pass my information onto them. I don't know if they tell the entire police force everything I tell them," he shook his head.

I took a step further back. "It doesn't add up..."

# The Doll House

"Do you really think I have something to do with all of this?" he asked, looking at me like I was crazy.

"It just doesn't add up... I suddenly get a job here the same time Zerox escapes to try and find me and we just happen to end up reviewing his case and you... You don't... You don't have any pictures up around your office and... I don't even know your name!"

He shook his head and looked angry now, he took another step towards me and I tried to step back but realised that I was already against the wall. When he spoke, his voice was stern and angry but level.

"My name is Dr Christian Reynolds. I do not have a close family, I do not have many friends, but I am good at what I do. I am passionate about what I do and that is the way I am happy living my life. I graduated from Durham university with an MSc in Clinical Psychology, I achieved my doctorate and published my thesis and continued conducting some significant research until I ended up here and was put on the Zerox case. I am the leading Clinical Psychologist in the area, the closest and the *best* psychologist near Sherwood hospital specialising in psychopathology and mental illness and so yes... It may be coincidental that you happened to be working for me but it is not even *slightly* coincidental that I am working on the case."

It all made sense. I was just being ridiculously paranoid and irrational and I was trying to find links in places where they didn't belong. This whole situation was getting to me.

"I'm sorry..." I whispered. "I just..." I didn't know what to say.

"You're clearly quite confused. You need to be careful, just remember what you said before."

I looked up at him confused, not appreciating the way that he was looking at me, as if I really was insane.

"What do you mean?" I asked.

"Well like you said, mental disorders can be triggered by stressful events and it does run in your family."

"I... I am *not* mentally ill!" I shouted.

I stared at him incredulously and he stared back silently.

"I quit." I sneered and stormed out of the office, ignoring the sound of him calling my name.

I stormed through the carpark trying to hold back my angry tears and when I saw my car my knees nearly buckled. It was covered in several bunches of lavender with a blue parcel placed in the centre of the roof. I walked over to it and picked it up slowly, my hands trembled as I untied the stupid blue bow. When I opened it, I was unsurprised to see a doll staring up at me. This doll was incredible. It was carved out of wood and then painted to look like me. It looked *exactly* like me. Its hair matched mine perfectly and she was wearing an outfit that matched an exact outfit I wore to work the other day.

I stood still and stared down at the doll in my hands and I couldn't quiet explain the way I felt at that moment. I was fed-up, frustrated, hysterical. None of those words felt strong enough. I felt like I was going crazy. It was all making me crazy.

I threw the doll on the ground with tears in my eyes and then looked around manically.

"Leave me alone!" I screamed and stamped on the doll. The few people around me turned to stare but I didn't care. I had reached breaking point.

"I know who you are, I know you're probably watching me, you sick freak!" I yelled as I stamped on the doll over and over, hearing it crack into pieces under my foot.

"Leave me alone, please just leave–"

Someone grabbed me roughly by the arms and span me around to face them. It was Caleb.

"No." I pushed him away. "You can leave me alone too."

He didn't loosen his grip. "Lila come on let's go and–"

I shoved him away from me as hard as I could. "Leave me alone!"

"Please, you need to calm down. I know you're going through more than I can even imagine at the moment but let me help you."

"No, you don't get to do that. You can't keep showing up, acting like Mr considerate and then disappearing!"

"Please just let me explain Lila."

His eyes flashed with pain and guilt as they flicked up to the stitches on my forehead. Flashbacks of the previous night came back to me and I swallowed hard, shaking away the images before I let them consume me.

I took a couple of deep breaths and all of the anger and pain suddenly rushed out of me. I was so tired, I was drained, I was exhausted and I just wanted all of this to end.

"I can't do this now Caleb. Do you not think I have enough going on in my life without you adding to it?"

"What, you don't think I have a lot going on in my life too?" He raised his voice. "You have no idea! I know you're going through a lot Lila but give me a break. You have no idea what is going on in my life."

I stood still in stunned silence before he huffed.

"For god sake, get in the car."

"Excuse me?" I said, shocked.

"Get in the car Lila. I can explain everything but I need you to come with me."

# Chapter Nineteen

I was completely taken aback. "You can't be serious?"

"Lila, I swear to God, if you don't get in the car I will pick you up and put you in there myself." His eyes flashed and I realised he was deadly serious.

"What... But..." I didn't know what to say. I huffed. "Fine. But I'm driving my own car. I will follow you."

He visibly relaxed, nodded and without another word he walked over to his van. I sat in my car and seethed although I realised I was more annoyed at myself than him at this point. After everything he had put me through recently, I was still doing as he asked. I was a sucker for punishment.

He pulled away in his van and I followed him with no idea where we were going. I almost slammed on the breaks when I recognised the road we were on and thought we were going back to that bar but then I remembered that Caleb lived around the corner from it. So, he was taking me to his house? I was probably being completely foolish to trust him considering my current situation but I didn't really care about much at this point.

He stopped the car and I pulled up behind him.

He climbed out, walked over to my car and I lowered the window. "Would you mind parking in the spaces over there? We only have enough space for one car and the idiot neighbours moan when we have cars on the path."

I nodded and he said, "I'll be right around that corner." He gestured with his head and I nodded wordlessly again.

I parked in the space he had told me to and sat in my car for a moment longer. I inhaled a shaky breath and let it out slowly in an attempt to calm myself down. I still didn't really know Caleb. I had no reason to trust him. I had countless theories running through my mind. There was no way Caleb and Samuel Zerox could have any relation to each other. He was far too young. This was completely unrelated and I was just being paranoid.

I considered driving away but knew I would regret it. No matter what happened, I needed some answers. I climbed out of my car and hesitantly

## The Doll House

walked around the corner. I saw Caleb standing by his van a few houses down. I could tell from where I was standing that he was nervous. I hated that I immediately softened. When I reached him, I put my hand on his arm.

"Caleb... What's going on?"

He looked at the floor, his usual playful expression completely replaced with anxiety.

"I..." he sighed. "Look, I like you Lila. You've got a lot going on in your life and it's a bit crazy. To be honest I have thought about walking away but... I can't. There is just something about you... I can't just walk away."

He met my eyes and brushed the back of his fingers against my cheek. He continued, his voice was so low I could barely even hear him. "You have let me into your crazy life and I do want to be a part of it but... I suppose it's now only fair I let you in to mine."

He locked up his van and we walked to the front door of his house. It was a terraced house in the middle of a row of at least 20 identical others. It was small and unassuming and the unruly garden needed a serious makeover. He took a breath and then walked in and I followed him through the front door which led to a small hallway. We walked through to the living room and I looked around.

It was incredibly small, but I instantly felt comfortable. It was decorated in warm colours with candles and lanterns and knitted blankets and soft cushions. Absolutely none of the furniture or colours around the room matched and yet somehow all worked together. Every space of shelving or wall was adorned with photographs of smiling faces. It felt like home.

"Jason!" Caleb called suddenly, startling me.

I heard footsteps and then a man walked through the door on the opposite side of the room. He was tall and had huge bulging arms that were covered all the way down to his fingertips in tattoos. He had dark hair and dark eyes and dark stubble and basically looked like a more serious and definitely scarier version of Caleb. This had to be his older brother.

He took one look at me and said, "Who's this? You don't bring girls home."

Caleb gave a brief and rushed introduction. "Yeah, this is Lila. Where's Mum and Daniel?"

Jason gestured his head towards the door that he had come through, his serious eyes studied me.

I looked between the boys and then when Caleb made to move towards the door I stuttered, "W-wait, I'm meeting your mum? You could have prepared me Caleb I'm not dressed for this."

With this, Jason's lips briefly twitched into a smile which vanished so quickly I may have actually imagined it.

Caleb put his hand in mine and led me towards the door. "She won't mind, I promise."

He pushed it open and we walked through into his kitchen, Jason following behind us. It was also exceedingly small, decorated with black cupboards and black and white tiles. It was cute, but I wasn't really looking at the décor.

"Hi Mum," Caleb said and walked over to the woman in front of us and kissed her on the forehead. Caleb's mother was in her dressing gown with her grey hair tied in a messy bun on the top of her head. She was also sat in a wheelchair.

Her eyes moved towards Caleb and she gave a moan and a slight smile.

"I know, I know," he said. "I never bring girls around but she is special and I wanted her to meet you." He looked towards me and I quickly tried to hide the look of surprise on my face.

"Hello, I'm Lila," I said with a smile. I almost held my hand out but I wasn't sure of her abilities.

"She was in an accident," he said. "A few years ago she was up and about, living her best life. She was skiing and there was an accident, she suffered serious brain damage."

He knelt down in front of her and smiled. "You know what's going on around you though, don't you Mum?"

She made a slight noise and then her eyes moved towards me and her hands twitched. Caleb smiled. "She wants to meet you."

My heart hurt at the situation. I was stunned at how amazingly Caleb was dealing with this and how awful it must have been for him to have watched his mother deteriorate so quickly. I swallowed the lump in my throat and walked over to where Caleb was kneeling in front of her.

"It's really lovely to meet you," I said. "I think you probably needed another woman in this house, it's a bit male dominant."

Her lips twitched into what looked like a smile and her head moved up and down. Caleb smiled. "She definitely agrees."

# The Doll House

I suddenly heard a high-pitched squeal from behind me. I spun around to see the most adorable little boy sat in a highchair. He had big round blue eyes, spaghetti sauce all around his face and in his hair and was waving his arms in excitement. He couldn't have been any older than one.

I looked between Caleb and the baby. He walked over to him and wiped his face and cooed, "Here's my favourite boy!"

My eyes widened, this was all a bit too much. I didn't bother to hide my expression this time and Jason looked between us and then cleared his throat. "I need to take this messy one up for a bath and it's time for Mum's favourite show so... We'll leave you to it."

With experienced ease Jason left the room with the baby in one arm whilst pushing his mother's wheelchair with the other.

Caleb sighed and sat at the little round table in the middle of the kitchen, it was only big enough to fit two small chairs around. I sat down with him. "Caleb I am so sorry about your mother... I had no idea."

"How would you have known?" He sighed again. "A lot has happened in the last few years. It all happened so quickly, none of us really knew what to do... We had a couple of carers in for the first few weeks but then we couldn't afford it so my brothers Jason, Matthew, Calvin and I took turns looking after her ourselves. It was okay to start with, she was still able to move, speak, feed herself and dress herself. Then Calvin and his wife Helena had Daniel, mums first grandchild and she absolutely adored him. He was her world, even more so than any of us."

He smiled sadly and then looked away and his eyes glazed over. "One night a few months ago I was babysitting Daniel whilst Calvin and Helena went for dinner. We thought they deserved it, they rarely had time to themselves. On the way back, they got into a car accident and neither of them–" He paused and cleared his throat and I placed a hand on his arm. "We couldn't do anything except take Daniel in, Mum wouldn't have had it any other way. She was devastated, we all were. One night, I think she heard the baby crying, she tried to stand up and... well, I don't really know but somehow she fell and knocked her head again and... she deteriorated to the way she is now. So, the three of us basically spend our time taking it in turns looking after mum and the baby."

He met my eyes and studied my face as if looking for a reaction. "So, there you go. Sometimes I'll need to rush back here. My family are the most important thing to me in the world, I hope you understand that."

I nodded and put my hands over his and blinked back the tears that had formed in my eyes. "Of course I understand that. I'm so sorry all of this has happened to you Caleb and I'm sorry that everything in my life is adding to it."

He smiled. "As bad as it sounds, it's actually a nice distraction."

I chuckled slightly. "Well I'm glad I can help."

Humour glinted in his eyes. "You thought Daniel was my son didn't you?"

"I'd be lying if I said the thought didn't cross my mind," I laughed. I had breathed a sigh of relief, I definitely didn't need any stepchildren at the moment. His eyes moved to my stitches and he reached up to lightly stroke the back of his finger across my cheek.

"I really am so sorry Lila. I was distracted, Jason had to stay late at work and so I had to deal with everything here but I shouldn't have left you in the bar on your own."

I shook my head. "A text would have been nice, but it's okay I do understand. Really. You weren't ready to explain all of this and anyway, you couldn't have known I was going to stay and get drunk and let myself get into that situation." I frowned and looked into my hands as I thought of what would have happened if Miles hadn't turned up.

"Hey, no," he said sternly. "It was *not* your fault. Being drunk is not an excuse to do… *that*. God, I'm surprised Miles didn't kill him." His jaw tensed.

"Well… I'm okay. That's all that matters, let's leave it in the past now okay?"

He nodded. I was just about to tell him about Zerox and everything that had happened over the last couple of days when he said, "Anyway, Jason's been here all day so I kind of have to start my *shift*. I would ask you to stay but…"

"It's okay I don't mind staying," I smiled. "I'm good with babies, I can help out."

He hesitated. "I really appreciate that Lila but… it just gets a little messy with my mum and to be honest I'm not ready for you to see all of that yet."

I hid my disappointment because I did completely understand. I smiled at him. "That's fair enough, I get it honestly."

"Thanks," he said getting up. I followed him to the front door and he walked me down to the bottom of the garden. It was only about 8pm but it was December so was almost pitch black already.

I shivered. "I love the winter. I hope it snows this year."

"I hate the cold," he shivered too. "I'd take a beach over the snow any day."

He stepped forward, looked me in the eyes and then leant down to kiss me. His lips were warm compared to the cold air outside. His kiss deepened and my hands wrapped around his neck. I waited for the spark or the usual pleasure I felt from his kiss but… nothing. A smash from the house followed by the sound of Daniel crying made us both jump. Caleb looked towards the house and then back at me.

"It's okay, you go," I forced a smiled.

He gave me a quick peck on the lips and then another one on the forehead. "I'll speak to you later, okay?"

I nodded and watched him with a frown as he jogged back towards his house. I stood there for a moment still a little bit in shock at everything that just happened. At least it had explained Caleb's unreliable behaviour. It didn't, however, explain the way I'd felt when he kissed me. I had a sinking feeling it had something to do with Miles. My mind flashed to the fierce and intense kiss we had shared at the gym.

A sudden cold breeze made the hairs stand up on the back of my neck and I realised how freezing it was. I walked back to the car, aware of how dark it was and I suddenly felt on edge. It felt as though I parked so much further away than I had thought.

I heard a crunch of stones behind me and I spun around. I laughed at myself, I was so paranoid. I turned back around to walk to my car when I felt a prickle at the back of my neck, as though eyes were watching me. I gently pulled the penknife from out of my back pocket and before I had time to feel completely ridiculous for doing so, I was yanked backwards by my hair and a leather-gloved hand slammed over my mouth.

Pain ripped through my scalp as I tried to pull back. I screamed against the hand, but I wasn't making enough noise. Before I could think or go into complete panic mode, I thought back to training with Miles. I gripped the knife and stabbed it as hard as I could into the leg of my attacker. He yelled out in pain. I wasn't stupid, I knew exactly who it was. Zerox had found me.

Even though I know the knife didn't do too much damage it had definitely hurt and caught him off guard and so he loosened his grip on my hair. I managed to pull away and tried to run towards my car but he was too quick. His hand grabbed onto my hair again and he tugged on it, painfully pulling me to the ground. He walked around and kicked me hard in the side and I yelled out in pain. He kicked me again in the same place and I looked up expecting to finally see the face of my tormenter but it was too dark to see anything. He was wearing a black hoodie that almost covered his eyes and had a scarf wrapped around the rest of his face. He lunged to grab me and I kicked upwards as hard as I could, straight into his groin. He doubled over and let out a sound as though all the air had just rushed out of his lungs. I quickly rolled over onto my front, pushed myself up and holding onto my side, I ran to my car.

I frantically patted my pockets and with sudden horror realised that I didn't have my keys. I must have dropped them. I bent down behind my car, breathing heavy jagged breaths whilst trying not to let him hear me. I needed to get back to Caleb's house somehow. I crouched down and looked underneath the car to where he was before, heart pounding in my chest as I realised he wasn't there anymore. I slowly tried to peer over the car and then let out a piercing scream as I was once again yanked upwards by my hair. I grabbed his hands on my hair and dug my nails in as hard as I could but he would not loosen his grip. I kicked backwards wildly but failed to make contact.

He pushed me up against my car and then slammed by head against the roof once, twice, three times. I screamed out in pain and could instantly feel the warm sensation of blood running down my face. Suddenly he span me round and his hands gripped around my throat, pinning me to the car. I thrashed and struggled, trying to make any sound, trying to breathe but I couldn't. He tightened his grip and my vision blurred and the world around me started to fade. Just before I was plunged into complete darkness he let go.

I fell to the ground and gasped for air, the metallic taste of blood bitter in my mouth, but I didn't have time to recover before he yanked me up by the neck of my shirt. His hand was back over my mouth and he dragged me stumbling across the road. I didn't know where he was taking me. I didn't want to find out. I thrashed and struggled and tried to scream but they were muffled by the gloved hand over my mouth.

Then, I heard a yell and I sobbed with relief.

"HEY!" I saw Caleb running towards us and Zerox stopped still before he shoved me harshly to the ground. I felt my knees and face crack onto the

## The Doll House

concrete road and then, for the second time in a week my vision blurred and my world descended into darkness.

# Chapter Twenty

I woke up in a panic and my eyes shot open. I had to squint because the room around me was so bright. I tried to sit up but the pain that shot through my head and body prevented me from moving. I laid still for a second and my eyes adjusted to the light and I looked around. I could hear the various beeps and buzzing from the machines around the room. I was in the hospital. I breathed a sigh of relief.

I thought back to the night before. I surely wasn't unlucky enough to have been the victim of two random attacks in the space of a couple of days. Zerox had found me, it had to have been him. Nobody else would have wanted to hurt me that much. I remembered that he was dragging me somewhere. I wondered where he was taking me. Thankfully Caleb had come to my rescue. I didn't know what would have happened if he wasn't there.

I frowned as I wondered where he was. And where were Steph, Miles and Tom?

Just as I was about to lean forward to press the help button I heard voices from outside my room. I don't know why, but I laid back down, closed my eyes and pretended to be asleep.

The door opened with a crash and I tried not to jump.

"You should have called us sooner!" I heard Stephanie's shrill voice. She was the sweetest, calmest soul usually but when she was angry she was a force to be reckoned with. I heard several sets of footsteps enter the room.

"I was a bit busy don't you think?" that was Caleb, his voice was raised but he didn't sound angry. "She passed out and she was bleeding and I had to call the ambulance whilst making sure she was okay!"

"Well she's not okay Caleb!" she argued back. "There is a crazy psychopath on the loose trying to get to her at any chance he gets and you let her walk back to the car on her own!"

"What are you talking about?" he asked.

"C'mon Steph calm down," Tom said. "It's not his fault, he probably didn't even know, did you mate?"

"No I –"

# The Doll House

"Seems a bit odd though," Miles said and I tensed at the thought of him and Caleb in the same room. His voice was raised too. "She's been attacked twice. *Both* times because you left her alone."

"What are you trying to say?" Caleb sounded angry now.

"I think you know what I'm trying t–"

"Guys, please, that's enough." I had meant for my voice to sound strong but it came out hoarse and weak.

Steph rushed over to me, tears in her eyes. "Shh don't try to talk, oh god look at you. Tom go and get the doctor!" She sniffed and he did as he was told.

"What happened?" I asked, although I knew most of it.

Caleb walked over to the other side of my bed and sat down in the chair. He stroked my head, not meeting my eyes. He winced as though he was in pain. I looked towards Miles who was staring at Caleb intently.

"You were attacked..." Caleb said softly. He was looking into his hands and I wished more than anything that he would look at me. "I came out after we spoke at my house... I had changed my mind and I was going to ask if you wanted to stay over and then I heard you scream and I... I ran around the corner to see you being dragged by this guy and I shouted and he just threw you..." He sighed and said thickly, "When I got to you, you were bleeding so badly I could barely even see your face and you weren't breathing right. I called an ambulance and the police but I didn't see who it was..." He looked around the room at the others but still not at me. "I should have been there, I know about everything that is going on and I should have been there, I'm sorry."

"No." I reached for his hands and squeezed them. "Caleb look at me."

He took a moment but then eventually he met my eyes. His were full of guilt.

"You did not know everything. We haven't told you everything. There was no way you could have known what was going to happen, this was not your fault." I looked sternly at Steph and Miles.

He began to speak, probably to ask what it was we weren't telling him, when the door opened again. We all turned our heads in synchronisation to see a doctor and a nurse walking through the door, followed by Tom.

"Good morning Lila. Glad to see you're awake. I'm Dr Stevens." he said. He was in a white medical jacket and had a stethoscope around his neck, he was tall and average looking, he seemed friendly but had a definite air of importance about him. "How are you feeling?" he asked.

"Um... I'm okay," I said.

"We're just going to do a few tests, okay?" he asked and I nodded.

He walked to the end of the bed and prodded the centre of my foot with a thin metal stick. "Can you feel that?"

I nodded and he smiled and said, "That's good Lila but I'm going to need you to answer out loud next time, okay?"

"Yes, sorry," I said.

"Can you feel that?" he asked, prodding my other foot.

"Yes."

"Good," he smiled warmly again and moved up the bed. He pulled out a small metal torch and said, "Can you follow the light with your eyes please?"

I nodded and he shone the light in my eyes. It was bright but I did my best to follow the light. He nodded and then asked, "Do you know what date it is?"

"How long was I unconscious?" I asked.

"Only overnight," he smiled.

"Then it's the... 18th December 2018."

"Good. Well, there's no sign of a concussion and your charts show no serious internal damage. You do have a couple of cracked ribs so movement might be difficult. You have severe bruising and swelling on your left knee which we have bandaged but I would suggest no pressure on it for a few days. You also have some quite bad bruising around your neck and it might be hard to speak or swallow for a while. We've had to put a few stitches in your forehead too. We noticed there were already stitches there and it was explained to us what they were from." He looked around at the others and then back at me and said softly, "It looks like you have a good support system, but you have been through a great ordeal, is there someone you would like to speak to? A professional counsellor?"

I looked around at the four concerned faces that were staring back at me and forced a smile. "No, I'm okay. Thank you though."

He placed a leaflet on the table next to me. "Well that's in case you change your mind. We're going to keep you in overnight and then you should be ready to go home tomorrow, okay?"

I nodded.

# The Doll House

"Okay," he said and walked to the door and then stopped and turned to face the others. "Lila has been through a lot, I'm sure you can all appreciate that she is going to need emotional support as well as physical support."

When they all nodded and gave their verbal agreements, he seemed satisfied and left us to it. I looked around at my concerned friends but I couldn't even bring myself to force a smile.

"Do you mind if I have a minute with Caleb, to explain everything?" I asked.

"Sure," Steph said. "We could do with some coffee anyway. Do you want anything?"

I shook my head. Steph and Tom left the room, Miles lingered in the doorway for a second before he followed them.

Caleb sat in the chair next to me, his eyebrows pulled together so tightly they nearly joined together. "In the space of a few days, you've been attacked twice." He shook his head.

"The first one was just bad luck."

"And what was the second one?"

I sighed. "Will you help me sit up?"

He stood and lifted me by the waist and stuffed some pillows behind my back and then he sat down again silently, waiting for me to explain. So I did. He knew most of it anyway, I just filled in the gaps.

"So that's it. I'm fairly sure Samuel Zerox killed my mother and blames me for something, so wants me dead too."

He pondered for a moment chewing on the inside of his lip.

"But he's been in your house. Twice. He's had the opportunity to hurt you and he hasn't."

I shrugged and then winced from the pain. "He is pretty sick. Maybe he was just enjoying tormenting me. If he is watching he's probably seen the police outside our house, maybe that's spurred him on to… Speed things up."

Caleb just looked at me, but I couldn't work out his expression. I reached for him, but he pulled back. He stood up and walked to the window, silently looking out with his back to me.

"Caleb?"

I saw his shoulders move up and down in a heavy sigh.

"Do you have a death wish?"

I frowned. "Sorry?"

He turned around to face me, jaw clenched.

"You knew all of this and you didn't tell me. You let me leave you in the dark to walk to your car, alone."

"I… It was a two second walk."

"Yeah and look what happened!" He threw his hands up and rubbed them through his hair. "Jesus Lila."

"Hey," I said softly, reaching for him but he stepped back. I frowned and pulled my hand away.

"Caleb... look, I'm sorry, I'll be more careful okay?"

He looked at me, his blue eyes filled with something I hadn't seen in them before. He looked away.

"I don't," he said softly.

"You don't what?"

"I don't have a death wish." He dragged his gaze up to meet my eyes once again. "I have so many people depending on me Lila. My mum a-and Daniel... I… Nothing can happen to me. It would be the end for my family, they need me."

Taken aback I said, "Nothing is going to happen to you Caleb it's me he's after, it's me that–"

"How long do you recon it will take for him to get bored of torturing you and move onto the people you care about? I can't take that risk."

I plastered a hard expression on my face and kept my voice level. "So what are you saying?"

"I'm saying I have to be selfish here Lila, for my family... I just... I think this has to be over between us, I think we need the distance."

I pondered everything for a moment and he was right. He was a coward, but he was right. He had so much depending on him, his mum and Daniel needed him more than anything. I didn't know if he was in danger by being close to me, but it wasn't worth the risk. *I* was not worth that risk.

"Can you say something?"

I sighed. "I don't know what you want me to say. I understand, it's shit but I get it, they need you."

He opened his mouth to say something then closed it again and stood for a couple seconds of awkward silence. I didn't have anything else to say.

"Sorry to interrupt Lila," DI Myers walked in followed by PC Pawlyn. "We just need to ask some questions."

"It's fine… I was just leaving," Caleb said, his voice thick with emotion. He walked over to me, but I didn't look up to meet his eyes. He gave me a light kiss on my forehead and without another word, he silently left the room as tears stung my eyes.

"I know it's difficult, but it is crucial that we find out as much as possible." DI Myers said, understandably mistaking my tears for trauma tears.

PC Pawlyn nodded in agreement. "Not only is Samuel Zerox a suspected murderer, he's clearly mentally unstable and that makes him even more dangerous."

She sat in the chair on the other side of the room.

"I spoke with your friends outside they said they would come back later. Now, if you're feeling up for it could you please tell us everything you remember?" she said with a kind smile.

I nodded. "I can… but I'm not sure how helpful it will be."

"That's for us to decide, please don't leave anything out." DI Myers said, standing by the door.

"Okay, well, I was walking back from Caleb's house to my car–"

"Where is that?"

"Crescent Avenue in Abingdon." I thought that was right.

She noted down the address. "We will check the CCTV in the area but there's no guarantee we will find anything. Please, carry on."

"I mean… that's kind of it. I was walking back from Caleb's and I was attacked from behind. It was dark, he had black clothes on, and his face was covered with a scarf or something. I didn't get a good look at him at all."

"Is there anything at all you remember about his detail?"

"Umm…" I tried to rack my brain. "He was quite tall, I think. When he… When he pulled my hair, it felt like he was above me. But not like big, not broad… Just tall."

"It's okay you're doing great." She gave me a kind smile then looked towards DI Myers, who took a step towards the foot of my bed.

"We wanted to talk to you about doing a press statement," he said.

My eyes widened. "A press statement?"

He nodded. "More of a public protection statement really. We're concerned that other women are in danger, considering his history, we aren't sure if it's just you he's targeting."

"Oh, of course, I hadn't thought of that."

My heart sped up as I realised I may have been completely selfish by not going to the police sooner. What if there were others out there being tormented the way I had been. It had nearly driven me insane already.

"You won't issue the statement of course. That will be left to us, but we needed to give you a heads up. We haven't got full authorisation, but we're hoping to issue the warning in the next few days depending on the progress of the investigation." She looked towards DI Myers and then looked away.

I frowned. "What is it?"

DI Myers swallowed and then said, "You see, we couldn't find any photographs of Zerox. We thought it was strange so it was thoroughly investigated... There are no childhood photographs, no photographs on his medical file, no booking photographs from when he was in police custody. There are no forms of social media linked to his name. It would appear Zerox is more intelligent than we were led to believe. We think he has infiltrated the systems somehow, either himself or he knows someone on the inside. Either way, all trace of him has been wiped."

My eyes widened shock. I shook my head in disbelief that this was all real life and I wasn't in the middle of a horror film.

PC Pawlyn stood up. "We're stationing a car outside your house for the meanwhile as he's now made physical contact. Hopefully that should keep him at bay until we find out where he's living."

Relief washed over me and tears once again filled my eyes. "Thank you," I whispered. Until that moment I hadn't realised how completely petrified I had been.

# Chapter Twenty-One

A few uneventful days passed since being in the hospital. Everyone in the house were walking on eggshells, being overly careful with me like I was a delicate piece of china balancing precariously on the edge of a table, threatening to drop and smash at any moment.

The police car outside seemed to be doing its job, for three days there had been no gifts, no letters, no strange noises. But none of us were relieved, none of us could relax. Because even though the policemen were keeping Zerox at bay he was still out there. It wasn't over yet. I knew we were all just waiting for the inevitable.

The police had kept in touch, updating us with their investigation but there wasn't much to update us with. The last time Zerox was on any records anywhere was in Sherwood hospital where he was with my mother. His listed address there was now preoccupied by new tenants who had never heard of him and that's where the trail went cold. No car, no sightings, they weren't even sure what he looked like now. The only picture they had shown me was some CCTV footage of him before he was sectioned, he was just a mess of hair and baggy clothes and I sure as hell didn't recognise him.

Me and Steph hadn't left the house since the hospital, she'd been signed off at work fully paid for a couple of weeks. They were very understanding apparently.

Miles and Tom continued going to work like normal. They'd all tried to come up to my room where I'd been hiding out, but I had ignored them. I left my room for food and showers and that was it.

Mostly, I was alone with my thoughts. I couldn't believe this was all happening. In the space of just a couple of months my life had completely turned upside down. I was stupid to not have gone to the police sooner. How could I *possibly* have thought it was my mother trying to reach out to me? She's got no reason to hide she would have just found me.

Zerox had taken so much from me. My mother was getting better, she was getting the right treatment. I could have grown up with a mother and he took that away from me. Instead, I grew up without knowing either of my parents. I wiped away the angry tears that formed in my eyes every time I let thoughts of my mother invade my mind.

I lifted myself out of bed, wincing as the pain shot through my ribs. I was still bruised all over. I swayed on the spot before I managed to steady myself, although I wasn't sure if that was from the pain or the strong meds I'd been taking in generous doses.

I walked over to the window in my bedroom and looked up and down the street like a paranoid guardsman, as I did every time I looked out. I could see into the window of the police car stationed outside our house, I couldn't see their faces, but I could see that they were laughing and enjoying some sort of fast food. They probably thought they'd hit the jackpot with this job.

It was all uneasily calm.

That was, until I heard a scream from my position by the window. It wasn't a scared scream though, this was more of an angry frustrated yell, and it definitely came from Stephanie's mouth.

I began to push myself away from the window ready to face whatever horror was waiting for me downstairs when I saw movement from the window that stopped me.

Steph, followed by Tom, stomped angrily towards the police car and banged her tiny hands on the window. A chill washed over me as she stepped back to let the policeman out and I saw she had something in her hands. I could hear shrill tones but not enough to hear what was actually being said so I took a deep breath and braced myself.

As I painfully hobbled down the stairs, I heard Miles' voice from behind me. "What's going on?"

I huffed, "I don't know I just-"

I paused as I had turn to speak to him and saw him following me dressed in only his grey sweats. I dragged my gaze away from his naked top half, cleared my throat and carried on towards Steph. He came up beside me and held my arm to help me down the stairs.

"I just heard a scream and saw Steph having a go at the policemen."

He sniggered. "This should be good."

We reached the scene outside where Steph was looking furious. I tried not to look at the perfectly wrapped blue parcel in her hands, but it was hard to tear my gaze away.

"It's just not good enough is it?" If Steph's voice had risen any higher, she'd have attracted all of the dogs in the neighbourhood.

# The Doll House

"What's going on?" I asked.

Steph's hands shook as she turned towards me and gave me the parcel.

"I was taking out the rubbish and when I opened our bin outside, that was inside," she said apologetically.

"How?" I frowned, even frowning made the stitches in my forehead ache.

"Exactly my question," she said and looked pointedly between the two policemen.

The younger looking one said, "It's impossible, we've been here the whole time. We've noted down everyone who has passed the house or even come onto the street the whole time we have been here. I swear."

I pinched the bridge of my nose. "*Obviously* not everyone, how could you miss this?"

Steph huffed. "I'm ringing DI Myers, hopefully he can swap these two morons for some actual competent police officers. I hope you enjoyed your lunch." She glared at them and then stormed away and I looked at Miles who had a very slight smirk on his lips and I knew he was thinking exactly the same as me.

It wasn't supposed to be funny; it was a serious situation and these incompetent morons had essentially put our lives in danger. But somehow, angry Steph was *always* a little bit amusing.

DI Myers arrived about 20 minutes later, unlike usual he was on his own.

"I can only sincerely apologise for what happened. We will be investigating exactly how this was placed in your bin and when. It could have been before we stationed a car outside."

"The bins were collected yesterday so that's very unlikely," I said, my tone a little more bitter than I had intended.

"Well as I said, it will be investigated and, in the meantime, we will be placing two new officers outside your house. You should feel safe with the car outside."

Steph scoffed at the same time as I rolled my eyes.

He pulls out two white gloves from his briefcase and Miles raised an eyebrow.

"Let's have a look at what he left this time then, shall we?"

Steph had insisted none of us open the parcel this time until DI Myers was there.

As he carefully untied the ribbon and peeled back the paper, I chewed my bottom lip and clenched my fists so tight that my nails dug painfully into the palms of my hands. Miles noticed and came to stand behind me, his hands comfortingly squeezed my shoulders, but I couldn't relax into his touch.

I grimaced as DI Myers lifted the lid from the box to reveal yet another doll. I felt my hand cover my mouth and my stomach screw in painful knots as I took in the details of the doll. This one was the sickest yet.

It was so sick I didn't even want Steph to see it, but it was too late. She gasped as she looked down at the doll and took in its features before she turned and cried quietly into Tom's chest. I glanced up at his face, but it was expressionless, he just rubbed a comforting hand over Steph's back, refusing to meet my eyes.

"That... is fucked up," Miles said.

DI Myers nodded. "Quite. Is there anything meaningful or relevant about this doll Lila? Anything that he could be trying to torment you with, like the lavender?"

I swallowed the lump that had formed in my throat and looked back down at the doll. Nothing particularly relevant stood out. It was just... sick.

The doll was completely naked. Disturbingly, it was anatomically incredibly detailed. There was one rope around the dolls neck, surrounded by cuts and bruises. Another rope, also surrounded by lacerations, tied its fragile wrists together. Even more disturbing however, were the gashes and bruises in the dolls most intimate areas. All of them.

I dragged my gaze up to the dolls face, dreading this part. It was always the most haunting part of the doll, the eyes were always somehow made to look terrified, screaming for help. Not this time. The dolls eyes were closed thankfully. However, across its mouth and wound round the back of its head multiple times to gag the doll was a strip of grey masking tape. It looked painfully tight against the doll's delicate pale cheeks, I almost wanted to undo it to relieve her.

I tried to speak but no noise came out so I just shook my head.

I saw him nod from the corner of my eye as I still hadn't managed to drag my eyes away from the doll. It was just so detailed, it was so... messed up. I suddenly wondered if this was a threat. Was this what he wanted to do to me?

"Oh god." Still weak from the other night's injuries I swayed on the spot as I thought about how grave the situation actually was.

# The Doll House

Miles caught me and pulled me tightly to him and whispered, "It's okay I've got you, that psycho isn't getting anywhere near you, that's a promise."

The chill that washed over me as I looked at the dedication it took to make this doll so intricately detailed told me that was not true.

Zerox was not going to stop until he got what he wanted.

After DI Myers had left, taking the doll with him as evidence, I had slid off to my bedroom to be alone.

I sat wrapped in a cosy blanket staring out the window, watching up and down the street. It had become my new favourite position. I wondered how long this was going to go on for. How could this mysterious Samuel Zerox evade the police for so long? Surely there were family, some pictures, some sort of CCTV or records or something? I didn't know how it all worked. I was sure the police were doing all they could, they kept ensuring us they were.

A light knock at my door made me jump as most things did nowadays and I rolled my eyes at myself.

"Come in," I said softly.

Steph poked her head round the door. "Can I come in?"

I nodded. "Of course."

I stole another quick glance up and down the street and then positioned myself next to Steph on my bed.

"I feel like we haven't properly spoken in ages." She sighed.

She was right, I'd been avoiding the house and their sympathetic eyes. I hadn't even told anyone that Caleb had ended things yet. I began to wonder how Miles would react but I shook that thought away before it got too serious.

"I know," I sighed back. "I just feel like everyone's treating me like I'm about to break. I'm stronger than you guys think."

"Hey, we know you're strong. That's why you haven't broken yet, if I was in your position I'd be a mess I don't know how you're still holding your head up."

"Well, I'm not really." I gave a sad laugh. "I've barely left my room in days."

"We need a girl's night," she said and I snorted.

"Yeah, we really do. That's the first thing we'll do after crazy psycho killer is found and locked up."

"No I mean soon, to take our minds off things. We should go to Joe's. He's not going to do anything there is he it's absolutely heaving 90% of the time."

I sighed again, it would be nice to get out of the house and just put all of this behind us for one night. It's not like we could even do anything, sitting here wasn't helping anything.

I felt a smile pull at my lips for the first time in days. "You're right. Let's do it, Friday?" That was in two days.

She smiled back. "Friday. It's a date."

She put her head on my shoulder and then sighed sadly again and began pulling at her fingers.

"They're going to catch him Steph, it won't be long. We're safe with the police outside."

"I know," she whispered. She sat up and fidgeted awkwardly and I frowned.

"I..." She looked at me. "I did something."

My frown grew. "What did you do?"

She stood up and sighed for the third time in about two minutes. She shifted and reached behind her and pulled out a small blue envelope from her back pocket and then handed it to me.

I looked up at her and she swallowed. "I wasn't sure what to do. I'm all for going to the police about things like this you know that but I don't know, I just... I can't explain it. I got a feeling you should look at it first. It was on top of the box I found in the bin."

I looked down at the shiny blue envelope, it was slightly rumpled from being in Steph's pocket but it looked like thick expensive stationary. Like a wedding invitation.

On the front written in black ink pen was some beautifully exquisite calligraphy that read:

"For the attention of Lila Beaumont, ONLY."

I swallowed and tried to steady my hands as the paper started to shake.

"Have you opened it?" I asked.

"No of course not... would you like me to leave?"

I shook my head. "No, stay. Please."

She looked relieved and sat back down on the edge of the bed and waited for me to open it.

# The Doll House

I took a breath and turned over the envelope. It was sealed with an actual wax seal, imprinted on it was a tiny bunch of lavender.

"He loves his theatrics," Steph said, but there was no humour in her voice.

I peeled back the seal and pulled out the tiny square of card paper that was inside. The writing was the same beautiful calligraphy that was on the envelope.

*"Lila,*

*I'm sure you know by now I love your mother. I always will. She has a special place in my heart. For that, you should trust me.*

*Something is going on in that place, Sherwood. It's not what you think and I'm not who you think.*

*It's all one big cover up. One big lie.*

*Your mother didn't kill herself.*

*She's safe, she's with me. We're together as a family and we want you to join us before they get to you too. We thought it would be safe for you but now you're too close to finding out the truth they will come for you.*

*Please, if you want to see your mother again come to the address below at 10pm on Thursday.*

*You won't regret it."*

Katie Masterman

# Chapter Twenty-Two

My heart pounded painfully in my chest as I handed the note over to Steph with a trembling hand. I tried to speak but I couldn't seem to form any words.

I watched her scan over the letter as she read the message multiple times before her wide eyes snapped up to mine.

"This is just one of his sick games…" she said, handing the letter back to me. "It has to be."

I read it again and looked at the address but I didn't recognise it.

"What if it's not?" I whispered.

"Lila, there is absolutely no reason for your mother to be alive and in hiding, she would come and find you herself not let this man torture you for no good reason."

She was looking at me panicked as if I was being completely insane.

"The note implies there's something bigger going on, what if it's not even him doing all of this to me… what if it's all a misunderstanding?"

She let out an exasperated huff. "Lila, this is ridiculous I should have given it straight to the police. It's obvious, come on you aren't that stupid surely. You're the one with all the psychology knowledge, he has been in a psychiatric hospital all these years for a reason surely this is a clear symptom?"

I sighed, she was right. "Paranoid delusions are one of the most common symptoms of schizophrenia."

I frowned and bit the inside of my cheek and her expression softened. She bent down in front of me and placed her hands on my knees.

"He wants you to go to that address because that's where he will be waiting for you. We don't know what his goal is or how dangerous he really is, but we know he's not well. No good can come from us not doing anything about this."

Tears stung my eyes and I swallowed the lump in my throat. "I know. You're right. Just imagine though, if it were your mother and there was a chance you'd get to see her after all these years of thinking she was dead. Wouldn't you risk it?"

She shook her head and looked at me sadly. "That's the thing though Lila... There isn't a chance."

I began to protest but she interrupted me. "If we go to the police with this they can go with you. They can catch whoever will be there and this will all be over."

My mind reeled with all the different options and possibilities and with the absolute absurdity of the situation and I realised she was right. Of course she was right.

But this was something I had to do.

I nodded. "Ugh you're right. I'm an idiot. There's just so much going on its messing with my sanity."

She nodded and her shoulders relaxed with relief.

We both stood up and I said, "I'll go sort this out."

"Alright, I need a shower." She sighed.

I pulled on my coat and hobbled downstairs, ignoring the painful throbbing that shot through my ribs with each step.

I could feel Steph's eyes watching me as I walked towards the car, so I faced forward and subtly slipped the note into the sleeve of my coat as I approached.

I knocked lightly on the glass of the window and the policeman inside reeled it down and gave me a friendly smile. I leant down on the windowsill and hoped from behind it looked like I was handing over the letter.

"Just wanted to see if you guys need anything, tea or coffee or a cold drink?"

He gestured to their takeaway coffee cups and wrappers from a recently eaten lunch.

"We're all good, just had a lunch break, thank you though."

"Oh that's good." I smiled but I could feel it didn't reach my eyes.

He frowned. "Is everything okay, miss?"

I gave a humourless laugh. "Aside from the obvious? Yeah everything's great."

He nodded sympathetically. "I can only imagine how you must be feeling."

"Have you seen anything suspicious?"

"Nothing unusual no, but rest assured, nobody's getting past us we promise you that. We'll find him soon enough."

"So everyone keeps saying." I nodded curtly as I turned to walk away. "Anyway, have a good evening."

Now I just had to convince Steph the police were dealing with the situation.

The next morning I sat at the breakfast bar in the kitchen with a coffee, wrapped in my dressing gown. I didn't sleep at all, I think maximum I must have dozed for an hour on and off. My eyelids felt so heavy it actually hurt to keep them open but I just couldn't sleep.

*"She's safe, she's with me. We're together as a family and we want you to join us."*

The more I read the note the more ridiculous it sounded. I doubted it was true. With all my heart I wished it was but there was no chance. Zerox was a maniac who was trying to lure me in. That or he was having one of his schizophrenic delusions and genuinely believed what he said was true. Regardless, I was going to get some answers and I felt the only way to do that was to go on my own. Even if he just wanted to torture me, at least all of this would end for everyone else.

I rubbed my now sweaty palms on my thighs that were bouncing up and down. I looked at the time, there was still 12 hours until I had to go to the address written in the letter and I had to keep Steph off my back that whole time.

"Morning," she chirped as she walked into the kitchen. "How are you feeling today have you taken your pain meds?"

I shook my head. "Not yet, I'm starting to feel better." I wasn't lying. The ache in my side had started to ease off and it was becoming much easier to walk on my bad knee.

Miles walked in and I frowned. "I thought you were opening at the gym this morning?"

"That's tomorrow, I've just got a couple of classes this afternoon."

He walked over to me and pushed the hair back that had fallen out of my messy bun. I knew the bruising on my head still looked bad but the headaches were less frequent.

"I'm fine. It doesn't really hurt anymore," I said before he could say anything.

He let a finger lightly trace down my cheek whilst Steph wasn't looking and my pulse quickened.

He smirked and then stepped back and turned to make himself a coffee. "Good, you'll be back in my defence class in no time then."

I snorted. "Fat lot of good it did, did you see the state of me?"

He turned to face me, his eyes turned serious as they met mine. "You're still here aren't you? After a grown man with pretty serious intentions attacked you. I'd say it did a lot of good."

Steph looked between us. "He's right. I can't believe you managed to get away."

"It was only because Caleb came out at the right time."

Miles' eyes flicked away and he stared intently at his coffee. "He shouldn't have left you in the first place."

I huffed not wanting to repeat myself and then began to tell them what happened with Caleb.

Despite everything going on, I wanted to see Miles' reaction to this information. This chemistry between us had appeared out of nowhere and it wasn't helping my sanity. I'd barely allowed myself to think about the kiss at the gym and torture myself over what it meant or the unexpected way that it had made me feel. I wasn't sure how much more drama could be added to my life.

Before I could tell them though Steph spoke.

"Did you speak to the police?" She asked and I stiffened. I didn't need Miles becoming another obstacle.

I gestured with my eyes towards Miles, indicating I didn't want him to know but he caught me.

"Speak to the police about what?" He asked, his eyes narrowed.

"Zerox left a note with that messed up doll that we hadn't noticed before. I let them know about it last night and they said they were sorting it out."

"Was it threatening?" He frowned.

I looked at Steph and then back to Miles. "No, it didn't make any sense it was just a load of gibberish," I said, hoping she wouldn't explain fully and thankfully she didn't.

"Sad fucker." Miles jaw clenched as he spoke. "He needs to be locked up in a straitjacket."

"I think that's the intention if they could find him. I don't think they'll have to look for much longer though." Steph smiled and I suddenly realised why she was in a better mood this morning.

She thought it was all going to be over tonight, the police were going to go to that address and catch him and the nightmare we'd been living was all going to end.

My chest tightened as I felt a huge wave of guilt.

This was just something I knew I had to do alone. Didn't I?

9:30pm came around incredibly slowly, I'd pretty much sat watching the clock like a child on Christmas Eve. Except this was a lot less exciting and more, you know, life threatening.

I'd been in a mental battle all day as to whether let the police in on my plan but I had decided against it. I was at that point where I was just so incredibly exhausted by everything. I was so sick of being tortured, so sick of living life on the edge with no answers at all. At this point, I didn't care what happened to me as long as it was all over.

I'd been plotting my escape all day.

The police were never going to let me leave at night without an escort as I was the main target. Miles and Tom however, had been going to and from work as usual.

I opened the door to my bedroom to leave and heard Steph's whisper, "What are you doing?"

I jumped out of my skin and held onto my ribs as the pain shot through them.

"Sorry," she groaned. "Are you going to that address?"

I tried to regain my composure. "Yes, and the police are going to be there hidden already waiting. They're probably already there now actually." I lied easily.

"Should I come with you?" She asked, her voice was full of concern.

"God no definitely not, he doesn't know I'm not going to be alone. He needs to believe it's just me."

She nodded and looked at me with a forced smile. "Okay well... Good luck. Let's hope it all ends tonight. I'll have the champagne ready."

I smiled back at her as she shut her bedroom door and then I snuck downstairs before I let the guilt consume me.

Quickly, before anyone else could see me, I grabbed Tom's black hoody from the hook in the hallway and slipped it on. I quickly snatched his car keys from the hook by the door and pulled the hood up.

I made my way to his car, preying the police wouldn't stop me and through the dark they'd just assume it was Tom going to do a late shift at Joe's.

I started up the engine, my hands trembled so much I wasn't even sure if I could change gear. I turned on the headlights in the car and pulled away with a shaky breath.

I made it out of the road without a hiccup.

I followed the directions I'd already pulled up on my phone to the address that had been written in the note. My pulse quickened as I left the bright lights of our town and pulled onto a windy country lane. It was pitch black except for the light from my car. I couldn't see anything at all except for the road in front of me and the trees surrounding it, hanging over the top almost making a tunnel.

Creepy didn't even begin to describe this scene. Haunting, terrifying, nightmarish. They came closer.

I followed the roads until I entered a slight clearing, and the directions on my phone said I'd arrived at my destination. I couldn't believe this was even a destination on the map.

There was nothing but a small rickety shed and open fields and trees and just, darkness.

Every fibre of my being was screaming at me to run.

I typed out 999 on my phone ready to call if I needed. I was an idiot, I should have called sooner. This was quite literally a scene from a horror film and I wasn't going to make it out of here.

I swallowed hard and my heart throbbed painfully in my chest. I looked around but there was still nothing. I kept the full beams on Tom's car to light up as much of my surroundings as I could but that was almost more terrifying. The trees rustled in the wind and every slight movement of the leaves or landscape in front of me made me jolt in fear.

I waited and waited for what quite literally felt like an eternity. I felt as though there was a huge weight crushing my chest and with each minute that passed, the weight became heavier and more unbearable. My internal monologue ran riot as the panic built.

What was I even waiting for? What was I supposed to do? Was it the shed? I silently prayed I didn't have to go into the shed. My mother wasn't going to be waiting for me in the shed. This was ridiculous, I should just turn back.

I looked towards the shed and swallowed, hard. It was the only entity in sight. It was completely derelict and looked like it hadn't been used in years.

*Shit.*

I shook out my hands in front of me and said out loud, "Okay it's okay. You can do this."

Before I could think about the situation too much I opened the car door, keeping my phone in one hand and my keys in the other. I chastised myself for not bringing some sort of weapon for protection.

The leaves and sticks crunched under my feet as I reached the shed. The wind whipped around my neck and I shivered, even though I wasn't cold. I should have been freezing but I was completely numb with fear.

I drew in a shaky breath and reached for the door handle of the shed. I was expecting it to be a struggle to open as though time had rusted it shut, but surprisingly it opened with ease as though it had been recently used.

I suddenly felt a prickle at the back of my neck as though eyes were touching me and I span around. I looked blindly into the darkness but couldn't see anything. Fearful tears brimmed in my eyes and I blinked them away turning back towards the shed.

Then I heard a sound. A sound that made every single hair on my body stand up.

From inside the shed came a voice saying only one word.

"Lila."

Goosebumps covered every inch of my skin as I stood, paralysed with fear.

"Lila."

It was a voice I recognised. A voice that caused my lips to tremble and the tears I'd been fighting to spill over down my cheeks.

It was my mother's voice.

I turned on the torch on my phone despite my hands shaking so much I could barely even keep hold of it. I pushed open the door and everything happened at once.

# The Doll House

As I leaned into the shed a light flickered on and I fell backwards painfully as a body of a woman suddenly dropped from the ceiling directly in front of me. As she dropped a toe-curling crack stopped her from hitting the floor.

I let out a blood curdling scream as the body swung back and forth by a rope wrapped around her neck. Her hair and clothes moving wildly as she swung.

I had no composure now, I sobbed as I scrambled backwards until I noticed the lavender headband balanced daintily on its head.

Was that... My mother?

I screamed again and I leaped towards the swinging body. I reached her and shone my light in its face and a sob caught in my throat when realisation struck.

It was my mother alright. Well, a perfectly accurate wax interpretation of her. I screamed again, more out of anger and frustration than fear this time.

That sick *freak*.

I had to get out of there.

I cried and practically sprinted to the car.

I quickly checked that there was nobody in the back of the car with me because I was determined not to be that dumb character in the films.

When I deemed it safe I launched myself into the driver's seat. I fumbled with the keys in my rush but eventually got the car started, turned the headlights on and got the hell out of there so fast my wheels span.

I sped down the roads that led me there until I saw the blissful scene of streetlights and houses. I sobbed with relief.

I couldn't believe I made it out of there. *Of course* he wasn't going to be there. Of course it was all an elaborate trick to torture me. He must get off on it, he probably filmed my reaction.

My only consolation was that even if the police were with me they wouldn't have caught him. I didn't mess up too much.

# Chapter Twenty-Three

I'd been sitting in the dark of this forest for an hour. I had to get into position with no risk of Lila seeing me. It would ruin everything. This was my show and I had front row seats. This was the best of my games yet.

Finally a car pulled up, it wasn't hers though it was her housemates. Tom's I think. Clever girl she is. I had wondered if she'd bring the police with her but seeing her in this car I realised she'd tried to evade them.

She wouldn't be able to see me from my position I'd made sure of that. I was too hidden in the darkness for her to see me. Although she could probably feel that I was here, somewhere.

That was my game. Always watching, always hiding in plain sight.

She sat in the car for a ridiculous amount of time and with every second that went by the joy building in my chest increased. She was scared, she was probably petrified in there, driving herself mad with the possibilities of what was going to happen tonight. I laughed lightly, this was exactly what I'd hoped for.

"The bitch deserves it." I heard a familiar voice whisper in my ear.

"She deserves everything she gets. You're making us proud." Another voice said from behind me. I smiled, assured I was doing the right thing.

My excitement bubbled up as the car door finally opened and she got out. I could practically see from where I was positioned that she was trembling with fear.

She made her way towards the shed, she was brave I'll give her that. Incredibly stupid though. What did she really think was going to happen, her mother was going to be waiting in there with a cup of tea? I had to force back a laugh. Stupid girl.

Suddenly Lila's head snapped in my direction and I held my breath. I was worried for a second that she could see me but then she turned back towards the shed.

Now the show could start.

# The Doll House

She opened the door slightly and I pressed play on the remote I was holding, linked to the tape recorder inside.

"Lila."

She froze with fear as she heard her mother's voice.

Ah, her mother. The *lovely* Kendra. I was doing all of this because of her. I lived for this. My soul purpose in life was to avenge their deaths.

I played it again.

Go on girl. Go inside.

She did as I willed her to and pushed the door open further. As she did, the wax work I'd so devotedly prepared swung down in-front of her and she fell backwards with such a terrified scream that I had to cross my legs and adjust myself. The thrill was overwhelming.

"Go, now!" The voice next to me hissed urgently.

I quickly moved out of my hiding position, whilst she was distracted and made my way towards the car.

With a gloved hand I opened the passenger door and slipped the files onto the seat that I'd been holding the whole time, waiting for my moment.

I looked up at her, I was so close to her. I could grab her easily and take her with me but no, not yet. I moved back into my hiding place in the darkness.

Our games had only just begun.

Katie Masterman

# Chapter Twenty-Four

As I pulled up into our road I still hadn't quite gained my composure. The sobs still racked my chest and tears streamed harshly down my face. I could barely see where I was going but I just had to make it home.

Through my blurred vision as I pulled around the corner with our house in sight I could see the blue flashing lights of police cars.

*Shit.*

I pulled up to the house and stopped the car and before I could even compose myself the door was ripped open and Miles had pulled me out and into his strong arms. He held me against his chest and I welcomed the comforting, although slightly crushing, hug. I sobbed against his chest and he stroked my hair.

"You're a fucking idiot," he said sharply, his voice not quite matching his comforting touch. "Steph told us everything when we noticed Tom's car was gone. Do you realise how stupid that was? He could have... You could have been... Shit, Lila!" I realised his whole body was trembling.

I couldn't speak just yet. I had so many conflicting feelings running through me I couldn't possibly string a sentence together. I was shocked, disturbed, embarrassed, terrified, frustrated, angry. Mostly though, I was disappointed.

How the *hell* had I let myself get my hopes up into believing my mother was alive. For one split second I has genuinely believed he'd abducted my mother just to hang her in-front of me. The image of her swinging back and forth would be forever imprinted into my mind.

I pulled back, sniffing, trying to force my body to relax. As I pulled away from him he kept a hand on my lower back and I looked up to see Stephanie standing in the doorway. Her eyes were red and full of tears, she was sniffling lightly and her eyebrows were pressed into a frown.

"He wasn't there anyway Steph, it wouldn't have been over tonight no matter who had come with me." I managed to choke out.

She didn't say a word before turning on her heels and walking back into the house.

"Are you okay?" I heard Tom's voice from behind me.

I nodded. "I will be. I'm sorry about taking your car I just... I needed to go there on my own."

He put a comforting hand on my arm. "Don't worry about it. We were just worried you weren't coming home Lila, Steph couldn't remember the address and she was beside herself with worry."

I nodded sniffing as the sobs began to build again. "I know I'm sorry, it was so stupid."

DI Myers approached me with a very stern look on his face. His lips were pressed into a tight line.

"I'm sure you know how reckless your actions have been tonight Lila, they've probably impacted the case. We're trying our best to find Zerox, not just for you, remember that."

I felt like the most selfish person in the world.

Miles' arm tightened around my shoulders as he pulled me into him.

DI Myers huffed. "Do you have the letter? We need to check the address he lured you to as there could be plenty of evidence at the scene. We also need to ask you a few questions regarding what happened of course."

"It's in Tom's car I'll get it," I said numbly.

I walked on shaky legs back to the car and opened the door, leaning in to get the letter. As I did I noticed a brown manila folder on the passenger seat that wasn't there before.

My whole body prickled in fear again.

He had been there, with me. Watching me. He'd put this in my car whilst I'd been distracted by his sick twisted little games. I reached over and it grabbed it and flicked through the pages. My eyes scanned over the words and my chest tightened. I hadn't thought the night could get any worse, I was so wrong.

It was the police report of my mother's suicide.

It confirmed she died by strangulation, she hanged herself, there was no note. I flicked through it, not needing anymore details until I came to the last page.

The crime scene photographs.

There she was, the real-life version of what I thought I had seen tonight. Hanging lifeless, suspended by the rope wrapped around her neck, with her eyes wide open.

I pushed harshly back from the car and threw my guts up onto the street.

Now *that* was the image that was going to be imprinted in my brain forever.

I wretched and threw up again and again.

I felt Miles' hand rubbing my back as I heaved. It was completely undignified but I couldn't have cared less at that moment.

When I was sure I wasn't going to be sick anymore I took a deep breath and stood up. PC Pawlyn hurried over and handed me a tissue.

"This was left for me in the car. I only just noticed it," I said, my hoarse voice barely even made a sound.

DI Myers took it and opened it up and flicked through the pages. PC Pawlyn looked over at the pages as he did. They both began to frown and he shook his head.

"I... I don't know how he would have gotten a hold of this information."

He flicked to the last page and his eyes widened. PC Pawlyn's horrified eyes flicked up to mine as she realised what I had just seen.

She looked at Miles on my one side and then gently took my other arm. "Come on, let's get you inside."

The police left after I answered all of their questions about the events of the night. Once Steph learned what had happened and what I had seen in the file all of her anger melted away and she stayed glued to my side. I had to practically push her out of the bathroom when I went for a shower.

I stood in the too hot shower for ages, as if the scolding water could wash away the horrors of the evening, but no water was that hot. My head fell back, my bottom lip started to tremble and my tears mixed with the water that fell over my face.

At least it put to rest any doubts in my mind about my mother still being alive, even if they were completely ridiculous. Apparently hope outweighs logical reasoning.

The images of her in the back of the file flashed into my mind and I squeezed my eyes shut and forced myself to think about something else. Anything else.

# The Doll House

He was there watching me. He'd set up this whole elaborate evening to torment me, but he could have hurt me. It was the perfect location, completely isolated with nobody around for miles, he could have done anything to me.

So why didn't he? What did he want?

Was his goal just to keep torturing me until I ended up the same way as him and my mother? Surely he was going to run out of ideas soon. What could I have possibly done in my life for him to think I deserve this?

I switched off the water angrily. I was so, so sick of this.

I laid in bed that night tossing and turning. There was no way I was going to be able to sleep. I kept telling myself that this would all be over soon. The police would find some sort of evidence in that place he led me to and they would find him. They had to.

My stomach almost lurched into my chest when I suddenly heard a noise outside my window. I looked at the time to see it was 2:30am.

I took a deep breath and told myself to stop being paranoid. It could be anything, the police were outside anyway.

I heard another noise and couldn't help myself. I jumped out of bed and held my breath as I peered out of my window.

I swear my heart actually stopped in my chest at the sight below me. It was dark so it wasn't completely clear, but there was definitely someone down there dressed in all black. I could see the silhouette moving.

I looked towards the police car in panic and could see the faint lights from inside. What the *hell*? Why weren't they doing anything?

My heart began to beat rapidly in my chest as I looked down again to see the silhouette slowly open up the bin. I saw a flash of blue as the moonlight hit what he was holding. He was putting something in there. He was definitely putting something in our bin. Another perfectly wrapped blue parcel.

They could catch him. What were they doing?

I began to open my window to scream to the police the person they were supposedly protecting us from was there when the silhouette came out of the shadows and hit a spot of light.

I gasped. I took a step back into my bedroom, shaking my head and grabbed the part of my chest where my heart was beating so hard I thought it was going to explode.

I was exhausted, I was emotional, probably a little hysterical. But I was not mistaken.

This was a silhouette I recognised all too well.

I sat in the dark of his bedroom. I sat there for what felt like hours. I knew what I saw. I was sure of it. I just didn't understand it.

I sighed and rubbed my hands over my tired heavy eyes and looked at the time on my phone. 2:42am. Where was he?

I knew I was right. I wasn't moving until I had some answers.

I looked around in the darkness, seeing only silhouettes and shapes of the room I knew so well. I heard a slight creak from the hall and my head snapped towards the door as it slowly and silently opened inwards. If I wasn't so hypersensitive tonight, I would have missed it. These were the movements of someone who didn't want to be heard.

I held my breath as the silhouette I had seen earlier silently creeped into the room and I swallowed the lump that formed in my throat.

The silhouette silently closed the door behind him and then stood still and leaned his head against it. I saw his shoulders slump, as if the whole world were weighing down on them. He sighed and pulled his hood down.

"Late night stroll?"

Tom startled violently and fumbled for the light switch by the door. The sudden bright light burned my eyes and I squinted until I could focus on his face.

He stared at me, eyes wide and terrified before he swallowed and plastered a neutral expression on his face.

"Yeah, I couldn't sleep. Nothing was working so… I went for a walk."

"And the police were okay with that?"

"I'm not the one in danger. I have a lot on my mind and… I just needed to clear my head. They said it was okay if I didn't go far."

"You're not even wearing a coat. It's freezing."

He stared at me.

"I guess I don't feel the cold that much," he said in a tight voice.

"Where did you go?"

"I just went–"

"Oh cut the crap Tom!"

He shook his head and put his keys on the set of drawers next to him.

# The Doll House

"I don't know what you're talking about Lila." He sat on the end of the bed, facing away from me. "Why are you in here anyway?"

"Tom, I've known you for years. We live together. We've grown up together! I know you. I know your shape, I know the way you move and I know it was you leaving that parcel in our bin."

He slowly stood up, still facing away from me, but didn't say anything.

"How could you? How could you do this to..." My voice broke and I willed it to come out stronger.

"Why?" I demanded. "What have I ever done to you?"

I had so many questions.

"Has it been you this whole time? What have you got to do with Zerox!?" My voice raised and he suddenly span and faced me.

I was expecting to see the Tom I knew, scared Tom, guilty Tom. Tom horrified with everything that he had done. I was not expecting to see this crazed Tom, his eyes wide and tortured and his jaw set in a hard line.

"You have to listen to me Lila." He took a step towards me and I instinctively took a step back, suddenly afraid.

He held his hands up. "Lila for god sake, it's me." He took another step towards me and I tried to take another step back but pressed against the wardrobe.

I didn't know what it was but something about the look in his eyes made my blood turn cold and I instinctively began to shout.

"MILE–"

But Tom was on me, his body pressed tightly against mine and his hand clamped over my mouth before I could scream for Miles. His hand was damp with warm sweat and I could feel his whole body trembling. His face was inches away from mine and I looked into the eyes of my friend I had known for so long and I didn't even recognise them. A noise resembling a sob broke out of my throat.

"Please Lila," he begged. "You have to listen to me. I would never hurt you, ever. I didn't want to do any of this, please just... Just give me a chance to explain."

I blinked and felt the tears drip onto my cheeks. I nodded slowly and he sighed, regarding me for a few seconds before he removed his hand from my mouth and backed away from me.

"MILES!" I screamed at the top of my voice.

"Shit Lila!" Tom looked around in a panic before Miles burst into the room wearing only a pair of shorts.

He squinted at the light. "What? What is it, are you okay?" His voice was thick with sleep.

When his eyes adjusted and he saw it was me and Tom standing there he visibly relaxed until he saw our expressions.

"What's going on?"

"Yeah, what's going on?" Stephanie appeared from behind Miles and walked into the room. "It's like 3am, what happened?"

I was frozen to the spot, but I swallowed hard and forced my trembling lips to move.

"Do you want to explain or shall I?" I said to Tom.

"Oh god." He let out a strangled groan and sat on the bed. He leant forward and put his head in his hands.

Steph reached out for him. "Tom, what–"

"Don't." I snapped and she froze. Her and Miles both looked at me with wide eyes.

"It's him," I spat. "I caught him leaving a lovely blue parcel in our bin. I'm just waiting for an explanation."

# Chapter Twenty-Five

## Tom

### One week ago

I had just finished the shift from hell. People are dicks and I never want kids, that's what I've learned from working in customer service. I desperately needed to get those job applications out, I don't know why I was delaying it. I knew I wanted to work in IT or coding or something to put my degree to use, and yet I was waiting on tables every night.

I sighed as I climbed into my car, determined the next day I was going to send out as many applications as I could and start achieving something with my life.

It was completely dark in the car park. I'd parked around the corner from the restaurant as there wasn't any space out front and there was no lighting back here. The car was pitch black.

I began to put my keys in the ignition to get some light to put my phone on charge when suddenly I couldn't breathe.

My hands reached up to my throat and I felt a rope strangling me from behind. I tried to gasp and grabbed and scratched at the rope around my neck in a panic but I couldn't take a single breath.

My vision became hazy and I was seconds away from completely blacking out when the rope eased.

I coughed and spluttered and gasped for air, holding my throat as I tried to fill my lungs.

Before I could do anything the rope pulled at my neck again, this time it wasn't strangling. I could still breathe but it was tight enough so that I couldn't move a muscle without being strangled.

My entire body was physically shaking with fear and I had never been more jealous of Miles. I wished I'd had his strength, physically and mentally.

"The quicker you calm down, the quicker we can get this over with." I jerked as a smooth voice came from behind me.

My eyes moved to the rear-view mirror to see my attacker but it had been covered in black tape. They were prepared for this.

"What do you want?" I strangled out.

"You're not stupid I'm sure you realise who I am." His voice was so calm and completely void of all emotion. It made the hairs stand on the back of my neck.

"Samuel Zerox," I stated.

"Quite the name isn't it? I know you like your superheroes. It's almost like when my mother took my father's name she wanted me to become a villain." The last word was full of venom.

How did he know anything about me?

I swallowed painfully as the rope pulled tighter against my neck.

"Let's cut to the chase shall we? I need you to do something for me. I've seen the police cars outside your house, obviously Lila couldn't deal with this on her own like the coward she is. She had to get the police involved, you can see how that makes things more difficult for me."

He paused as if waiting for me to respond but I had no idea what to say.

He continued. "Now I wouldn't want all this work to go to waste. You see it's all part of a plan, it's all building up to the "endgame" as such."

He was making fun of me, making another superhero reference.

"In the back here are some gifts for Lila, a lot of effort has been put into these so it's imperative that she gets them. In the order that's written on them as well else it just won't make sense, I'm a logical man."

"I can't do that." I willed my voice to come out strong but it sounded like more of a whimper.

There's no way I could do that, these gifts had been torturing Lila. I couldn't put her through that.

"If you don't, you won't have any of your little friends left alive to play with anyway and it wouldn't be quick. I can assure you they'd suffer. Lila is mine anyway, Miles doesn't look like he has a lot going up there-" He sharply tapped my temple with a gloved finger. "-so I doubt he'll be missed and Stephanie..."

I stiffened and my blood ran cold.

"Beautiful Stephanie, now that would be a waste wouldn't it?"

# The Doll House

He pulled the rope even tighter against my neck and breathing became difficult but not impossible.

I jerked as I felt his breath right next to my ear as he leant in and whispered, "I don't want them though, not really. So they're safe as long as you do as you're told."

I nodded and I felt him lean back away from me although his hold on the rope never wavered.

"And I'll know if you don't do it or if the police are involved, trust me. There are certain requirements in the gifts and I will know if Lila has received them."

Before I could even blink, the rope was whipped away from my neck and the back door opened and slammed shut.

I span around in my seat to try and put a face to the name but I couldn't see a thing.

I glanced at the three parcels on the back seat and turned around and punched the steering wheel as hard as I could over and over. Then I did something I hadn't done in years.

I put my head in my trembling hands and I cried.

# Chapter Twenty-Six

Tom finished telling us what happened. I had slid down the wardrobe and onto the floor as I listened. Guilt overwhelmed me to the point where I couldn't speak.

"I'm so sorry Lila," Tom said and I looked up at him, his voice was thick and tears shone in his eyes.

"I never would have done anything to hurt you or put you in any danger, I swear."

Steph's hands moved over his shoulders comfortingly and I realised where she stood with the situation.

Miles scoffed angrily. "Wouldn't put Lila in danger? Was it you who left that fucked up doll in the bin with the note that led her to that place?"

Tom nodded and before we could react Miles had launched forwards and grabbed him up by the scruff of the neck.

"Miles!" Steph and I screamed at the same time. We jumped from our positions to try and pull Miles off but he was too strong.

He slammed Tom up against the wall and yelled in his face, "Do you realise how that could have gone? He could have killed her, he could have done any amount of fucked up things to her out there on her own. Do you know what she saw?"

"He knows Miles!" I yelled and yanked at Mile's arm as hard as I could and thankfully he let go.

Tom looked absolutely horrified.

"What alternative did I have?" He yelled back. "Let him kill you all? I didn't know what was in any of those parcels, I didn't know there was going to be a letter with an address in it. I thought it was all just going to be stupid dolls!"

"You should have told us," Miles argued.

Steph and I looked at each other sadly, the whole situation was overwhelming. I didn't even know if I was angry or not.

"I couldn't take that risk. I don't know how he knows us but he does, he knows us well. He knew how I felt, he used my weakness and it worked,

# The Doll House

okay? I would do anything to protect Steph, Miles, just as you would with Lila." Tom said strongly. His eyes instantly widened as if he'd said something he shouldn't have.

Steph looked between us all and Miles took a step towards Tom again. His eyes were fuelled with fire, his jaw tight and his fists clenched.

Tom took a step back but then Miles swore, turned on his heel and left the room.

A few moments of stunned silence passed.

I shouldn't have been surprised that Zerox had threatened my friends and attacked Tom. My chest physically hurt with the guilt I felt, this really wasn't just about me. I'd been selfish and stupid, this wasn't about getting answers anymore, we needed to end this before anyone got seriously hurt.

Tom sniffed and stepped towards me, placing a hand on my arm and I didn't move away.

"Lila, I'm so sorry. I really did think I was doing the best out of all the options I had."

I nodded as my eyes filled with tears. "I know."

It was almost 6am when I poured myself a coffee and looked out into the garden. It wasn't even light yet and I hadn't slept at all, how could I have?

I was dreading the tension in the house today. On my way downstairs I had I poked my head into Steph's room to find it empty so she'd obviously stayed in with Tom. I didn't blame her for not being angry with him. I didn't even blame him, what could he have done?

I'd done similar things by not going to the police when I should have, I'd be a hypocrite to hold a grudge.

Miles had always cared about me but the protective way he'd been acting recently was definitely different, stronger. I knew there was the added threat of a crazy psycho killer which would increase anyone's concern, so maybe I was just looking too much into things. But then there was that kiss at defence class, I'd be lying to myself by pretending it didn't stir something in me that I hadn't realised I'd felt for him.

As if the Gods were completely against me, my phone rang at that thought and I looked down to see it was Caleb.

I frowned as I wondered why he would be ringing me so early.

"Hello?" I answered.

"Hi, sorry I know it's early. Did I wake you up?"

"No, I haven't been sleeping too well."

I heard him sigh down the phone. "Good that's what I was hoping. I mean, that you were awake, not that you hadn't been sleeping well."

I raised my eyebrows. "Is everything okay Caleb?"

"Well I was just driving to work early because I couldn't sleep either and I don't know why but I took a detour passed your house and then saw the police and got concerned." He sighed again. "Basically, I'm outside and was hoping we could have a coffee or something."

I internally groaned at his timing. He was the one who had ended things, and for good reason too now I knew what had happened with Tom.

I also knew I looked like a complete mess in my small pyjamas and bed hair. I sighed. "Sure, you can come in for a coffee," I said as I quickly scraped my hair into a bun on the top of my head.

I went to the door and opened it quietly, not wanting to wake anyone up. I could see Caleb in his van being questioned by the police, they looked over to me and I waved and smiled gesturing it was okay. They nodded and went back to their car.

He walked over to where I was standing in the doorway, looking as gorgeous as ever. "They made me show them ID, very thorough. Is that because of the incident outside of my house?" He asked, as if there was no awkwardness at all.

I huffed out a humourless laugh. "One reason of many. Turns out a lot can happen in a few days."

I shivered at the cold and turned and walked into the dark house and headed into the lit-up kitchen. I kept my voice hushed as I asked if he wanted a coffee so he'd get the hint that the others were still asleep.

"I just wanted to check on you," he said, his voice matched my hushed tone. "Your stitches look like they're healing. How do you feel?"

"Physically? Fine. Mentally? Not so much." I answered truthfully.

"I'm sorry," he looked down at the coffee in his hands. "I should be here for you. I've been selfish, I know you need me."

I shook my head. "I have a perfectly good support system here actually."

I didn't mention the fact that one member of that support system had inadvertently almost led me to my death and another was in bed with him.

"I know that, but I want to be a part of it Lila. I made a mistake ending things with you. I haven't stopped worrying about you and thinking about what you were doing."

I softened at his confession but then instantly realised I hadn't actually thought about him at all. Surprising, considering only a couple of weeks ago I thought I was head over heels for him. Stupid Miles getting in my head.

Distracted by my thoughts I barely registered Caleb moving towards me. His body pressed against mine and he placed a hand either side of me on the counter I was leaning against.

"I miss you."

He gave me his signature smirk as he leant down and kissed me lightly on the lips. He went to pull away but I pulled him closer, strengthening the kiss. I wasn't too sure why, maybe to prove something to myself, maybe just because I'm a bad person. Either way, he didn't complain and enthusiastically kissed me back until we heard a throat clear.

I span around clutching my chest and stared straight into the profoundly serious expression on Miles' face.

I forced out a nervous laugh. "Christ Miles, you scared me."

"Please, don't let me interrupt." I waited for his signature humorous smirk but it didn't show.

I turned back around to Caleb. The kiss had answered my questions.

"You should probably go."

"Lila, can't we talk about this?"

I wished Miles wasn't in the room.

I pulled Caleb to the front door by his arm and opened it, the sun was just starting to rise.

"This hasn't changed anything Caleb. There's even more going on than you realise at the moment and you were right. It's too much of a risk. It's not the right time for me to be in a relationship."

He looked into my eyes with a defeated expression and I almost faltered. I did like him but just not enough. I knew I was doing the right thing.

"This will all be over soon. I'll still be here," he said, and he leant down for a kiss but I tilted my head so that he caught my cheek. He looked at me sadly and then turned and walked away.

I prayed that I was only imagining the feeling of Miles' eyes boring a hole in the back of my head. I closed the door silently and turned around, but then gasped and jumped back at the sight of him.

"Please stop doing that, you idiot!" I snapped.

He stepped towards me with his signature playful smile, a dangerous look in his eyes.

"Miles..." I stepped back but my back pressed against the door.

"Look Miles, I'm not sure what you think is going on here but I just want things to go back to normal." I lied. He nodded, still smiling and took another step towards me.

"I'm serious. As if things aren't complicated enough in my life I don't need you complicating thing. You know that. I need you Miles, as a friend." I pointed a finger into his hard chest.

His gaze softened and he paused for a second before he took yet another step towards me, close enough so that he was towering over me but not touching me. He placed a hand either side of my head on the door and I swallowed hard as he leant until he was an inch away from my face.

"I think you need me for more than that."

His gaze went to my lips and he leaned in slowly. My body betrayed me as my pulse quickened and my chin turned up so he could kiss me for the second time.

But he leaned down past my lips to whisper in my ear, "Next time I kiss you, it won't be seconds after another man has had his lips on yours."

Then he suddenly pushed himself off the wall and jogged up the stairs towards his bedroom, faintly laughing as he slammed the door.

I leaned my head back on the door and groaned at the state of my life.

# Chapter Twenty-Seven

"It's Friday." Steph sheepishly poked her head into my room where I'd been hiding from everyone. I couldn't face Tom for obvious reasons and Steph had been glued to his side since the other night.

I couldn't face Miles because he was just making things more complicated.

I'd resigned to the fact that I had feelings for him, strong feelings that had appeared out of nowhere. But we were such good friends, the house dynamic worked perfectly, if anything were to go wrong it would mess everything up. Knowing Miles' dating history, it would go wrong. He wasn't looking for a relationship and I wasn't looking to be used. So that was the end of that, I had to avoid him until these arbitrary feelings went away and we could all go back to normal.

"It is Friday yes." I looked up at Steph.

"We have a date."

I rolled my eyes. "I'm not really in the mood to go out. I don't think it's the smartest thing to do at the moment anyway, I'm surprised you even want to."

She sat down on the bed. "I've spoken to the police outside, they think it's safe to go to Joe's as they don't believe anyone is watching the house and Joe's is always busy. They'll be staying watch here and Miles and Tom are going to be here all night and they're staying up until we get home."

My lips twitched. "You really want to go out?"

She put her hands on her hips and raised her eyebrows and I knew instantly that I'd lost this battle. "Yes Lila. We need to go out before we go crazy. No talk of anything serious either, we're going to pretend that it's three months ago and we're going to drink alcohol and have a worry-free evening."

I held up my hands in defeat, not being able to help the smile that had formed on my lips. "Alright you win. I'll start getting ready."

She nodded, satisfied with her win and bounced off to get ready as well.

I knew there was absolutely no way that the evening was going to go the way Steph wanted it to, life was just not that simple, but I played along for her sake.

Miles dropped us off at Joe's that evening. He looked me up and down when I got out of the car.

"You sure you don't want me to come in? I could use a drink and you could use a bodyguard." He flexed his muscles jokingly and Steph pretended to gag.

"No way," she said sternly. "We need a girl's night. We need to gossip about boys and feelings and stuff."

He grimaced. "On that note, don't talk to any strangers and remember our training."

He looked at me in the eyes and opened his mouth as if he wanted to say something else but then he pursed his lips and drove away without another word.

Steph linked her arm through mine as we walked into Joe's and to our table. We ordered a bottle of red wine and some nibbles, olives and bread.

Steph put her hands on the table in front of her and blew out a breath. "Okay, I know we aren't going to talk about anything serious tonight but I just need to say one thing."

I prepared myself for a Stephanie ramble.

"I haven't taken sides regarding the whole Tom thing, I know I've been... Close to him recently but I know what he did was wrong and stupid and he could have got you hurt but he really did think that he was doing the right thing. He's so sorry Lila, he feels awful and—"

I held up my hand cutting her off. "I'm stopping you so you can take a breath before you pass out."

She smiled sheepishly and I continued.

"I know what you're saying and I understand how you can forgive him, I really do. I'm not angry at him, I just haven't had the energy in me to have a conversation about what happened. I feel guilty more than anything, that he was put in that position because of me so, we will be fine don't worry about that."

She relaxed as if that was the main problem in our ridiculous lives and sighed with relief. She then looked down and picked at her perfectly polished nails in a very un-Stephanie manner.

"That's great because I love you, you know that, you're my family but... I love him too. And not in the same way."

My heart felt like it actually swelled at the admission and I smiled the biggest and most genuine smile I had done in a long time.

"I think you were the last person to realise it but good, I'm happy for you guys, genuinely."

She smiled back. "Where's Caleb anyway I haven't seen him since the hospital?"

I sighed and began to explain when the wine and nibbles were brought over. I watched as Steph poured us both a glass with the most relaxed expression I'd seen on her face in weeks. I didn't want this to turn into a sympathy filled evening.

"I know life's just been hectic hasn't it."

She snorted. "That's one word for it."

The rest of the evening was perfect. It had been just what I'd needed without realising it. I had needed to take my mind off everything, a night with just Steph by my side. We drank wine and chatted and giggled about meaningless crap all night, never letting the conversation get too serious.

The taxi dropped us off outside the house and we both shivered and wrapped our coats tighter. We gave the police officers a quick wave to let them know we were home okay as we hurried inside out of the cold.

"It was nice to have a girl's night like old times, no boys, no... Drama." Steph smiled at me.

"By drama do you mean creepy murderous psychopaths?"

"I wasn't quite sure how to word it," she said dryly.

I shivered as I glanced up and down the road before closing the door.

"Come on don't think about him tonight," Steph said. "More wine?"

I tried to shake the anxious feeling that had abruptly made its home in the pit of my stomach. The evening had gone too well.

I headed past her towards the kitchen. "Definitely more wine."

I peered into the living room on the way past and saw the flashing lights of the TV in the dark room, at least the boys were home. We walked into the kitchen and I flipped the lights on.

At the exact same time we both let out piercing screams.

Steph gripped my arm so hard I thought her nails pierced my skin but I couldn't pull away. I was rooted to the spot with the type of instant fear that makes your blood run cold. We both stared straight ahead unmoving.

In front of us, stood in the garden leaning against the double glass doors was a woman. The light from the kitchen glowed against her pale face. Her wide terrified eyes stared directly into my soul, screaming for help. She stood in nothing but a ripped bloodied shirt, with two bloody hands pressed against the glass.

I was frozen with fear until my eyes properly adjusted and I realised the woman was completely devoid of life, making no movements at all. I stepped forward an inch and frowned.

"It's fake, it's a doll," I breathed to Steph as Miles and Tom rushed in behind us. The dolls were getting increasingly lifelike.

"Those fucking useless cops." I could hear the fury in Miles' voice as he stormed outside. I hurried after him, leaving Steph and Tom in the kitchen.

"Miles!" I shouted, but he had already reached the police car and was pulling on the door handle, which was inevitably locked.

The policeman wound down a window, he was young with a fresh face, no facial hair whatsoever and he looked at Miles like he was about to beat hell into him.

"Sir if you'd just take a step back then I can talk to you."

Miles apparently realised he was a young policeman and did as he asked although the fury was still in his eyes and his fists were clenched so tightly his knuckles turned white. The young man and another police officer who incredibly looked even younger both got out of the car.

"Why have they left you two children to watch over a house targeted by a fucking psychopath?"

"Sir we are fully trained and fully capable and we've not taken our eyes off–"

"Stop talking," Miles snapped as he pinched the bridge of his nose and I saw his jaw tense. "Follow us."

The policemen looked at each other and followed us inside the house and into the kitchen. I saw the panic in their eyes as they saw the woman and went through the same thought process as we had.

"Shit." The younger looking one said and pulled out his phone to call it in.

# The Doll House

I stared at the doll's lifelike features and I frowned, taking a couple of steps forward. It did look incredibly realistic. Closer up I could see cuts and bruises on the woman's arms and legs, although the face looked doll like, the cold skin and fresh wounds just looked so... Real.

As I stepped forwards I heard one of the policemen say, "Miss, please don't touch anything it could be—"

"Just wait." I snapped.

I reached a shaky hand to the door handle and slid it open. A rancid smell hit me instantly and I gagged. The room was silent behind me as I held my breath and reached forward with trembling fingers to lightly touch her arm. I flinched at the touch and I fell backwards, bile rising in my throat. I scooted myself away as quickly as I could before I gagged again.

I felt Miles sit down behind me before he pulled me onto his lap and stroked my hair. "Shh Lila it's okay, we're not going to let anyone hurt you. I'm not going to let anyone hurt you. This will all be over soon."

I tried to speak through sobs but couldn't catch my breath.

"It's... It's..."

"Holy shit."

I looked up to see the younger police officer stood by the doorframe, arriving at the same horrifying realisation I just had.

"It's real skin."

# Chapter Twenty-Eight

In no more than ten minutes PC Pawlyn and DI Myers arrived as well as two other uniformed police men, two men in suits and a woman in a full white forensic suit.

I was still sitting in the same spot and Miles hadn't moved from his position behind me. More and more people were rushing around the kitchen in a blur, talking to me but I didn't register much. A faint buzz, my name.

"Lila... Lila."

I snapped out of my bubble when I heard Miles' voice in my ear.

"They need us to move Lila this is a crime scene now. Come on." Miles stood and pulled me up with him and I followed him wordlessly out of the kitchen and into the living room.

Steph was inconsolable, she rocked back and forth on the sofa whilst Tom attempted to calm her down.

Miles sat me down on the sofa and crouched down in front of me, his hands were placed comfortingly on my thighs.

A crime scene. That was real skin, I knew the second I'd touched it. The smell... I tried to hold back another gag at the thought. I felt dirty, the smell and the feel... I looked at my hands. I had touched it.

"I need a shower," I croaked out.

Miles followed my gaze to my hands and nodded. He left the room and I stood up but he returned a few seconds later.

"They just need to ask a few questions first."

I sighed and sank back into the sofa, I'd expected no less.

That was *real* skin.

The four of us sat in the living room in a deafening silence before PC Pawlyn, DI Myers and a non-uniformed man I didn't recognise entered the room.

DI Myers spoke first. "We understand this has been a traumatic night for you all so we will try to make this quick."

He nodded towards the man next to him who stepped forward and cleared his throat. He smiled a friendly "let's get down to business smile" that didn't quite meet his eyes. He was clean shaven which only accentuated his age lines and dark circles under his serious but kind eyes. He had an air of authority and importance about him.

"I'm Detective Chief Inspector John Porter, I will be performing the role of Senior Investigating Officer on this case from now going forward. As DI Myers said I know this has been a rough night but I just need to ask some questions. You young men were in the house all night yes?"

I looked towards the boys who both nodded.

Miles said, "I got home from work around half 5. I dropped the girls off at Joe's at around 7 and was back here by 7:15 and Tom was home from work around 8."

"Okay and you didn't hear anything suspicious at all?"

They both said no in unison.

"And Lila and Stephanie what time did you get home?"

I looked towards Steph who looked so pale I could practically see through her skin so I cleared my throat, "Um about half 11."

"And you saw the assigned police officers stationed outside your house?"

We nodded.

"Okay, can you please tell me exactly what happened."

"We went out to dinner, we got home, we walked into the kitchen, we turned on the light and *that* was staring back at us. That's it." I shook my head, physically trying to get rid of the image that had forced its way back in my mind.

"I understand this is difficult, I've been reviewing the case and we have to face the fact that this was Samuel Zerox again as he appears to have targeted you in particular Lila because of your mother can we agree?"

I nodded

"They were at Sherwood Institution during the same time correct?"

I sighed. "We've been through all this yes they were together, I've given you all the letters from my mother she explains there about his obsession with dolls and with her, that's the extent of what I know it's all in there."

He nodded. "Yes I know, I've read them."

He paused looking around. "Do you recognise the victim outside?"

I blanched at the word victim and looked at Miles who had also paled.

He looked back at me and then to DCI Porter and swallowed hard. "So, that was a real woman out there?"

"The gruesome truth as you will have to know," DCI Porter said, "is partly, yes. It appears to be a wooden mannequin, with a completely wooden and fabricated head however, the body is covered in real skin yes which escalates this to a murder case."

As he used the words we'd all been avoiding since turning on the lights in the kitchen I felt like I'd been punched in the stomach.

Murder.

Victim.

"Oh god," Steph put her head in her hands and began to cry again as Tom rubbed her shoulders.

"So was there anything you recognised, anything of significance at all like the lavender and the poems from before?"

I shook my head, tears forming in my eyes.

"Do you know... who it was?" I asked

"Not yet, forensics will do an exam and then we will do a search of all missing people in the area and hopefully we will be able to get an identification."

"Sorry sir but... how did this happen? With two police officers outside and us at home?" Miles asked.

DCI Porter looked at his watch then said, "The perpetrator has evidently made a pathway leading to the back of your house through the trees and made an opening in your back fence, it looks as though it's been used a couple of times."

I felt sick.

DI Myers said, "But we have eyes on all areas of the house now, we are aware of the increased threat and you are well protected."

We might have been now, but someone out there... Some innocent victim, was killed, skinned and beheaded just so that sick bastard could get at me.

I couldn't help but feel like this was all my fault.

It took hours for different officials to examine the crime scene and take photographs and ask all the same questions but finally the house was empty and cleaned up and they took away the... body? Was that the right word? The skin covered mannequin. The rest of the body was out there somewhere else. I shuddered.

# The Doll House

Me and Steph had both taken showers hot enough to burn through our skin, but I still felt dirty.

The four of us sat in the living room. Steph checked outside the window for the 12th time in half an hour that the police were still keeping watch and then sat down on the sofa next to Tom.

Miles was stroking my hair with my head laid on his lap but nobody had said a word, it didn't look out of ordinary, just like any decent man comforting his best friend.

Steph chewed her nails and bounced her knees up and down. "This feels so weird, what are we supposed to do now just carry on like normal? I feel like I'm constantly just waiting for the next horror show."

I knew exactly how she felt.

"That's what he wants," Miles said, his hands still moved comfortingly through my hair. "He wants us, especially Lila, to be tortured. We have to just go on like normal else it's letting him win."

She nodded and I agreed, but it was hard to do that. What if was one of us next, it wasn't even worth thinking about.

"They'll catch him before anything happens anyway," Tom said quietly.

Steph looked at him hopefully. "You think so?"

He nodded although his eyes looked sad. "Sure, it's been escalated to the Major Crimes Unit, they've got all the highest people and resources on the case now, he's not going to get away for much longer, he can't."

She nodded and her knees stopped bouncing, and in spite of everything I felt the corner of my mouth twitch. Tom always knew what to say to make her feel better.

She looked towards me. "Do you think you should call Caleb and let him know what's happening?"

Miles' hands still didn't stop moving but I felt him tense.

"I should have probably told you this before but we broke up, in the hospital."

Now his hand did stop still.

"What?!" Him and Steph both said at the same time.

I sighed and sat up, even though everything hurt. "He thought being with me was too much of a risk with everything going on."

Steph gaped. "I can't believe it, that *dickhead*." I blinked as Steph swore which was completely out of character.

Miles looked at me. "What about yesterday in the kitchen?"

"What happened yesterday in the kitchen?" Steph asked.

"Nothing happened he just–"

Miles interrupted. "I walked in on them kissing."

I held up my hands and huffed. "I was testing a theory okay, it doesn't matter. It's definitely over."

She shook her head. "What a coward."

"Steph come on you know he's right."

"None of us would ever abandon you now when you need us most."

I stood up. "Look I really don't want to talk about this but, he's got people depending on him okay? His mums sick, he's got a young orphaned nephew he looks after... and you know I thought he was being thoughtless but after what happened with Tom and then tonight I don't blame him at all. I'm not worth that risk."

Without another word I took myself off to my bedroom and climbed into bed, wrapping my duvet around me tight enough to shut out the cruel world.

I felt my bed sink as someone sat down next to me and Miles' scent washed over me. I opened my eyes and frowned when I glanced at the clock and saw it was 3am, even though I wasn't asleep. I didn't think I'd ever sleep again.

I sat up and looked at him. Through the darkness I could just about see he'd got that serious expression again, the one that still didn't look right on his face. I reached over and flicked on the lamp that was placed on my bedside table.

He studied my face and his glazed eyes look so intently into mine I couldn't look away.

"You are to me," he said, softly.

"What?" I frowned.

My pulse quickened as he placed a warm hand on my cheek and gently brushed his thumb over my bottom lip

"You are worth the risk to me. You're worth any risk."

I had a sudden rush of feelings, such a sudden intense need to be close to him, one that I had never felt with Caleb, that I couldn't help myself. I grabbed his face and pulled it towards mine and kissed him as if my life depended on it. He kissed me back just as enthusiastically, his strong hands slid over my back and down to my waist. I ran my hands down his chest and grabbed the bottom of his top and started pulling it upwards. He complied with a smirk and pulled his top off and gave me one second to admire his incredible body before he crushed it down on mine. His lips found mine again and I ran my hands over every inch of his bare skin that I could reach, his shoulders, his arms, his chest, his back…

Caught up in the moment and full of emotions I pushed his chest slightly and reached my hands down to his belt buckle.

He chuckled and put his hands on mine stopping them.

Breathlessly he said, "As much as I want to do that, you're pretty vulnerable at the moment. It would feel wrong."

I frowned feeling rejected. "I'm fine."

I kissed him furiously again to which he reacted the same but then seemed to sober and he softened the kiss. He pulled my hands back once again from attempting to undo his belt buckle and he pinned them either side of my head.

He kissed me slowly now, so softly and so tenderly and full of meaning that my stomach tensed with pleasure.

He pulled back and looked into my eyes and said, "I want to do this right with you and now is not the right time. Don't try again because I'm not going to be able to stop a third time."

I huffed but didn't move and he chuckled again and rolled off me. "C'mon I'm being the good guy here and you know it."

I did know it. He stood up and surprised me by unbuckling his jeans himself and I raised an eyebrow.

"Don't get any ideas, not even a psychopath could sleep in jeans and socks."

He undressed down to just his boxers and climbed into bed with me and I didn't complain. He laid down on the pillow and pulled me into him and stroked my back lightly with the tips of his fingers.

My mind was still reeling from the events of the evening but gradually to the rhythm of his chest rising and falling and his fingers tracing patterns on my back I started to relax.

He pulled me closer and cleared his throat. "When I saw you after you were attacked… I knew then I'd never let anything happen to you Lila."

I believed him, and with that thought in mind that I surprised myself by finally drifting off to sleep.

I jolted awake with the images of the night before haunting my dreams. I sat up breathing heavily and looked at the time, 7am. It felt like I'd barely even slept.

I remembered Miles was next to me when he pulled me back down and cuddled me into his chest.

"Shh you're okay," he said, thickly. "Need more sleep."

The painful thudding of my heart against my chest eased as I relaxed into him. I closed my eyes and breathed deeply, as he rubbed my back each muscle gradually relaxed.

Until I heard the bedroom door open and I stiffened and sat up again suddenly.

Steph was standing in the doorway, wrapped in her dressing gown, make up smudged all over her face. She looked like she hadn't slept a wink.

She raised an eyebrow and then shrugged and said, "I know I know it's not what it looks like."

She shuffled slowly over to the bed and began to climb in with us.

Miles chuckled with his eyes still closed. "Actually, it's exactly what it looks like."

I groaned and laid my head back down on the pillow, hiding my face in Miles' neck and I pulled the duvet over us. I felt the duvet being ripped off my body, exposing us to the cool air.

"Lila?" Steph gaped.

I huffed and turned to look at her. "I know I should have told you, although there wasn't much to tell I didn't really know what was going on... I still don't to be honest we haven't um..." I trailed off.

The heat rose to my cheeks and I saw Miles smirk even though his eyes were still closed. I rolled my eyes and then reached for Steph but she moved away.

"I'm sorry, I know I tell you everything normally but with everything going on—"

"You think I'm annoyed because you didn't tell me?" She shook her head and looked between us but then slowly she smiled.

"I'm annoyed because, with everything going on in the catastrophe that has become of our lives, this is a good thing. We've all needed a bit of good news at the moment, it's a healthy distraction." She reached for my hand and gripped it tightly.

Tears glistened in her eyes and she abruptly changed the subject.

"I can't stop thinking about it," she whispered. "That innocent person. It's just so cruel, so... sick. I thought everything was messed up, I thought Samuel Zerox was a crazy man who wanted to tease you but this is just..." She covered her mouth as her tears spilled over.

I felt the hot sensation falling onto my cheeks as my emotion matched hers.

Miles' reached over and squeezed her leg comfortingly. "I don't know what the crazy bastard wants but he's not coming anywhere near either of you. He'll be laying low now, he got too brave and now the police are onto him. They'll find him before he does anything, nobody else will get hurt."

Steph nodded as if that made sense. I appreciated him trying to comfort us but somehow I didn't think he was quite right. Samuel Zerox didn't give a damn that the police were onto him, it was probably all part of his game. His torments were escalating, getting worse and more disturbing each time.

Miles' eyes briefly met mine. Zerox was leading to something big and we both knew it.

PC Pawlyn had checked in on us every day over the weekend, updating us with their investigation and generally checking that we were doing okay. She had taken on the role as a sort of family liaison officer. She was obviously not enough of a senior rank to be involved in the actual investigation, but I knew we all appreciated her presence. She was friendly and capable and I didn't think it would take long for her to go through the ranks.

Sunday night the four of us sat in the living room. Tom and I hadn't really spoken but we weren't avoiding each other and it wasn't awkward. I was cuddled into Miles' side staring at whatever programme was on the TV but not really absorbing anything. Steph was sat in the same position with Tom on the other sofa, she had red rings around her eyes and a box of tissues in her lap. She'd been on and off crying all weekend. I felt too numb to cry.

I had to keep my emotions behind some sort of wall to keep functioning. If I let out exactly what I was feeling I didn't think I'd ever stop. I was going crazy stuck in the house. It was like we were all just sat waiting for the next scene of the horror film and I couldn't take it anymore. My hands constantly trembled, every noise outside made me jump out of my skin, I'd barely eaten or slept. I was going to end up the same way as my mother if I let this eat at me any longer.

So, I'd made a decision that I knew the others weren't going to be happy with.

"I'm going back to work tomorrow," I said quietly, my eyes fixed on the TV.

I felt Miles tense next to me and saw Steph's head snap in my direction.

"You can't be serious?" She said.

"I've sorted it all out. I've emailed Dr Reynolds and he's happy for me to come back and PC Pawlyn said it would be fine, the police escort car is going to be outside the office during the day whilst I'm there and then come back here in the evenings."

Tom and Miles had taken some time off work, Miles was self-employed anyway so he was just going to go in every now and again and Joe's had been incredibly understanding with Tom, just as Steph's work had been with her. That was why I didn't mind going back to work, I knew they'd be here in the day with Steph.

I'd emailed Dr Reynolds the evening before. I'd apologised for my behaviour and time off and explained the situation as briefly as I could, although he knew the case anyway. I'd asked if I could come back into the office Monday and resume my position, I'd basically sucked up big time. I couldn't let this affect my career as well as the rest of my life.

He'd responded quickly and pretty briefly.

"Yes I understand, we will discuss this more in person. I will see you Monday at 9am."

Steph groaned. "Lila, I really don't think that's a good idea."

"Me being there is no different to me being here. Either way I'm going to have the same police protection, if anything the office is more secure, you can't even get in the building without a pass."

She sighed but I could tell she wasn't going to argue any more.

I looked up at Miles, we still hadn't even had a conversation about what was happening between us and for some reason it didn't feel like we needed to. But because our dynamic had changed I felt like I needed him to be okay with me going back to work.

"You don't need my permission." He smirked and then looked back at the TV. "But if it were my choice I'd keep you prisoner here with us until that creep was behind bars."

"I just need to get out of the house," I explained further. "I'm going crazy here waiting for them to find him."

They all nodded in understanding and nothing else needed to be said. I didn't tell them that one of the main reasons I wanted to get back in that office was to get information from Dr Reynolds.

He was the leading clinical psychologist in the area and I knew he'd been brought in on the case. There may have been something he knew that would help us find him, maybe I'd recognise something. I just felt like I needed to do something more productive than sit at home waiting on the inevitable to happen and I felt like his psychiatric case was the best place to start.

Just as we were all about to head up to bed my phone rang.

"Its PC Pawlyn," I said frowning. "Why would she be calling me this late?"

Any colour left in Stephanie's face drained completely and she whispered, "I don't know but it can't be good. Answer it."

I swallowed hard as I pressed the answer button. "Hello?"

"Hi Lila, it's PC Pawlyn. How are you this evening?"

"Umm, okay as I can be, thanks for asking," I said. "I don't mean to be rude but can we just cut to the bad news?"

She cleared her throat. "Well, we have identified the body and thought you ought to know. It was Edie Fairview, do you recognise that name?"

"Edie…" I frowned. Where did I know that name from? "Edie…"

It was only when I saw Tom's concerned eyes snap up to meet mine that it clicked.

"Did she umm, work at the hospital where my mother was?"

"Yes that's her. She was the gardener. It seems he broke into her house the other night, you don't need to know any more details than that."

I blinked back tears and swallowed the lump that had formed in my throat as utter guilt began to consume me. "No and I don't want to."

# Chapter Twenty-Nine

Monday morning I arrived at the office 15 minutes early. The two police officers assigned had driven me to work and parked in the car park so I didn't feel too worried. My body was in a constant state of anxiety but I was confident I'd be okay at work at least.

I gave Annie a smile as I buzzed myself in and she took in my appearance. I was still limping slightly although walking was a lot easier and although the main bruising on my face had cleared up, it was still quite bad around the stitches on my forehead. Her eyes widened.

"Gosh I wondered why you hadn't been here in a while, I thought Dr Reynolds was going to have to hire a new assistant! What happened was it some sort of accident?"

"Yeah." I smiled weakly. "Something like that."

She held her hands up. "Say no more, I'll mind my own business. If you need anything you know where I am." She smiled kindly and I smiled back in thanks and headed upstairs.

My stomach clenched when I reached Dr Reynolds' office. I was quite hysterical when I'd left his office last. I was actually surprised he hadn't already replaced me.

My phone buzzed in my hand and I quickly checked it before I entered. It was Miles.

"Good luck on your first day back at work, don't suck up too much to Dr Jackass. I'm taking you for lunch, I'll be at your office at 12."

A broad smile spread across my lips to match the butterflies in my stomach and I knew then exactly how I felt about Miles. This wasn't just physical and it was nothing like I'd felt for Caleb. I wiped the smile off my face and pushed away all thoughts of my love life. It was not the time.

I knocked lightly and then opened the door slightly, poking my head round.

"Ah Lila, come in." Dr Reynolds smiled at me.

I smiled back in relief, it was rare he smiled. He gestured to the chair opposite where he was sat at his desk and I took his invitation to sit down.

"Gosh, what happened to you?" He asked, his expression full of concern.

I let out a humourless laugh. "I'll explain everything I just first want to say thank you so much for giving me my job back, Dr Reynolds. Things have been so hectic I'm not sure you will even believe half of what has happened."

He smiled again and I couldn't help but smile back.

"I did hold a couple of interviews but I was holding out in case you wanted your job back, you've got real potential in this field Lila." I felt my cheeks begin to blush as he continued. "You ask all the right questions, you just need to not let your personal life take over."

He didn't understand how impossible that had been. Looking at his features close up now I could see the dark circles under his eyes, he was still attractive but he looked tired. His hair wasn't as pruned to perfection as usual and he had grown a slight beard.

"Thank you so much. It's complicated though. It's very coincidental actually, it's all to do with Patient Zero, Samuel Zerox."

"I know," he sighed. "It's very coincidental we were looking at his case when he was in the same institute as your mother. I'm sure that brought back a lot of memories, I do apologise for not being as sympathetic as I should have been."

I raised my eyebrows, I'd not expected an apology. "Well, it's more than that actually. The police asked you to review his case to get a psychological perspective to help find him didn't they? Because he escaped. He's dangerous Dr Reynolds, I have no doubt at all now that he killed that poor girl he was seeing at university. He's..." I paused. I hadn't been planning on pouring my heart out so soon but now I was here I had to have the answers. Maybe Dr Reynolds knew something that would help. "He's been tormenting me and my friends." I said quietly.

"What do you mean?" Dr Reynolds frowned.

"I didn't know it was him at first. He started off gifting me these creepy dolls, they were hideous honestly and each one got more messed up." I sighed. "Then he started linking the gifts to my mother and they got worse and more terrifying."

He leaned forwards on his elbows, "Well I have to say from a psychological perspective it's all very intriguing. Did he do this to you?" He gestured to my bruises.

I nodded and looked at my fingers as I pulled at them. "Yes, I think he'd followed me one night when I was out. It was the last day I worked here actually. I don't know what he wants but he's targeting me. He lured me to the woods just to torture me with another stupid doll and show me my mother's case file but he didn't hurt me then when he could have so it doesn't really make sense why he tried to before. The last one though was... horrific." My voice caught as I thought back to that poor woman. "Sorry it's a bit gruesome."

"Nothing I haven't heard before in this industry unfortunately," he said sombrely.

I nodded. "Well, he killed the woman that used to give my mum her favourite flowers at the hospital and then he... skinned her and put it on a doll in our garden."

I expected a gasp or at least a look of horror but Dr Reynolds gave nothing away.

Suddenly his eyes flicked to the corner of the room. I followed his gaze but there was nothing there. I frowned and looked back at him.

He dragged his eyes back to mine and said, "He seems pretty dedicated. Why is he targeting you specifically?"

I shook my head and shrugged. "I read some letters my mother had left and I think he was a bit obsessed with her before she died. He made her all the creepy dolls as well but I'm really just not sure what he wants with me."

Dr Reynolds looked deep in thought. "It really is remarkably interesting, maybe it's a form of flattery? Perhaps he's developed the same obsession with you as he had with your mother? It would appear that way from him leaving the dolls and the lavender, things she enjoyed."

I shook my head, "I don't think so, the ones at the end were more threatening than anything and—"

I stopped suddenly and stared at Dr Reynolds.

He picked up his mug of coffee and took a slow sip. "Lila?"

I swallowed and said slowly, "I never told you he left lavender."

Dr Reynolds swallowed his coffee. "You just did, you said the woman he killed used to give your mother lavender."

I shook my head and a feeling of unease started to wash over me. "No, I said she used to give my mother her favourite flower, I didn't say what that was."

His grip tightened on his mug to the point where his knuckles began to turn white. "It must have been in the case file somewhere then, I'm sure I read it somewhere."

"Can I see the file?" I tried to keep a steady voice despite the fact my body was beginning to tremble. Something felt off.

"I suppose it wouldn't hurt." He said, as he stood up his eyes never left mine. He turned slowly and took a step towards his cupboard and I quickly pulled my phone out, clicked on Miles' name and slipped it back into my pocket. *Please answer.*

Dr Reynolds eyes snapped again to the corner of the room where he stared intently. I again followed his gaze to see there was nothing there.

A chill washed over me.

I looked back up to him as he cleared his throat. He stepped forwards weakly with his right leg and then quickly moved back onto his left as if he were in pain. My thoughts shot back to the other night and I swallowed hard.

I had swung that knife into Zerox's leg with all the strength I could muster.

Without a second thought and ignoring the pain that shot through my body, I leapt up and bolted for the door.

I pulled it open about an inch before it was slammed shut and I was spun around. Dr Reynolds stood pinning me to the door with a hand either side of my head. My mind reeled.

*What the hell?*

The second I looked into his crazed, manic eyes I knew it wasn't Dr Reynolds. I was looking into the eyes of Samuel Zerox.

He laughed an actual joyful laugh and rested his forehead against mine breathing heavily, the joy gleamed in his eyes. I flinched away from him, my heart pounding.

"Well," he chuckled. "This definitely escalates things but that's fine. We can adapt."

I forced myself to speak. "You're Samuel Zerox, how is that even possible? H... How have you even got in this position, Dr Reynolds is a real psychologist I've studied his work, does he know you're here?"

He rolled his eyes dramatically. His entire persona had changed from the stiff, awkward one of Dr Reynolds to an expressive madman.

"Of all the questions I know are running through that brain of yours what a boring one to start with. But no matter, we aren't holding a Q&A right now anyway so you have time to think of a better one." He winked.

I opened my mouth to speak but no words came out. I was completely speechless. This was just insane.

He grabbed my upper arm painfully and yanked me over to his desk where he pulled out a small gun and my legs began to tremble.

He chuckled again. "Hopefully I won't have to use this." He spun me round and jabbed the gun into my lower back. "You're going to go exactly where I tell you and do exactly what I tell you else you'll end up with a bullet in your spine."

He reached into my pocket and pulled out my phone. "You won't be needing this," he said as he threw it and I heard it smash somewhere to the side of the room.

He put his lips so close to my ear I could feel the moisture from his breath. I tried not to flinch. I didn't want him to know exactly how terrified I was at that moment.

"Alert anyone and I'll hunt down everyone you love and put a bullet in each of their brains. Understand?"

My lip threatened to wobble but I wouldn't let it. I forced myself to stay strong. I simply nodded. He chuckled and then slowly began to nibble on my earlobe. The sensation made my stomach churn and I forced myself not to recoil away from him. He finally pulled away and chuckled once again. There was nothing friendly about his laugh.

"Oh my dear Lila, this is going to be fun."

I just had to do as he said. I wasn't going to allow anyone else to get hurt. So I complied when he pushed me towards the door and told me to make my way to the car park. I realised the moment he said it that the police car was there, there was no way they'd let him take me anywhere. Everything was going to be okay.

I led the way down to reception, fully conscious that Zerox was following behind me with a gun hidden in his jacket. We didn't say a word as we made our way downstairs.

My mind was reeling. He was right, I had so many questions. The man I had been working for this whole time, Dr Reynolds, was also Samuel Zerox? It didn't make any sense. How could he possibly get away with having two

# The Doll House

identities? Why had he targeted me this whole time, just because of my mother? What was he planning to do to me?

I needed to think of a plan quickly.

The police were outside in the car park. As soon as they saw me they'd know something was wrong I was sure of it. I just had to get to them.

We rounded the corner to reception and my heart nearly leapt into my throat.

"Caleb?" I gasped and felt Zerox move closer to me. I thought back to his words in the office. If I alerted anyone he'd hurt all the people I cared about, I didn't doubt that for a second. He was evil enough.

I planted a smile on my face, praying he couldn't tell how much my whole body was shaking. "I thought you'd finished working here?" I asked, my voice set at the wrong pitch.

He looked between me and "Dr Reynolds" and said, "I have I've just got to sign some paperwork about payments I'm just waiting for Annie to get back. Are you going somewhere?" He frowned.

Zerox stepped up beside me. "Yes we have a research meeting to attend, we're actually in a bit of a hurry." His voice had lost all its animation and he was back to his stiff psychologist persona. I think they'd misdiagnosed him, it was more like multiple personality disorder than schizophrenia. That or he was a damn good actor.

Caleb looked between us again and I mentally pleaded with him.

*Don't do anything stupid Caleb please just don't say anything.*

"Are you sure that's wise with everything going on? Is the police escort okay with you going?"

I stiffened. Something *exactly* like that.

I was never going to get to the police now that Zerox knew they were there.

"Oh yeah we've cleared it with them don't worry Caleb. That's not your job anymore," I said, hoping he'd take a hint.

He looked at us for a second before Annie came back holding a folder. She smiled at us all.

"Sorry hun the photocopier was playing up! Just need you to sign these and then we're all done."

Caleb nodded and then turned his attention away from us and onto the paperwork. I let out the breath I hadn't realised I'd been holding.

As they were both distracted Zerox subtly but painfully gripped the top of my arm and pulled me over to the door.

He leaned into my ear and hissed, "You thought you'd get away with that didn't you, you little bitch. Here's what you're going to do—"

"Holy shit!" I heard Caleb's voice from behind us.

We spun around to see him and Annie staring in horror at the TV screen that constantly showed the news. The screen displayed a Breaking News message. From here I couldn't see the words but next to them clear as day were two photographs of the man standing next to me.

*Shit.*

Zerox sighed and shook his head. "Today just isn't my day, is it?"

He gripped my arm even tighter and pulled me to his side. He swiftly pulled out his gun and pointed it at my head. I let out a small whimper but didn't struggle against him. Annie shrieked and jumped behind her desk.

Caleb took a step towards us and Zerox moved the gun away from my head and pointed it straight at him.

"No!" I screamed. The panic built in my chest. "Please, I'll go with you I'll do whatever you want!"

"You're never going to get anywhere with the police outside anyway," said Caleb and he took another step forward.

"Caleb stop, please," I pleaded.

Zerox sighed. "I really don't care if I have to kill you, you'd just be more collateral damage. I've done a lot worse."

Without thinking or giving Zerox a chance to react I suddenly jabbed my elbow as hard as I could into his ribs. I grabbed the wrist of his hand holding the gun and span my entire body around, twisting his arm with me. He grunted in pain and let go of the gun which dropped to the floor with a thud.

We both leapt towards it at the same time but he easily barged me out of the way, winding me in the process. I fell to the floor and rolled over onto my front and pushed myself forwards. I had just about reached the gun when–

BANG

I squeezed my eyes shut as a sickening gunshot rang in my ears. I looked around and relief flooded through me when I realised the gun was still on the floor. Had the police arrived just in time?

The feeling didn't last long.

Caleb grunted and my head snapped towards him as he held his side which began to pour with blood. He dropped to his knees and I let out a scream. Zerox roughly pulled me upwards and said breathlessly, "Annie darling, what wonderful timing. But the police would have heard that so we have to go. Now."

Pure confusion and shock racked my whole body as I stared at Annie, overly friendly, chirpy Annie, as she held a gun pointing at Caleb. Her eyes were wide and her hands were trembling.

"I'm sorry I didn't know what else to do," she said, looking at Zerox and then lowered the gun and hurried over us.

"What the *hell*?" I shrieked. "Annie?"

I struggled and screamed and tried to get to Caleb but Zerox had both arms around me as he dragged me towards the door.

Annie walked in front of us, gun still in her hand and buzzed the front door open. I tried to look back at Caleb, who had now fallen to his side on the floor.

"Please!" I cried. "I just need to see if he's okay, please!"

I was pulled into the car park where the two policemen were already running over to us.

"We called for backup when we heard a gunshot, what happened? Are you all okay?"

Annie cried, "We're okay but he's still in there with a gun and someone's been shot, you've got to help him!"

The policemen looked at each other in a panic. They weren't armed so I knew they were supposed to wait for backup. If I let them know what was going on whilst both Zerox and Annie had guns I would be putting them at risk.

"We don't have time for this, backup is going to be here soon and then that really would just ruin my day." Zerox sighed. "What's a couple more to add to the list?"

I screamed as he whipped out the gun and lightning fast, before either of them could react, he shot each policeman in the stomach. They both fell to the ground with agonised grunts.

"You said nobody else was going to get hurt Sam," Annie said. I looked at her incredulously as tears streamed from my eyes.

"You were the one who just shot Caleb!" I screamed and launched myself at her.

Zerox pulled me back. "Now, now ladies, let's not fight. We've got a big day ahead of us. I've been planning this for a long time Lila, I can't wait for you to see your final *gift*."

"HELP!" I screamed at the top of my lungs. "PLEAS–"

Zerox slammed his hand over my mouth and started pulling me by the hair. "Well I suppose this wouldn't be nearly as fun if you didn't put up a fight."

We reached his car, a brand-new silver Audi, and I knew I had to fight for my life. I knew that if I got into this car, chances were I'd never be seen again. I kicked and screamed and held onto the side of the door for dear life.

Annie looked around frantically and hissed, "She's making a commotion Sam somebody's going to notice."

He huffed and then suddenly yanked my head back by my hair and slammed it down on the car. I wasn't usually a fainter, but now for the *third* time in only a short space of time, my world once again descended into darkness.

The Doll House

# Chapter Thirty

*My mother was cooking pancakes as I watched from the table. She was smiling, this was one of her good days. There was suddenly a loud, angry knock at the front door and my mother turned to me and frowned.*

*"Stay there darling," she said. I did as she asked as she left the room but I could hear the muffled sounds of raised voices.*

*"This isn't the right time."*

*"Kendra, she's my daughter too! I have the right to—"*

I gasped awake suddenly as pain shot through my head. Was that a dream, a memory? Where the *hell* was I?

I looked around frantically and as my eyes adjusted to my setting a chill ran down my spine. My eyes widened with a sudden fear that crushed my lungs and stopped my breath.

I was in a house, a very peculiar house. I swallowed hard as I looked at the mismatched furniture around the room. A bright pink sofa pointed at a fake television on the wall that displayed a painting rather than a digital screen. Every single window had been covered with paintings of the blue sky.

I was sat on one chair of four, at a bright pink dining table with my hands tied behind my back. On the table in-front of me was a pink tea set made up of a pink tea pot and matching teacups and saucers.

On the other three seats around the table were sat three life sized mannequins that were unmistakably identifiable as Steph, Miles and Tom.

I was in an actual, life sized, doll house.

My body trembled as I heard slow footsteps approach from behind.

"Impressive isn't it?" Zerox said as he moved into my vision. He stood behind the chair that "Tom" was sitting on opposite me and patted a hand on his shoulder, as if they were friends.

"ISN'T IT?" Zerox bellowed so loudly I nearly jumped out of my skin.

I nodded quickly and tried to keep a steady voice. "Y... Yes, very impressive."

He pulled up a chair and sat at the table. I watched in absolute dismay as he poured all four of us imaginary cups of tea.

He watched me so intently I felt naked under his gaze. "You still don't know who I am, do you?"

I forced myself to stay strong. "You're Samuel Zerox. You were at the hospital with my mother."

He nodded and his lips turned up into a sneer. "You took everything from me."

"I know you loved my mother but I read those letters. She didn't want to leave you, she just wanted to leave the hospital. She

wanted to get back to her life, that was all. You must understand that?" I pleaded.

He scoffed. "Your mother was nothing but a slut, I could never love someone like her. I wish that could be said for all members of my family."

I frowned. "What are you talking about?"

He shook his head and stood up quickly, he reached me in two long strides and pulled me upwards.

"It's almost story time but first, I must introduce you to the stars of the show."

He pulled me with him and I had no choice but to follow. I needed answers but he seemed determined to drag this out.

He yanked open what looked like a cupboard door and I peered into it, down a set of wooden steps. I swallowed hard and tried to take a step backwards at the thought of being taken down into the darkness of the basement in-front of me.

I stumbled as he dragged me down the steps and then shoved me harshly onto a chair. He flicked the lights on and I looked around at the room, elaborately set up to resemble a bedroom. There was a huge wooden wardrobe to the left of the room, a gold framed mirror hung next to it on the wall. There was a double bed in front of me with soft looking silk sheets I prayed I would never get to touch. Abstract paintings adorned the walls and vases filled with lavender sat on every table and shelf possible.

I dragged my eyes to the object in the room I had been trying to avoid. My entire body started to tremble uncontrollably. There was yet another life-sized doll in-front of me. This one was wearing a floral dress and was hanging from the ceiling fan by a rope tied around its neck. Its long black hair flowed down past its shoulders and I looked away quickly, I couldn't bring myself to look at its face.

In the corner of the room tied to a wooden rocking chair was another one, made up like a man dressed in grey pyjamas. It looked bloodied and beaten and incredibly realistic. It coughed suddenly and I jolted.

Zerox walked over to him and smacked him harshly in the jaw and then looked at me.

"Oh how rude of me sorry, Lila Beaumont meet Dr Reynolds."

My eyes widened and my jaw dropped.

"Oh yes," Zerox chuckled. "He's been immensely helpful these past few weeks. I'm not sure I could have kept up the act without his help."

"Is... Is he okay?" I stammered.

Zerox bent in front of Dr Reynolds and tilted his head. "Hmm... I doubt it."

He stood suddenly and walked over to the hanging doll, this one I was sure wasn't real. He brushed a hand over its dress and sighed adoringly.

"This is who I've been just dying for you to meet. The only woman I have ever and will ever love. My dear sweet mother." He looked at me and rolled his eyes. "Of course it's not actually her I'm not completely insane, but this is my way of having her here with me forever."

I swallowed hard.

He looked at me now, his eyes were filled with pure hatred. "This all ends today Lila, you're going to get what you deserve just like your mother did but first I just need you to understand why, else what's the point?"

My eyes filled with tears. "My mother... Did you...?"

"Did I kill her? Yes, I thought that was quite clear by now, it was surprisingly easy to make it look like suicide. They don't question suicide too much when you're supposedly insane."

I held back a sob. "If it weren't for you, I'd have grown up with a mother!"

He laughed. "You have no idea how ironic that is."

I was completely defeated. I looked up at him through tearful eyes and whispered, "I don't understand any of this."

He smirked and then roughly pulled me up off my chair and over to the extravagant gold framed mirror hanging on the wall. He stood me in-front of it and I stared at my reflection. Blood had dried all down the side of my face but the cut on my forehead had been patched with a butterfly stitch.

"That was Annie, bless her, I think she felt guilty for shooting that boyfriend of yours."

My heart jolted. *Caleb*. I prayed the police would have gotten to him by now. He'd be okay. He had to be.

I looked up to meet Zerox's eyes. "Annie... I don't understand?"

There was so much I didn't understand.

He sighed. "I had to get close to you. She was my way in."

"But why?" I pleaded. "Why me? Just because of my mother?"

He gripped my face roughly and pointed back to look at our reflections.

"What do you see?" He sneered.

"I..." I didn't know what he wanted me to say.

"Good looking pair aren't we?" He ran the backs of his fingers over my cheek softly and then suddenly grabbed me by the neck and whipped me to the ground. My elbow made a sickening crack as I slammed painfully down onto the floor.

"You weren't always part of the plan. I'd taken my revenge against your mother and I thought that would be enough. I thought I'd just find you, out of curiosity and when I saw you–" He rubbed his hands through his hair. "Agh it just made my blood *boil*. How dare you, walk around leading your happy little life when you'd ruined mine?"

He pulled me up and sat me back in the chair. Every part of my body ached and he was throwing me around like I was one of his dolls.

"I knew I had to get close to you." I guess now was story time. I pulled my wrists slightly apart. Where he'd been throwing me around the rope had come loose. I thought I might be able wriggle them out of their hold, but I knew I couldn't let him notice.

"It wasn't actually that hard." He laughed. "I looked you up, such a unique name like your mothers it wasn't difficult to find you on Facebook and who was in your profile picture? Stephanie. Stupid girl has her workplace on her page. Very chatty, overly sweet, actually I liked her but *Christ*, FOUR suits I had to buy before she mentioned your "passion" for psychology."

This had been going on even longer than I realised. My heart beat painfully in my chest, I didn't know how this was going to end but I was almost relieved I was finally getting some answers. I stayed silent, letting him continue.

"I did some research and can you believe my luck? Our dear friend Dr Reynolds over here was moving to the area for work. No friends no family so he wouldn't be missed. Except his brother." He laughed again. "Can you believe his brother works for the Cybercrime unit in the police? It's like the universe was helping me. A picture here or there of Reynolds with a bloodied face or gun to his head and his brother was putty in my hands. He helped with everything I needed him to I'm sure you don't need the details, you're a clever girl."

The missing photographs, Dr Reynolds identity, working at Chambers, the police file of my mother's death. Everything had all been worked out from the beginning.

"I thought it would be easier to have someone on the inside of Chambers so I made friendly with the receptionist."

He bent in front of me and looked around dramatically, as if he were about to tell me a secret. He whispered, "She's a bit unhinged if you ask me but she made it easy for me."

If the situation weren't completely insane, I'd have laughed.

He stood up straight again. "She's ever so fickle, craves male attention. A few compliments here and there, a few promises of a future and I didn't have to worry about pretending to be a psychologist in the office, she was on board with everything. Fake meetings, fake assignments... Fake interviews." He smiled at me meaningfully.

My job... My career... Nothing was real.

"I thought you'd realised it was me that night I was in your room, I was looking for those damn letters. But then you just came to work like nothing had happened and I realised I'd lucked out, again!"

I shook my head in disbelief. I had actually been working with this maniac.

"Then you quit and I have to admit I panicked, I acted rash."

I thought back. "That was the night you attacked me, outside Caleb's house."

He nodded. "Indeed. I knew I wouldn't be able to keep you close if we no longer worked together. But everything happens for a reason. It gave me more time to prepare."

"But why didn't you just kill me straight away if that's what you wanted? Why torture me and my friends and kill that poor woman?" I cried. "Why drag this out for so long?"

"Because Lila, I'm an artist. I wanted to get close to you, look at your features, I needed it all for the dolls. That and I was just having too much fun."

He slapped his hands on his thighs. "Anyway, we'd better get to it before the police arrive."

He turned to a wardrobe next to him where he pulled out another doll. It looked *exactly* like me. She was scarily accurate, like a piece of work from Madame Tussauds and she was wearing what I wore the day of my interview. He whistled eerily while he pulled a rope out of the same wardrobe and tied it round the neck of the doll and my pulse quickened.

I pulled my wrists apart again whilst he was distracted, wriggling them almost free from the rope. I was so close.

His head suddenly snapped towards the hanging doll of his mother.

"I know I know, I'm doing it," he said.

I looked between him and the doll, completely bewildered as he continued.

"No, I don't need to hurry up mother. This is going to be perfect, just for you."

He was completely insane.

I pulled at my wrists again. He turned and walked over to me and I stopped struggling. He bent and cupped my chin as he looked into my eyes. "It's almost poetic. I'll hang you both next to each other, just like I hanged your mother. Just like my mother hanged herself."

I recoiled, not quite registering the meaning of his words as I focussed on the rope he was trying to tie around my neck. I struggled and fought to get away, falling off the chair onto the ground. He straddled me and slapped me across the face and I could taste the metallic flavour of blood as it seeped into my mouth.

"Please don't do this!" I screamed and tried to shove a knee upwards into him when there was a loud crash from upstairs.

Zerox's head shot upwards in the direction of the sound.

Through gritted teeth he said, "That better not be Annie I told her I needed to be alone for this." He leapt off of me and bounced up the wooden stairs we had come down, slamming the door behind him. No doubt he'd locked me in but I had to try.

I pushed myself upwards off the floor and yanked my wrists over and over again until they finally broke free painfully. I hobbled up the stairs. I

# The Doll House

was fairly sure I had a couple of broken bones and I was definitely going to need a few more stitches.

I reached the door and pushed and pulled at the handle, of course it was locked. I stumbled back down the stairs, there had to be something here, *anything*.

Dr Reynolds coughed again in the corner and I startled. How could I forget he was here? I hurried over to him.

"Oh god I'm so sorry this is all my fault," I trembled. "Can you hear me? Are you okay?" That was a stupid question, he was an absolute mess. His face was completely covered in cuts and bruises, some old, some fresh, some had only just begun to heal. His eyes were completely swollen shut.

He coughed again and tried to clear his throat. "In... the... war..."

"I'm sorry I don't understand?" I rushed out; we didn't have time for this.

"Wardrobe." He groaned with the last of his energy and his head slumped forwards as he passed out again. I heard another loud crash from upstairs and wondered what was going on up there.

I swallowed and leapt to the wardrobe searching frantically when I noticed a box in the corner. I bent to open it and found a beautifully sharp knife. At least I had more of a chance with this. I stood up about to turn around when a strong sweaty hand slammed over my mouth.

I began to scream although it was muffled by the hand when I was spun around to meet a pair of panicked eyes.

"Miles!?"

Katie Masterman

# Chapter Thirty-One

### Miles

Even though I was taking Lila for lunch in a couple of hours I was in the kitchen making a bacon sandwich for breakfast. We hadn't spoken about anything that had happened and I knew that was my fault. I never took anything seriously and Lila knew that, that's why I was taking her for lunch. I needed to tell her exactly how I felt. I'd always liked Lila and I'd always thought she was gorgeous. She was confident and fierce and had a wicked sense of humour like mine and yet she was kind and compassionate at the same time. I knew I'd started to fall for her when she went on a date with Caleb and my insides felt like they were on fire with jealousy. Then when I saw her in that bar with that man... I knew I'd do anything to protect her. I knew I loved her. I'd never done this before; I'd never had a relationship that lasted longer than about a week but I knew it was time to become a man. I wanted this with Lila.

I had just laid down two rashers of bacon into a hot frying pan when my phone rang. Speak of the devil. I smiled at my phone like a teenager with a crush. God, if Steph could see me now.

I answered the phone. "Just can't get enough of me can you?" I cringed, why was I always such a dick?

There was no answer on the other end, thank god maybe she hadn't heard me. "Hello?" I waited.

"Hellooo, Lila?"

Still nothing.

I sniggered. She must have pocket called me. I placed the phone on loudspeaker on the counter purely because I'm a nosey bastard. Nothing to do with the fact she was in an office with someone Steph insisted on calling Dr Sexy.

I began to butter a slice of bread when there was a sort of scuffling from down the phone. I frowned. She was probably just sitting on her phone but with everything that had happened I was on edge.

There was silence again and then muffled tones. I frowned towards the phone. I think she sounded distressed. I shook my head, I was being paranoid. I picked the phone up off the side and hung up.

I began to butter the other slice of bread for my sandwich and then sighed and picked the phone back up and called Lila. It rang continuously but there was no answer. I turned the hob off.

I couldn't shake the feeling that something wasn't right. I didn't care if I was wrong, I'd rather be safe than sorry and at that moment after everything who'd blame me?

I grabbed my keys, got in my car and sped to Lila's office not caring about any speed limits. I almost halved the 15-minute journey.

I don't know what I had been expecting to see when I pulled into the car park but it hadn't been Lila's two police escorts lying on the floor in a pool of blood.

"Shit."

My blood ran cold. Where was Lila?

I skidded to a stop about to climb out of the car when the passenger door was yanked open and in climbed a blood covered Caleb.

I stared at him eyes wide open. "What the *fuck*?"

He gasped for air as he held onto his side. "No time," he grunted and appeared to use all his strength to lift his arm and point at a car speeding away. "Silver Audi, he's got Lila."

I didn't hesitate before slamming the car into gear and speeding after the car.

"What the fuck happened Caleb? Who's got Lila?"

He drew in ragged breaths. "Who the fuck do you think? It was her boss the whole time I don't know how but he's dangerous you can't lose that car."

"Dr Sexy?!" I said without thinking. He stared at me as if I was the crazy one and I shook my head. "I need to drop you off somewhere you need to get to a hospital."

I sped onto the wrong side of the road and overtook two cars as I tried to catch up with the silver Audi. I refused to lose sight of that car but I knew I had to stay a few cars behind else he'd know I was following

He coughed. "No I'm fine it's just a flesh wound it just fucking hurts."

He said so and I believed him, I didn't have time to worry about that. Lila was my priority and knowing all the things that sick creep had done... My stomach clenched. I couldn't even bare to think about what he'd do to her.

We pulled up two cars behind the Audi at a set of red traffic lights. I tapped my hands on the steering wheel and bounced my legs. Where was he taking her?

"You've got to call the police," I said. "At least just dial and put them on loudspeaker."

"I've got it," he said and dialled but put the phone on speaker anyway.

"999, what's your emergency?"

"Hi, yeah, that man on the news Samuel Zerox he's just shot two policemen at the Chambers Psychology place in Oxford, he's been acting as a Dr Reynolds and he's taken our... Friend. We're following them now he's in a silver Audi."

Caleb rushed out his words not giving the operator a chance to speak. "Shit, I can't see the number plate but we're heading down the A34, he's just turning off. We're in a blue BMW-"

His phone made a loud beeping noise and then the line went dead.

"Your phone just ran out of battery didn't it?" I said through gritted teeth.

He nodded and grunted in pain as he sat forward. "Where's yours?"

My heart sank as I pictured it on the side at home.

"I rushed out without it. Shit!" I braked hard and followed as they turned off the main road. I followed at a distance as we left the busy roads and pulled into country lanes. It felt like we'd been driving forever in the middle of nowhere.

"Hurry up you're going to lose them," Caleb said as they turned a corner and left our sight.

"He can't know I'm following them else he'll try and lose us and I can't risk that. I also can't just pull up behind him when he stops. He clearly has a gun and I do not."

"It's not just him, it's the receptionist too. Annie."

I looked at him. "What?"

"I don't know, she was the one who shot me."

I shook my head, this could not get any crazier. I looked back at the road, I could just see the back of his car as it headed round the corners

# The Doll House

of the windy country roads. I was pretty certain he didn't know I was following them.

"What if he's already... What if she's already..." Caleb started but I cut him off.

"No way you haven't seen half of the stuff that sick bastard has done. There's no way he'd end it quickly, he'll want to drag this out." I swallowed hard, ignoring the bile that was threatening to rise up from my stomach. I couldn't think about that. I'd get there in time.

The car in-front finally started to pull down a tiny lane and slowed to a stop. I stopped back behind some trees and strained my neck to see through the leaves. We were in the middle of nowhere but there was definitely a house there.

"What are you doing?" Caleb hissed. "They're stopping we can get her."

"They have guns genius. I may be advanced at a variety of martial arts but I still haven't quite mastered the skill of becoming bullet proof," I hissed back. "We rush in there he shoots us both and then probably Lila. We have to wait for the right moment."

I looked at him as he drew in ragged breaths through blue lips. "And for fuck sake don't pass out on me."

# Chapter Thirty-Two

"Miles?!" I gasped as he pulled me up into a crushing hug. He pressed his lips onto mine for only a second before he pulled back and placed his hands on my cheeks. He wiped at my bloody forehead and then rubbed his hands on the back of his jeans.

"I thought... God..." He shook his head.

"How are you even here?" I gasped.

"It's a long story I'll explain when–"

He was cut off by a series of loud thuds and a pained grunt. I looked to see Caleb had been thrown down the stairs and had landed in a pile at the bottom. He was covered in blood with his face turned away from us. He wasn't moving.

"Caleb?!" I yelled and looked at Miles. "What the *hell* is going on?"

He didn't have time to answer before hurried footsteps followed Caleb and Annie appeared holding her gun from earlier. Zerox was behind her, also holding his gun.

Miles pushed me behind him and I clung onto his top. Zerox pointed the gun at us with a clenched jaw.

"This has not gone according to plan at all. That's one more casualty you've caused Lila, how much blood do you really want on your hands?" He sneered.

"You don't have to do this."

"I do!" He roared, waving the gun madly. Annie flinched by his side. "You and your filthy mother took everything from me!"

Miles turned his head to me although kept his eyes on Zerox. "What's he talking about?"

"I don't know." I trembled. "He keeps saying it."

Zerox strode over to us and grabbed my hair. Miles tried to pull me back but Zerox pointed the gun in his face. "Make one more move like that and I won't hesitate to blow your brains out."

I pushed away from Miles, I couldn't live with myself if something happened to him.

# The Doll House

"Annie!" Zerox snapped and gestured to Miles. "Shoot him if he moves."

Annie lifted her gun and pointed it at him.

Zerox pulled me over to the mirror once again.

"What do you see?" He sneered into my ear.

"I... I see us?"

"Look closer Lila. Look at your features, your nose, your eyes. What do you see?" He pushed my head forwards, the tip of my nose barely an inch away from the mirror.

I looked at myself, dried blood down my cheeks, wide terrified hazel coloured eyes, a round button nose, bow shaped lips swollen and bruised.

"Now look at me," he spat and gripped my face, pulling it harshly to look at his face. I took in his features.

Wild and crazed hazel eyes, a slightly rounded nose, bow shaped lips... I frowned, realisation sinking in.

He laughed. "She's got it. She's got it!"

He pushed me away and I stumbled backwards.

No, no.

He couldn't be?

As he said his next words my blood turned ice cold.

"Nice to properly meet you, little sister."

"I... What are you... talking about?"

"25 years ago, I was only 16. The same age as your mother. Her and our philanderer father started up their little affair. Little did they know, nine months later you'd come along."

I shook my head. He was wrong, he had to be.

"Do you know what that did to my mother!?" He shouted. His voice was trembling and his hands were shaking. "It CRUSHED her! She doted on my father. She thought they had everything, a happy marriage, the perfect life with their smart, happy son. That's all we needed. Then she found out about you and the affair and something tripped inside her head. I came home from school to find her, hanging from the ceiling. Our family was destroyed."

I began to hyperventilate. So that's why he was doing all of this? My mother destroyed his family.

He continued. "She left me behind with nothing but a note that read "I'll always be with you" and a doll she'd beautifully crafted to remind me of her. I inherited my artistic skill set from her you see."

He wandered over to the doll of his mother that hanged from the ceiling. He sighed as he played with the hem of her dress and looked wistfully at her face. The room was deadly silent.

I flicked my eyes towards Miles who kept his focus on Annie. I could see the cogs in his mind spinning from here. He was weighing up his odds, he knew he could take Annie down easily but there was a chance he'd get shot in the process. I wanted to shake my head at him. She'd already shot Caleb, it wasn't worth the risk.

"Anyway, that's it," Zerox sighed. "It's over. It's almost underwhelming but it's finally time for you to get what you deserve the same way your mother and our father did. This was the part I was looking forward to the most."

He picked up the rope from earlier that he'd tried to wrap around my neck and the breath jilted in my throat. He tied the rope in a noose and then looped it through some sort of metal contraption on the ceiling that I had no doubt he had built to hold the weight of a person. I suddenly remembered the knife in the wardrobe that I had stupidly dropped when Miles had showed up.

Zerox began to make his way over to me with the rope when Miles obviously made his decision and launched himself at Annie.

A gun shot pierced through the air and I screamed. Please, no.

I tried to reach Miles but Zerox grabbed me from behind and shoved the rope over my head and around my neck. I watched as Miles fell to his knees, blood began to seep from his side.

"No!" I shrieked.

With trembling hands Annie dropped the gun to the floor and stepped back. "Samuel please," she pleaded. "Sam... We've gone too far. We've got to go."

"Annie darling don't be naive, not a single one of us will be leaving this room today. This is just something I have to do first." He pulled at the rope and I was dragged backwards.

Annie's eyes widened in panic, she bound up the stairs and pulled at the door that was clearly locked shut. She screamed in frustration as she continued to pull at the door and then ran back down to us.

"Sam why are we locked in here, what are you doing!?"

He ignored her and pulled out a Zippo lighter from his pocket. He flicked it open and without hesitation, threw it into a pile of blankets in the corner of the room. The way they went up in flames it was clear they'd been doused

# The Doll House

in some sort of flammable liquid and it dawned on me that this was his plan all along. The flames built higher, terrifyingly quickly and started to spread. I watched as they reached the wardrobe when Zerox yanked at the rope again and I frantically grabbed and scratched at it as it pulled painfully around my neck, but it was too tight.

He pulled on it until it was taught and my neck was strained upwards. Panic built in my chest. He was going to hang me. This was how I was going to die. Either hanged or burnt alive.

"Please, I'm so sorry for what my mother did to your family," I begged.

From the corner of my eye I saw Annie creeping towards the gun on the floor but despite his injuries Miles reached it first.

Zerox noticed and lifted his own gun and before I could even blink, he shot Miles in the leg. I screamed again as Miles let out a sickening yell. Zerox dropped the rope and left my side to stride over to Miles and grab the gun from him and I knew I had to think fast.

The only thing I could reach from here was the hanging doll of his mother. Was this the one she'd left him all those years ago?

I grabbed at its ankles and pulled hard, creating a loud tearing noise. Zerox' eyes snapped towards me. "What are you doing?"

I pulled again and the dolls neck began to tear from the pressure against the rope.

"Stop it!" He yelled frantically and moved towards me I pulled again.

"Make one more move and I'll rip her head off."

He stopped still and looked between me and the doll. Then his eyes narrowed and his lip turned up into a sneer. "They're all going to be destroyed anyway."

But his hesitation had given Miles just enough time. Despite being in obvious agony, he used the last of his strength to grab Zerox whilst he was distracted. Miles twisted his arm, grabbed the gun and slammed it into the back of Zerox' head over and over until he fell to the ground.

Miles limped over to me and pulled at the rope around my neck but it was still too tight.

"The wardrobe! There's a knife in there!" We both looked towards the wardrobe, completely engulfed in large flames that were spreading rapidly around the room. We had to move fast.

He made to move to the wardrobe when the rope suddenly snapped free from my neck. Annie stood holding a knife, tears in her eyes.

"What have we done?" She whispered to herself in horror, but I just ignored her. I untangled myself and leapt to Miles' side.

"We've got to get out of here," he groaned.

"I know, I know. Caleb and Dr Reynolds, we've got to get them out too."

"Well let's just focus on getting out first."

I swallowed and bent carefully over Zerox avoiding his face.

He was my *brother*.

I felt around in his pockets and relief flooded through me when I felt a key. I ran up the stairs and unlocked the door then made my way back down to Miles. We all started to cough as the flames began to whip round the whole room. Me and Annie pulled Miles up the stairs, gasping for air. He slumped on the floor and grabbed my ankle when I turned to go back downstairs.

"Lila, you'll never make it, it's almost completely in flames down there!"

"I have to Miles!" I yanked my ankle away. "I'm the reason they're down there I can't just leave them!"

I reached Caleb first, he was still laying lifelessly at the bottom of the stairs. I looked around the room, I couldn't even see Dr Reynolds through flames and smoke.

I put my arm over my mouth and tried to hold back my coughs as I bent over Caleb. Blood pooled around him and completely covered his top half. His face was deathly pale and his lips were blue, as if there was no life left in him and I was petrified it was too late.

I pulled him upwards but he was too heavy. Even pumped full of adrenaline there was no way I could get him upstairs.

I shook his shoulders. "Caleb!"

His eyelashes fluttered and my heart raced. "That's it, Caleb it's me, come on you have to get up."

He groaned slightly and I pulled my arm back and slapped him as hard as I could across the face. His eyes opened but didn't focus on anything. All I needed was a bit of strength to get him upstairs. "Caleb just stay with me please."

I pulled him again with all my strength, this time was easier. He was incredibly weak but not a complete dead weight. I managed to get him standing up at the bottom of the stairs, I couldn't contain my coughs now.

"Just step Caleb that's all you have to do, just step!"

He did as I said and stepped clumsily upwards as I pushed him from behind. I pushed and pushed as he stepped and it seemed to take forever

# The Doll House

before we reached the doorway and I shoved him forwards. He fell next to Miles who was now passed out, his chest moved up and down in ragged movements. I looked around, there was no sign of Annie.

I looked down the steps towards the basement as smoke started to flow through to this level of the house. I couldn't leave the real Dr Reynolds down there, it was only because of me he was down there in the first place. He was a complete victim in all of this.

I made my way down again, flinching as the flames crackled loudly. I looked towards the corner of the room where Dr Reynolds had been, it was completely engulfed in flames. I covered my face and let out a sob. I wasn't going to make it to him.

I had to at least get the others out of the house. I turned and made my way up the stairs, coughing wildly as smoke filled my lungs.

I just reached the top step when I was suddenly heaved backwards by my ankle. I landed painfully on my front with a crash and spun my head around.

Zerox was crawling up the stairs behind me, a wild and crazed expression on his face.

"You don't get to leave me here you bitch. We go down together."

I pulled my leg back and kicked as hard as I could, aiming at his face, but he grabbed and pulled at my ankle and we began to fall down the stairs together. I rolled onto my front and scrambled upwards, heaving myself up the stairs as I felt him climb on top of me from behind. I screamed.

Suddenly a silhouette appeared in the doorway in front of me. I looked up to see Annie, holding one of the guns. She pointed it downwards and I squeezed my eyes shut as she pulled the trigger. The weight of Zerox on top of me released and I looked up as Annie lowered the gun with a trembling hand as tears streamed down her face. She reached down and pulled me up into the house.

I looked at her in complete incredulity and dropped to my knees, completely drained.

I lay myself down onto my back breathing heavily, in and out. I closed my eyes as sirens wailed in the near distance.

It was over.

Katie Masterman

# Chapter Thirty-Three

### Two Weeks Later

"How did it go?" Steph asked as I walked through the front door to our home.

"It was a beautiful service," I sniffed and she walked over to pull me into a hug.

"This was not your fault. You have to remember that."

I just nodded in response. I was always going to feel guilt over the death of Dr Reynolds. Even if I wasn't personally responsible, I was part of the reason and I wasn't sure the guilt would ever fade.

"How's our patient?" I asked when the lump in my throat had disappeared.

"As demanding as ever," she chuckled. "I've been in the kitchen with music on pretending I can't hear him."

I shook my head and walked into the living room where Miles lay on the sofa. He'd had to have surgery to remove the bullets from his abdomen and thigh but there was no long-term damage. He just had to stay on bed rest until he healed, which of course he was thoroughly enjoying.

I slid on the sofa next to him, carefully avoiding the cast on his leg and leant down to give him a kiss. He smiled up at me although his eyes looked sad.

"How'd it go? I wish I could have been there with you."

"It was fine, quite small. He didn't have many friends or family it seems," I sighed. "Caleb was there though, he's doing okay."

"How is that bastard up and about whilst I'm still on bed rest?" he asked.

I shook my head but I couldn't help but smile at him.

"You know he didn't need surgery, he had a lot of wounds yes but they were all broken bones and flesh wounds."

# The Doll House

He had been in a wheelchair being pushed by his brother, with one arm and a leg in a cast and stitches in various places. They both gave me friendly smiles at the service but then sat away from me, not saying a word. I hadn't expected him to. I was only glad he was going to be okay.

We all were.

Miles reached down and picked up his bell, he rang it obnoxiously with humour in his eyes. I chuckled as Steph barged through the door with her eyes narrowed.

"Lila take that bell off him before I shove it up his—"

"My glass is empty," Miles interrupted.

I swatted him on the shoulder and then laughed as he pulled me into him tickling my ribs.

Steph softened as Tom appeared behind her and wrapped his arms around her, planting a kiss on the side of her cheek.

"Fine I'll get the drinks in, nothing alcoholic for you though Miles of course, whilst you're on medication," she said sweetly and her and Tom headed to the kitchen.

"Battle-axe!" Miles called after her and I swatted him again.

I looked down at him. My stomach always screwed in knots when I thought back to how close I'd been to losing him. He looked up at me seriously.

"I know what you're thinking Lila." He placed a hand on my cheek. "I'm okay, we all are. Samuel Zerox is well and truly dead, we can go on living our ordinary lives."

That he was. Samuel Zerox, my half-brother, was dead. It hadn't quite sunk in yet.

Once the police had realised from Caleb's phone call that Zerox was living under the different alias they'd managed to find everything; various cars, a home address and the address of the doll house, all registered under the name of Dr Reynolds.

The police had investigated everything once they'd had all the facts and the missing files given to them by Dr Reynold's brother. It was all true, my mother and his father... Our father, James Zerox... Had an affair and had me as a result. It had devastated Samuel's mother who hanged herself, leaving her son only a doll as a parting gift. It had triggered his psychotic break and the onset of his schizophrenia diagnosis and definitely his obsession with dolls and ropes. I shuddered.

"I know we're okay now. Still, I can't get the thought out of my head. Mental illness clearly runs in my family, what if—"

"Don't even say it Lila, you're nothing like him or your mother." He pulled my head down and I laid it on his chest as he stroked my hair. "Regardless, I've got the straight jacket ready just in-case."

I pulled up to look at him with my mouth open.

"I'm kidding!" he said with wide eyes. "Too soon?"

"Way too soon!"

His eyes turned serious as he gazed into mine and he said suddenly, "I love you Lila, you know that don't you."

I smiled the biggest, most genuine smile. There was no feeling of unease, no dreading what was going to happen next. There is no darkness so dense that it could not be overwhelmed by the light.

"I love you too."

# About the Author

Katie Masterman grew up in Oxford. She spent six years of her life studying psychology, achieving a Bachelor of Science in Psychology with Criminology and a Master of Science in Forensic Psychology. It had always been a dream of hers to author a novel and after two back to back maternity leaves (one during a pandemic) she published her debut novel, *The Doll House*.

*If you enjoyed this book and found some benefit in reading this, I'd like to hear from you and hope that you could take some time to post a review on Amazon and it would be really nice if you could share this book with your friends and family.*

*Your feedback and support will help to greatly improve my writing craft for future projects and make this book even better.*

*Thank you.*

Printed in Great Britain
by Amazon